Broken Halos

BESTSELLING AUTHOR
AIMEE NICOLE WALKER

Dedication

To the fur babies who come into our lives and
make our world a better place.

Other Books by
AIMEE NICOLE WALKER

Only You

The Fated Hearts Series

Chasing Mr. Wright, Book 1
Rhythm of Us, Book 2
Surrender Your Heart, Book 3
Perfect Fit, Book 4
Return to Me, Book 5
Always You, Book 6
Any Means Necessary, Book 7

Curl Up and Dye Mysteries

Dyeing to be Loved
Something to Dye For
Dyed and Gone to Heaven
I Do, or Dye Trying
A Dye Hard Holiday
Ride or Dye

Road to Blissville Series

Unscripted Love
Someone to Call My Own
Nobody's Prince Charming
This Time Around
Smoke in the Mirro

The Lady is Mine Series

The Lady is a Thief
The Lady Stole My Heart

Coauthored with Nicholas Bella

Undisputed
Circle of Darkness (Genesis Circle, Book 1)
Circle of Trust (Genesis Circle, Book 2)

Standalone Novels
Second Wind

Prologue

Oliver "Ollie" Knight

"**D**O YOU HAVE A SOLID PLAN FOR WHEN YOU'RE RELEASED from jail?" Pastor Randall Givens asked.

I looked into the kind, dark eyes of the older black man, knowing he would lose interest in saving my soul when he learned I was gay and that I had no intention of apologizing for who I was or who I loved.

"Why do you care?" I asked, not trying to hide the bitterness in my voice. "Do you earn extra points with God for showing up here each week and trying to convert us to Christianity?"

"Is that what you think I'm doing?" he asked in an unflappable, calm voice. "I assure you I'm not trying to convert you to anything other than a happy life free of crime. I want to show you there is another way."

"Then why do you work Bible verses into your lessons?"

"Like with Hallmark cards, there's a verse for every occasion," he teased. A warm, deep chuckle rumbled from his chest, reminding me of the actor James Earl Jones.

I leaned forward and looked him square in the eyes. "Pastor Randall, I think you're a good man, and you mean well. I also thought the same about the members of the church we attended growing up. I saw them more than I did my cousins and loved them just like family.

I learned the hard way their love, as well as my so-called family's, was nothing more than hollow words, and they use their Bible to preach hate instead of love. I've had enough religion to last me a lifetime. Ha. Make it two lifetimes. You're wasting your time with me because God has no room in his heart for me. I'm queer, and nothing and no one can change me. I wouldn't want to even if I could. I like who I am." I lowered my eyes to stare at my hands resting on the table between us, not wanting to see his kindness turn to scorn. I hated the way the garish overhead lights made my olive-toned skin look pale and dull. I nearly cringed when the words olive-toned crossed my mind. As usual, it triggered memories I wanted to forget.

"Oliver has inherited his father's Greek genes," my mother used to say when people wondered how a blonde-haired, blue-eyed woman could claim someone with skin, hair, and eyes as dark as mine. *"I bet he inherited his father's way with the ladies too,"* she added when I hit puberty.

"You're making an awful lot of assumptions based on the actions of one group of church members." Pastor Randall's deep voice pulled me back to the present, but I still couldn't meet his gaze.

"Don't forget my family," I added sullenly. "They tried to convert me, and when I refused to cooperate, they kicked me out of our home. Do you know what it's like to be homeless at fifteen years old with no money and no safe place to rest your head at night?"

"While I can't say that I personally experienced rejection and homelessness, it happened to someone I loved dearly," Pastor Randall said solemnly. "I wasn't in a position to help him at the time, but I can help you. There is a better life waiting for you outside the walls of this jail. It might take a while for people to see the good in you that I see, but it will happen. Oliver, I'd like for you to look at me so I know you're listening to what I have to say next because it's very important." I raised my eyes and was surprised to find his gaze warm and inviting instead of the chilly disdain I expected to see. "God does love you just the way you are, Oliver. He's not going to stop loving you because you love men, but he will want you to stop stealing things." Pastor Randall smiled wryly and added, "Some might call you a modern-day Robin Hood, but a crime is still a crime. You took things that didn't belong to you and sold them, there's no way around it, even if you used the money to feed other homeless people."

"Not just homeless people, Pastor Randall. Hungry kids discarded by their families just like I was. I didn't want them to sell their bodies on the streets to have money for food or turn to drugs to escape their misery."

"Like you did?"

I looked away again because my shame made it impossible for me to hold his gaze, but I nodded because ignoring his question didn't seem right.

"This is your chance to turn your life around, Oliver. I know it's hard for you to have faith, but if you can learn to trust me, I will show you there is someone who loves and believes in you."

"You?" I asked

"Okay, make it two people who will love and believe in you. Me and God, Oliver."

I wanted to believe. I ached to have a better life. I spent the first three weeks of my six-month jail sentence going through withdrawal as my body detoxed from the poisons I put into it. I kept thinking to myself there had to be more to life than bone-deep loneliness and highs that only took off the sharp edges of my pain. "What will you require of me? Attend your Bible study here at the county jail?"

"I'd love for you to attend, but I will settle for one-on-one meetings like this one."

I thought about it for a long time, debating the pros and cons of putting my faith in a stranger. "Why are you different?" I finally asked. "Why are you willing to say being gay is okay?"

"I'm going to be really honest with you, son, because it's the only way I can earn your trust." Hearing someone refer to me as a son and not a disgraceful bastard started to thaw my heart the tiniest bit, even though I knew he meant I was God's son and not his own. "I was raised to believe homosexuality was wrong, and I held firm to those beliefs for many years. Like in your situation, my family turned my older brother away when they found out he was in love with another man. This was 1965 and men didn't love other men, especially African American men. I felt so much conflict in my heart because John was the best person I knew. He was so kind-hearted, loving, and dedicated to our family. He was my hero, and I worshipped the ground he walked on. Yet, I didn't stand up for him when my family turned their backs on him. It didn't matter that I was a seventeen-year-old kid; I should've told him that I would always love him no matter what, but I didn't. I was afraid my family would turn on me too. John knew it; I saw the truth in his eyes when he winked at me before he left."

"What happened?" I asked, although, I could tell by the solemn tone in his voice there wouldn't be a happy ending to the story.

"He wrote me a letter as soon as he was diagnosed with AIDS in 1989, and I boarded the first Greyhound bus to Philadelphia. I wasn't sure what to expect when I arrived, but seeing my brother and so many others crammed into this quarantine room shocked me to my core. The room was cold, sterile, and without windows or hope. They didn't even want to grant me access to my own flesh and blood." Pastor Randall narrowed his eyes like the memory still angered and possibly haunted him. "It was for my own good, you see. They still were ignorant as hell about AIDS, but I wouldn't let my brother die alone. There was this one nurse who I swear was an angel on earth. Her name was Christina, and she fought hard for me to see my brother. I ended up signing paperwork that I wouldn't hold the hospital liable if I contracted AIDS. She spent as much time as she could with the men, reading newspapers or books to them, and she wasn't afraid to touch them. She'd place her hand over theirs or press the back of her cool hand against their fevered foreheads. She encouraged me to simply be myself around them, and together, we made sure my brother and the other patients felt love before they died. I have so many regrets about the years I lost with my brother. He was only forty-four years old when he took his last breath."

"I'm so sorry, Pastor Randall," I said solemnly.

"My brother never lost his faith. Right up until the end, he knew he was going to heaven to be with the angels. I use the Bible as a guide to do good things with my life. I use scripture to guide me and enlighten those around me, but I also accept the Bible was written more than thirty-five hundred years ago, Oliver. It has been translated so many times there's no way to know the true word of God unless you can read and speak Hebrew."

"And you can?" I asked.

"I cannot, but I've read many articles from people who can, and it all boils down to this: God does not discriminate. He loves all of his children equally and without favor."

"You really believe that?"

"I do."

I stared into his eyes, looking for any sign of trickery but found none. He looked and sounded sincere, and I wanted to believe in him. I needed a champion, a mentor, to show me life wasn't all bad. Pastor Randall was willing to be that for me and only asked for one thing from me in return: to try.

"What time is Bible school?" I asked after several minutes.

"One o'clock in the afternoon."

"I'll be there," I said, earning a smile. Little did I know how much the decision would alter my life.

Chapter One

Ollie

"**F**OURTEEN YEARS AGO TODAY, WITH THE HELP FROM A GREAT man, I chose to stay clean and sober. I was eighteen and in jail serving a six-month sentence for breaking and entering and selling the stolen items." I paused for the typical gasp from new meeting attendees. "I had zero potential for a happy life. My body had already started to detox from the poisons I'd put into it for the past two years. When I looked into the late Randall Givens' eyes, I knew he was my only hope at redemption. I wanted it very badly. There was never a day living on the street where I didn't crave a better life for myself, I just never thought it was attainable. I had given up believing in miracles. I'd stopping waiting for a hero to come along and rescue me from a miserable life. But Pastor Randall did come along, and he made me believe again. He restored my faith in humanity and the god I was convinced could never love me as I was—gay and proud of it."

One of the newcomers looked away and squirmed in her seat. It was never my goal to make anyone uncomfortable, but I always started out with the same story when someone new arrived just in case they didn't thoroughly read the pamphlet their counselors gave them. I wasn't going to deny my sexuality or my faith, because there were plenty of other chapter meetings they could've chosen. My mission in life was to provide a safe place of worship for the rainbow community and a Narcotics Anonymous chapter designed with LGBTQ+ persons in mind because they had additional needs and issues their straight counterparts didn't. It wasn't like I hung up a sign that read: No Straights Allowed, but I made it abundantly clear in all my signage, descriptions, and even with my rainbow logo that this was a safe place for my community.

"Don't worry," I said jokingly. "I'm not going to preach to anyone, and I'm not here to convert you to a religion. My only goal is to help you stay clean and sober." The woman met my eyes once more and smiled slightly. "I took the chance Pastor Randall gave me and never looked back. I had many hurdles and temptations to overcome, but my need for a better life outweighed the desire for drugs. I want to help you reach that point too. The first way to do it is always to be honest. Pretending you aren't having cravings isn't helping you and standing up here and talking about your struggles could help someone else who isn't ready to talk about theirs yet."

I caught and held a particular member's eyes for a few seconds before glancing around the room again. Keeton had been attending meetings for months but had never felt comfortable enough to stand up in front of the group. When he had first arrived; angry, bitter, and so very alone in the world, he made snide remarks when someone shared their story. So, instead of seeing his silence as a negative thing, I saw it as a victory.

"Speaking in front of the group is always voluntary, and I'm available for private counseling an hour before each meeting. Other arrangements can be made in emergency situations. You'll also pair up with a sponsor who you can reach out to any time. We're a family here, we care about one another, and we're in this for the long haul. Are there any questions before I step aside for someone else to come up and speak?" No one raised their hand or asked a question, so I asked for a volunteer to come up and give testimony. Rebecca raised her hand.

"Come on up, Bec," I said and returned to my seat.

"Hello, everyone. My name is Rebecca, but my friends call me Bec."

"Hello, Bec," almost everyone said to her.

"This is my third attempt to get clean and sober." She gasped and looked at me with wide, panicked eyes before continuing. "My lack of success has nothing to do with Ollie or his program. This is only my second time attending one of his meetings. Maybe I should back up to the beginning."

I nodded at her encouragingly then listened as Bec talked about deciding to quit on her own after she was nearly beaten to death by her pimp. Her sobriety didn't last long; she returned to prostitution and was arrested a few months later. The judge had offered her rehab over jail, and she'd chosen wisely. A stint at rehab isn't the cure-all everyone thinks it is. Sure, you get medical attention and therapy while your body detoxes, but you're on your own most of the time after that unless the court mandates meetings. In Bec's case, she was required to attend meetings and chose mine because she didn't want to be harassed at other meetings when her sexuality came up in conversation.

Only straight people thought sexuality shouldn't be a factor in anything because they'd never had their own used against them as a weapon. A person's sexuality is a huge factor in teen homelessness, drug addiction, depressive disorders, and suicide. I couldn't change the world by myself, but I could build an army of people who could combat hate and intolerance. Instead of using bullets and machines to kill, we'd use words to heal and educate. It all started right here in this room with acceptance, love, and encouragement.

"The second time, I came here to one of Ollie's meetings and felt hope for the first time in decades. Everyone was so nice to me, but I guess I wasn't ready yet. I went back to rehab for sixty days where Ollie visited me weekly and let me know how welcome I'd be when I was released. And here I am. I'm not sure if I'm ready to talk about the things that led to my addiction, but I do want to say you've all chosen a great program if you're serious about getting help." I noticed her gaze connected with the new lady who'd looked so nervous when I introduced myself, and she didn't shift away for a few seconds. It felt like a host of things were being communicated between them during the brief interaction.

"Thank you, Bec," I said from my chair. "Who's next?"

"I'll go," Paul Windsor said.

Some meetings were over with quickly, and others took longer because we had more speakers. Most of the time, I wouldn't be upset if meetings lasted hours because people were free to come and go as they pleased, and I didn't want anyone in the group to feel rushed. After the meetings ended, a small group of us usually went out for burgers, fries, and milkshakes before going home, but lately, we started going to Queen City Divas after dinner to watch drag queens perform.

It probably wasn't something many pastors did in their free time, but I would never be considered a *normal* pastor, nor did I want to be. I didn't try to stifle my sexual desire, because to do so felt unnatural to me. Loving God didn't mean I couldn't love my body, and those of other men, or had to give up sex. I wasn't a priest for crying out loud.

Andy, one of the guys in the group, dated a performer, so that's how our weekly field trips started. It was during one of those late nights at Queen City Divas when Milo introduced me to his former drag mother, Archie White, who was responsible for the antsy feeling in the pit of my stomach as I tried to keep an eye discreetly on the time. Archie had retired from drag to run an HIV transition home he named Ryan's Place to honor his friend who'd died from complications of the disease, and the drag revue was hosting a charity event to raise money for the home. The owners at QCD decided to donate a huge portion of the profits every Wednesday to Ryan's Place, and Archie showed up to emcee the event. His previous life as a drag queen and his ownership of the transition house were the only things I knew about the man I couldn't get out of my mind because he kept me at arm's length every time I tried to get close enough to ask questions. He preferred not to be in the same room with me at all, but it hadn't always been that way between us. For a brief, shining moment, Archie looked at me with keen interest and longing, until he found out about my profession.

"Ollie," Keeton nudged me. "No one else has anything to share tonight." Dang. How long had I tuned out? "About twenty minutes," Keeton said.

"I asked that out loud?" I whispered.

"No, but you have this dazed look on your face and the question in your eyes. Don't worry, no one else noticed with that serene smile slapped on your face."

"I bet he was thinking about a certain someone with mesmerizing green eyes and pouty lips designed to kiss and suck." The comment came from Tyler who was a CFO for a major corporation whose headquarters were in Cincinnati.

"Ew," Adam said. He was a pediatrician at Children's Hospital. "He's a man of the cloth."

"Beneath the cloth beats the heart of a man," Brent said. For an engineer, he sounded romantic at times. "And the heart wants dirty, back-clawing sex with a man he can bend in half and—"

"Guys," I whispered, cutting him off before he could finish. "You don't usually get crude until we go to dinner. Let's not change that now."

"Besides," Andy said, "Archie is one of Milo's best friends. I'm not cool with hearing this."

"Mr. Sensitivity," Keeton teased.

I ignored them and walked to the podium to close out the meeting by expressing my gratitude they all came and my hope to see them again the following week. Some of the veteran recovery addicts attended meetings biweekly or monthly, but most showed up weekly. As I explained many times, it was good to connect with people who understood and related to your daily struggles.

Afterward, we drove over to Janine's for the best burgers I'd ever had. Andy liked to argue and claimed a place called Gemini's was better, but I thought it was more to do with the sentimental value the place held for him and Milo. Gemini's didn't have the 1950s diner feel or serve hand-dipped milkshakes and fresh-cut fries, so I wasn't interested in giving it a try. We all ordered our usual and settled in for conversation while we waited for our food.

It wasn't customary practice for an NA chapter leader to show favoritism toward certain members of the group, or form deeper, personal relationships with them, but I was drawn to these five men, or maybe they were drawn to me. Whatever the reason, there was a spark and bond between us that went deeper than my sponsorship. We ate together on Wednesday nights and caught an occasional movie together or bowled against one another for fun.

The Frat Boys, as Milo dubbed Adam, Tyler, and Brent because they dressed like it, rarely spoke about their jobs, which was understandable since they all had confidentiality agreements. Instead, they talked about hobbies or what was happening with their families. Some were blessed with involved, loving families and others were in various phases of discord with theirs. I hadn't spoken to my parents or sibling since I was fifteen, and on occasion, I'd feel a twinge of pain because of it, but mostly, I was grateful for my chosen family. I smiled because I realized it would make a great subject for a future sermon.

I realized the conversation around me had stopped, and everyone was staring at me with various expressions stamped on their faces. Adam, Tyler, and Brent looked smug as if they assumed I was thinking about Archie which was fair because I thought about him a lot. More than I should. Keeton looked annoyed like I'd let him down somehow. Andy looked content and maybe hopeful I'd find the same for myself.

"How's the house coming along?" I asked Andy. He was a master carpenter who specialized in rehabilitating and renovating older homes. It was the perfect job for a gentle giant with a caring nature.

"It won't be much longer now. The walls downstairs are painted and the floors are sanded and ready for stain."

"You work fast," Keeton said.

"I wouldn't say fast, but I take a methodical approach. For instance, it's extra work if you sand the floors first then try to paint. Floor sanders make a mess, even though they have bags attached to collect the sawdust. You can wipe down the walls a dozen times before you paint, but I promise you the roller will still manage to pick up dust from somewhere you missed with the naked eye, and you end up with textured walls no one planned for. What about you, Kee," Andy asked. "I bet your job never slows down."

"Nope," he said, shaking his head. I was sure confidentiality was a requirement for a fire medic, but I suspected his unwillingness to talk about his job came from a deeper issue. The young man revealed next to nothing about himself except a sharp mind and an even sharper tongue.

"What are the odds Archie finally acknowledges Ollie's existence tonight?" Tyler asked.

"Fifty to one in favor of fuck no," Adam replied.

"It's better than one hundred to one," I said, trying to stay positive.

"Does that mean you're feeling lucky?" Brent asked.

"Can we not hear about the padre getting his love jones on?" Keeton asked, looking and sounding extremely uncomfortable.

"He's still a man," Adam said to Keeton.

"A man with needs," Tyler added.

"I said 'feeling lucky' not getting lucky, brat," Brent said, hooking Keeton around the neck and pulling him closer so he could rub his knuckles over Keeton's head.

"Knock it off," Keeton said, elbowing Brent in the ribs so he could get away. I noticed his face was a nice shade of pink, but it didn't appear to be from displeasure, fear, or exertion.

"You sure didn't blush like that when you took your clothes off for the annual fireman's calendar," Adam said to Keeton. "Or did they photoshop it out."

"I had clothes on," Keeton protested.

"You had on a pair of work pants, and they were unzipped at the top," Tyler countered.

"Someone manscapes," Brent said, trying to pull Keeton close again.

"Knock it off, B," Keeton said. *B?* When did that happen?

"Since when did you give one of us a cutesy nickname?" Adam asked with a pout.

"Just now, I guess," Keeton said with a shrug. "Normally, I think of you as Saint, Bruiser, Nerd 1, Nerd 2, and Nerd 3."

"Oh, which one of us is Bruiser?" Tyler asked with wide, innocent eyes. "How do you know what we're packing anyway? None of us stripped down to become spank bait."

"Speak for yourself," Brent said, waggling his brows. "You have no idea what I get up to when you guys aren't around."

"Oh, I bet he goes live cam when he jerks off. How many subscribers do you have, Bruiser?" Adam asked.

It never failed to surprise me just how fast things could get out of control. "Knock it off, guys," I said firmly. "It's obvious as hell *I'm* Bruiser." That got a laugh out of all of them.

I noticed Brent had removed his arm off Keeton's shoulder but propped it on the back of Keeton's chair instead of dropping it back in his lap. Keeton was aware even if he didn't let on. I was glad no one else pointed it out either, and by the time our food arrived, we were too hungry to do any more talking.

By the time we arrived at Queen City Divas, the club was packed with energetic fans who loved the carefree atmosphere and exciting entertainment the queens delivered with every show. Andy's relationship with one of those queens guaranteed us a reserved table front and center of the stage. Many people grumbled when we arrived, but none dared to sit in our seats unless they wanted to be called out and embarrassed during a performance.

Mistress Vixen was on the stage giving her best Etta James performance and the words to "At Last" resonated within me because I knew I'd met someone truly special the night I looked into Archie White's eyes. Then the man in question stepped onto the stage after the song was over to excite the crowd for the next queen. He looked sexier than he had a right to in his skinny jeans and white lacy shirt giving me, and everyone else, a tantalizing view of his cut abdomen and perky, dark pink nipples. The lacy shirt stopped a tantalizing few inches above the top of his jeans, and I was dying to see if his ivory skin was as soft as it looked. Archie's green eyes looked even lighter beneath the spotlight, his black lashes even longer. His mouth looked shiny and plump from whatever lip gloss he wore. Was it flavored? I wanted so badly to find out. I ached to climb the stage and slide my hands into his immaculately styled hair to see if those black strands were as silky as they looked. The only thing hotter than an August summer day in the Queen City was Archie White, leaving my throat dry and feeling parched. I was desperate to quench my thirst, and only he would do.

"I need a volunteer for the next performance. Any takers?"

I would've liked to blame the devil for my next action, but it was a pure act of desperation. I wanted, no needed, Archie to look at me and really see me, so I stood up and yelled, "I'm your huckleberry." At least those vivid green eyes locked on mine.

Chapter Two

Archie White

IN ALL THE DRAG JOINTS IN ALL THE TOWNS IN ALL THE WORLD, HE WALKS INTO *mine.* Why couldn't Oliver Knight, make that Pastor Ollie, take a hint and realize I wasn't interested in him? Liar! Okay, why couldn't he understand I wasn't interested in him any longer? My interest was a fleeting thing, lasting a mere thirty minutes before someone from his congregation stopped by his table to say hello. Only I would get a raging boner looking into the eyes of a man who devoted his life to religion, a religion which had no room for me and my kind. His kind too. It was shocking how quickly my hard-on deflated when God or religion was brought up in a conversation.

Ollie knew it too; I could see the dawn of recognition in his eyes. Of course, me jerking my hand off his thigh like it had been bitten was a pretty big hint. If that hadn't given me away, my expedient departure from the table or my refusal to return his phone calls or text messages in the following days should've done the trick. If nothing else, I learned not to give my fucking phone number out so damn fast to strangers, because the messages he'd sent still haunted me a month later.

Come on, Archie. I don't bite. Unless you want me to.

I don't know why you're pretending not to be attracted to me. Or is rubbing your hand up and down a man's thigh your usual way of saying hello.

I dreamed about you last night…

A wise sinner would delete the shit off his phone and forget the man who sent them. Not this dumbass. I used the images they stirred to masturbate twice a day. Ollie was the first and last thing on my mind every fucking day for a month. I wanted to hate him for it, but his earnest, dark eyes wouldn't permit it, especially the worshipful way he looked at me like I was the altar he wished to kneel before.

Damn it! I just had another image to add to my growing collection. Me sucking him off beneath the table, Ollie biting my neck as he fucks me aggressively from behind, him waking up hard and wanting and reaching for his cock to ease the ache. Now, I'm kneeling before him and sucking his cock…how? Under his robes? Did he wear robes? Did I think the robes were sexy? Was he naked under there? What if he wore the black pants and black shirt with the white collar? Oh, that was for sure sexy. He'd leave the collar on while I gave him head. I'd see it, but it would be out of focus because I wouldn't be able to look away from his demanding eyes.

Fuck! My skinny jeans were two sizes too skinny and were already threatening to cut off the circulation to my boy parts. How long had I stared gaping at him after his dorky but adorable attempt to volunteer? I could almost expect a Boy Scout salute or even a Katniss Everdeen tribute salute, but Val Kilmer quotes from Tombstone? It seemed Pastor Ollie was an endless source of surprise for me.

"Well then," I said sassily. "Come on up here, Huckleberry." Ollie's mouth fell open like he hadn't expected me to agree to his offer, or maybe he was still shocked he'd made it to begin with. "Don't be shy now. Mistress Gracie Lou Fullbush won't hurt you. Well, maybe a little, but some people are into a little pain. Does it get you off?" *Oh, fuck! What was I doing?*

"I'm up for just about anything," Ollie boldly stated then began making his way to the stage. How dare he look so delicious in his pressed, button-down shirt? The stark white fabric made his skin, hair, and eyes look darker. His jeans were tighter than I'd expect a pastor to wear. The dark fabric had a velvety sheen, and it clung so beautifully to his muscled thighs and lovingly cupped his crotch. I wanted to lovingly cup his—

"Here I am," he said, standing before me. How had he arrived so fast? What magic did this man possess to ensnare and enslave my interest when I intellectually knew he was all wrong for me. "Reporting for duty."

"A glutton for pain, are you?" I asked, dramatically quirking a brow.

"Apparently." He stared me right in the eye, and I knew he was referring to the way I'd ignored him the past month. "A real pain slut," he added.

My shocked gasp turned into a sputtering cough. Who was this collared man, and why did I suddenly want him to wear a different kind of collar? One attached to a chain holding him in place while a mysterious, masked man took a riding crop to his firm, round ass. I didn't need to shout, "You there; take off that mask and reveal yourself," because I knew who was hiding behind the mask and what he didn't want anyone, especially the kneeling man, to see. Consuming want. Debilitating need. If I weren't careful, I'd make a fool of myself and reveal the emotions he stirred inside me.

Ollie matched my raised brow with one of his while we silently stood there staring into each other's eyes. I needed to find a dark-eyed stranger to fuck so I could work him out of my system. The smile slowly spreading across his face indicated he knew just how far he'd thrown me with his words and actions. I was never one to surrender the final word to anyone, not even a worthy adversary like Pastor Fuck-Me Eyes.

"You're in for a real treat then," I said innocently, but my wicked smile gave me away. "Everyone…" I said, turning away from Ollie to face the audience. My words died because there wasn't a single soul moving in the crowd. They were raptly watching the exchange between us. Could they feel the electricity arcing between us? Could they see my white-knuckle grip on the microphone and the way my other hand was glued to my hip because I was seconds away from dropping the act, and the mic, and reaching for Ollie? "What the fuck are you all staring at?" I demanded in my best drag voice. Ollie flinched beside me. Was it because of my gruff voice or my crude language? "Who wants to see Mr. Goody Two-Shoes here learn a lesson or two in submitting?"

The crowd went wild, especially his group of friends sitting front and center. I looked back at Ollie to give him a chance to change his mind, but I saw he'd accepted the challenge. In fact, he appeared to relish it.

"Gentlemen," I said, signaling the stagehands to bring out the plush spanking bench covered in purple velvet. It looked like something a kinky Victorian would've kept in their home. The fellas turned the bench sideways to give the audience the best view. They'd see every blow Gracie Lou landed on his ass while I'd be standing off to the side of the stage where I'd see every expression crossing his face. It would be torture, but I had to accept my punishment just as he would.

Ollie proudly walked to the bench then winked at me once he was in position. "Comfy," he said, leaning his chest against the curve of the bench designed to support his upper body while his ass was up in the air.

"Glad you think so." I strolled over to the bench and squatted down. Ollie lifted his head up and looked into my eyes while I pulled open the small drawers built at the bottom of the chair that discreetly hid the padded cuffs. "Do I have your permission?" I asked, rattling one of the cuffs. It wasn't part of Gracie Lou's instructions to me before the show, but I couldn't seem to stop myself. Was it my desire to touch him once more? Was I that big of a masochist? "Do I have your permission, Oliver?"

"You do," he said, daring me to do it. "Will I need a safe word?"

"Do you want to have a safe word?"

"How about Archie?" he asked me. And, of course, I couldn't stop my mind from imagining him calling out my name in ecstasy while riding my cock. Damn him. Damn my horny brain. Damn the fucking world.

"Fine. You shout my name as loud as you want, and I'll come rescue you from Mistress Gracie Lou." I set the microphone on the stage so I could use both hands to secure Ollie. I bit my lip to keep from crying out when my bare skin touched his. He electrified every molecule in my body, and I was certain the mic picked up the sound of precum dripping in my briefs.

"Perfect."

"There's my cue to exit the stage. You'll want to hold onto your cocks during this performance, but I advise you to just hold onto your hats so we don't get shut down for lewdness."

"What about you?" someone asked from the audience. "Jacking off in the shadows?"

"Maybe," I said coyly, earning delighted cheers from the crowd. I blew Ollie a kiss and exited the stage.

The loud techno beat of Christina Aguilera's "Keeps Gettin' Better" began, and Mistress Gracie Lou Fullbush took the stage wearing a black leather bustier, the tiniest leather boy shorts I'd ever seen, and matching leather, lace-up boots that came up to her fishnet-covered thighs.

"Spank him! Spank him!" the crowd chanted.

Milo approached where I stood in the shadows. "What the hell are you doing?" he hissed. I turned to look at him and noticed he was only half dressed as Peach. "Ollie is a very good friend, Andy's sponsor, and a pastor. Why the hell did you allow him to get tied up and—" His voice was drowned out by the audience cheering when Gracie Lou mimed fucking Ollie's pert ass. Unwanted jealousy rose swift and hard, making me want to march out there and free Ollie for... What did I want to do with him? To him? For him?

Whack! Gracie Lou didn't hit him hard, but it sounded like she'd smacked him a good one. Ollie flinched a little before a wicked smile danced on his lips. I needed to turn and address Milo, but I couldn't tear my eyes off Ollie, and neither could he look away from me.

"I don't even know why I'm bothering," Milo groused beside me. "Don't play games with him, Archie. You're a better person than this."

Usually, I would've agreed with him, but right then, all I wanted was to know Ollie's taste—his lips, his skin, and his cum.

"I know you don't get out much with all the responsibilities you have, but Ollie isn't the kind of guy you scratch an itch with. Find someone else to fuck and forget, Archie."

"Yeah, okay," I said, dismissing him. He offered sound advice, but I could fuck a hundred brown-eyed guys, and I'd still want Oliver Knight. Milo stomped off in a huff because he knew I was blowing him off.

My eyes stayed locked on Ollie's during the entire performance. I felt every playful slap Gracie Lou landed as if I was the one leaning over the bench. I stood far enough in the shadows there was no way Ollie could see me, yet he knew I was there. He felt my presence as surely as I felt his. When the song ended, I was supposed to go out onto the stage and let everyone know there was a twenty-minute intermission between the first and second half of the show, but I stood as still as a statue as Gracie Lou freed Ollie while telling bawdy jokes about his arousal and whimpering sounds of need.

I was seconds away from coming in my pants. Maybe Gracie Lou picked up on the vibes between us before she walked onto the stage because she took pity on me and made the intermission announcement while Ollie made a beeline straight for me.

"Loverboy, your seat is that way," Gracie Lou said. "He must need a bathroom break to"—she mimed jacking off with her right hand—"before he returns to his friends. Wait for me, honey," she called playfully but exited from the opposite side of the stage as the crowd roared with laughter.

The DJ started playing music to entertain the crowd during

intermission. "Dirrty" started playing just as Ollie stopped in front of me. I didn't act coy and ask what he wanted, I took him by the hand and led him to the prop closet down the hallway.

"This means nothing," I said when I pushed him up against the closed door. "I'm not sending you flowers tomorrow. I won't be answering your texts. I won't think about you another second after tonight."

I didn't give him a chance to answer me; I crushed my lips against his. I loved the fact we were nearly the same height. No one had to strain to reach anything. We fit together so fucking perfectly. Ollie parted his lips, maybe to welcome me or maybe to gasp in surprise, but either way, I took advantage to slip just the tip of my tongue inside his mouth to tease and tantalize. Ollie rounded his mouth and sucked my tongue deeper inside his mouth.

A needy whimper purred in my throat, and my hands fisted his crisp, white dress shirt on either side of his waist. Ollie didn't choose to place his hands in a chaste place as I had, he placed them at the gap between the bottom of my lacy shirt and the top of my skinny jeans, circling the bare skin with his fingers before slipping a hand under my jeans to tease the crack of my ass through my underwear.

Ollie ripped his mouth off mine and stared at me with dazed eyes and a gaping mouth. "You're wearing lace underwear too?"

"Matches my shirt," I said in a "duh" tone of voice. "We only have twenty minutes."

"I probably only need two," Ollie huskily said before he leaned closer and licked a trail from my collarbone up to my chin, stopping only to suck my Adam's apple into his mouth. "We could always wait and do this after the show when you're not pressed for time. I'd really love to draw this," he illustrated his intentions by circling my pucker with his finger, "out for as long as you'll let me."

"This is all I can give you, Ollie." I claimed his lips again before he could protest.

Ollie didn't appear to object to anything but the clothes between us because he moved his hand from the back of my jeans around to the front to attack my fly.

It was then when my conscience clubbed me over the head. Milo's words echoed in my ears even louder than my thudding heart.

"Don't play games with him, Archie."

"You're a better person than this."

"Ollie isn't the kind of guy you scratch an itch with."

"Find someone else to fuck and forget, Archie."

"Archie?" Ollie softly asked when I pulled back from our kiss suddenly. I took several steps back and turned so I wasn't looking at him. I required distance between us to say what I needed to. I couldn't do it while staring into eyes that showed me how badly he craved my touch. I couldn't push him away while looking at the way his dick rose stiff and hard for me. I'd caught a quick glance of the outline of his erection pushing against his white underwear through the gap in his open jeans. Only Ollie could make those boring briefs look so damn sexy. Fuck me. I wanted to drop to my knees and rub my nose against it, learning his smell before I learned his taste.

"This won't work," I said firmly. "I can't do this."

"You're right. You deserve to be treated better than this." Ouch! He'd just turned the invisible knife I'd driven into my own heart. "This isn't the place—"

"The location has nothing to do with it," I firmly said, cutting him off. "It's you."

"Me? You mean my profession?"

I turned around to face him once more. "What kind of pastor sends the dirty texts you do? What man of God looks at me the way you do?"

"How do I look at you?" Ollie calmly asked me.

"Like you want to fuck from sunset to sunrise, nap, and start all over again."

"You're not wrong, but you might be exaggerating my stamina a bit."

"I'm not joking, Oliver."

"Nor am I, Archie. You should know, there's more I lust for than to know you physically."

"You want to know me philosophically?" I challenged, raising my head.

"I want to know everything there is about you, Archie. I'd like to know why you're pretending you don't want the same thing."

"You're wrong, Oliver. I want to feel your dick in my ass or shove mine in yours. I don't want to take long walks down by the river, knit, or meet your folks. All I can offer you is a quick, dirty fuck right here, right now."

Ollie released a long, sad sigh then began closing his pants. "That's a shame. I had hoped to explore these feelings between us."

"I offered—"

"You offered your body, Archie. I want more. You should demand I want more too."

"Who are you to know what I should or shouldn't demand? You know—" I shook my head. "Ollie, I need you to stop sending me wet-dream-inducing texts and staring at me with such naked want and desire when you come in here. I'd rather you not come back here at all, but I don't have the right to ask or insist on it. I don't want to see you anymore."

"You'll see me in your dreams and every other time you close your eyes. I know this because you'll be waiting for me when I close mine."

"You are without a doubt the worst pastor I've ever heard of," I said, borrowing and tweaking my favorite line in *Pirates of the Caribbean.*

"But you have heard of me." He gave me a jaunty, two-finger salute and left me staring into space long after the door closed.

"I'm so fucked."

Chapter Three

Ollie

MY FAVORITE MONTH IN OHIO WAS SEPTEMBER WHICH STARTED off with a lingering heat from August but teased the promise of fall weather with every passing day. September was the start of football, hoodie, and pumpkin spice season, and although I loved all of those things, nothing made me happier than the beginning of the Queen City Rogues Bowling League mid-September of each year. I couldn't remember a time I was more excited about the team I assembled. This time last year Andy was still pining after Milo, the Frat Boys "had better things to do," and I hadn't met Keeton or Milo, who was the best bowler out of us.

So, every Tuesday, I had an extra pep in my step because it was bowling night, but on this particular Tuesday, I was extra peppy with excitement for our first league night. I wasn't going to let anything bring me down, not even missing Archie.

I'd honored his wishes and stayed away from Queen City Divas on Wednesday evenings and stopped calling or texting him. I tried to delete his number from my phone at least two dozen times over the lonely month of separation, but I couldn't do it. I wish I could say my dreams and fantasies about him disappeared too, but a pastor didn't lie. I might crave the touch of a man who didn't want me, and sometimes the numbness an illicit substance could give me, but I wouldn't lie about their existence. I wouldn't say my craving for one fueled the desire for the other, but they were equally as powerful, and both would cause me irreparable harm if I gave in. It was best if I just left well enough alone and avoided running into him.

"Hello, is this Pastor Oliver Knight?" asked a timid voice when I answered my cell phone.

"Yes, this is Pastor Ollie. How can I help you?" I was expecting the man to ask about NA meetings, but it wasn't the reason for his call.

"Is HIV a plague God has placed on gay men? Does he hate me?"

I have to say the question caught me by surprise, not because I hadn't heard the claims before, but because the man sounded so fearful of my answer. I knew this was a pivotal moment in the man's life, and I couldn't mess it up. I needed to speak with conviction, not only to reaffirm my beliefs but maybe to help him believe too. I didn't expect my answer to be a cure-all, but maybe a step away from the ledge.

"What's your name?" I asked gently.

"I…um—" His words broke off like he was afraid to tell me.

"You don't have to say, or you can just give me your first name if you like."

"My name is Henry, Pastor Ollie."

"Henry, HIV isn't a plague God has placed on gay men, and he most certainly doesn't hate you."

"My mother doesn't agree, Pastor Ollie."

"Forgive my boldness, but your mother sounds like an ignorant woman. Does your mother have the direct phone number to dial up God in heaven?"

"Uh, she believes her Bible is her direct line to God."

"Perhaps she's not interpreting the scripture correctly, or perhaps some ignoramus has done his or her part to guide your mother in the wrong direction. To me, misrepresenting God's love is the biggest sin of all."

"How do you know God loves me?"

"Let's pretend the scripture doesn't spell it out, even though it does. I know God loves you, a gay man, because he loves me. I feel his love in my life; it uplifts me and gives me hope. If God hadn't wanted gay people, then there wouldn't be gay people."

"So, he wants war and cancer and serial killers too?"

"Are you honestly comparing healthy, loving relationships between consenting adults to war, cancer, and serial killers? Do you think that's an apple-to-apple comparison, Henry? I sure don't."

"Okay, you make a good point, but you didn't necessarily answer my question."

"Well, it's not an easy question to answer."

"So, you don't have an answer then. You're like my mom who spouts her beliefs without anything to back them up."

"No, I do have answers, Henry. Its just not something I can surmise in a few sentences. Are you willing to sit down and talk to me in person?" I felt Henry needed more than just a phone conversation. It felt like he was on the verge of...giving up. "I can meet you anywhere, and I'll bring coffee, tea, or anything you'd like to drink."

"Um, I don't know," Henry answered after a long pause. "I feel silly."

"Were you recently diagnosed with HIV or did you just recently inform your mother?"

"New diagnosis and I came out to her because of it," he said softly.

"Henry, it's very possible she'll come around once the news has time to settle."

"Not likely, Pastor Ollie. Her preacher advised her to throw me out so she wouldn't catch it too. Do you believe people are still so ignorant?"

"Unfortunately. I'm also aware of how ignorant many clergymen are when it comes to homosexuality and HIV. Listen, Henry, I don't want you to feel like I'm going to pressure you into believing something you don't want to, and I don't have a prepared sermon to share with you. I will, however, offer you friendship and an ear to bend. I'm a great listener. I also know of some excellent support groups which can help you. I know receiving an HIV diagnosis is scary, but it is not a death sentence, Henry. You can live a long, happy life as long as you do what your doctors tell you to."

"Wow, you sound a lot like Dr. Kent."

"Dr. Kent probably wants you to live your best life, and I know I do."

"Why? You don't even know me?"

"I would like to know you if you'll let me."

"I don't own a car, but I have a few dollars left to take a cab or hire a Lyft."

"I'll come to you," I assured him. "Save your money. All I need from you is the location you'd like to meet and what you'd like to drink. It doesn't have to be a warm beverage. I'm sure there's a coffee house near you, and I can bring you an iced coffee or one of those frozen, flavored numbers."

"Claire's is around the corner from where I'm staying. She makes the best white chocolate mocha and banana nut muffins." I heard the wistfulness in his voice and decided to add the muffins to the order. Henry rattled off his address, and I jotted it down on a sticky note pad I found hidden under the open Bible on my desk.

"I'll be there within the hour, Henry. I'm just wrapping up the sermon I'm planning for Sunday."

"Okay." I detected a note of uncertainty like maybe he thought I wouldn't show up. I'd prove him wrong and show him some people could be counted on.

I set my phone aside and finished my sermon notes within thirty minutes then started out the door to meet Henry. I looked at my reflection in the mirror as I passed it by and worried the stark black shirt and clergy collar might put Henry off and make him feel uncomfortable. I changed out of my church clothes and put on a pair of soft, weathered jeans and a cream flannel shirt with various shades of blue crisscrossing with thin lines of deep purple and pale aqua. It was the softest shirt I owned and my favorite. My outfit said I was a man like any other rather than an uptight clergyman sent from heaven to be judge, jury, and executioner. I wanted to put Henry at ease, not make him feel worse than he already did. I hoped to find out the name of his mother's preacher by the end of our conversation so I could send the impostor a scathing letter.

Claire's wasn't too busy at two o'clock in the afternoon; I was in and out in fifteen minutes or less with a salted caramel mocha for me, a white chocolate mocha for Henry, and a dozen mixed muffins for us to nibble on. I'd leave the extras for Henry because the last thing I needed was to wolf down half a dozen muffins or more. I didn't google the property owner of the address Henry gave me, but I recognized it as a residential area. I wished I'd done my homework when I parked my car in front of the large, two-story structure and saw the wooden sign in the yard that said: Ryan's Place.

"Lord, help me," I said out loud. What exactly did I want the lord to do? Give me strength not to make a fool of myself in front of Archie by popping an erection or dropping to my knees and begging him for…anything?

I promised Henry I would meet with him, and I would never go back on my word. It didn't mean my palms weren't sweaty enough to drop the drink carrier as I made my way up the sidewalk leading to the house or prevent me from nearly tripping on the final step before I reached the porch. I inhaled a calming breath and slowly exhaled before I rang the doorbell. I tried to convince myself I didn't want Archie to answer the door, but the disappointment when an older lady opened the door proved how wrong I was.

"You must be Pastor Ollie," she said cheerfully. She was the tiniest thing. I bet she wasn't even five feet tall, yet the joy and happiness she radiated made her seem like a giant. "I'm so glad you're here."

"What gave me away?" I asked, looking down at my clothes.

"The goodness in your character. Henry called in a time of need, and you answered. Please come in. I'm Mrs. Grimaldi, but you can call me Esther or even Mrs. G if you'd like."

"Thank you, Esther."

The great hall was neat and tidy with polished wood floors, a warm, soft gray paint on the walls, and a staircase leading to the second story. Esther led me past the stairs toward the back of the first floor. We passed two large, open rooms on either side of the long hall. One was a large dining room featuring two rectangular tables with eight chairs tucked around each one. The other appeared to be a living room with older furniture that looked both comfortable and inviting, or at least, the three men lounging around watching a popular soap opera helped give it the appearance.

"She's going to take the asshole back," one of them said.

"Of course she is," the other two replied.

Esther snorted when she overheard the conversation but kept on walking, so none of the men were Henry. We passed two closed doors with signs that read: Private Residence and Manager's Office. I knew the two rooms across the hall from each other were Archie's private domain without asking Esther. The urge to open the doors and discover something about the tempting man was strong, but I wouldn't invade his privacy.

As I expected, Esther took me to a cozy kitchen with cheerful yellow walls, white cabinets, and modern appliances. "This is my domain," she proudly said. "I retired from nursing five years ago after more than forty-two years on a hospital floor. It turned out you could take this old nurse out of the hospital, but you couldn't take the nurturer out of this old nurse. I got to spend three wonderful years devoting all my love and attention on my Morty before he passed away." She gestured for me to take a seat at the small table tucked in the corner, so I did. "It was about the same time Ryan passed away, leaving this big ole house to his friend, Archie. I'd never seen such opposite friends in all my life, but their friendship was a work of beauty. I still feel their connection every day when I walk in here."

"You work here every day?" I asked. The lady had to be pushing seventy years old.

"I *volunteer* here six days a week, only taking Sunday off. I love fixing the food and helping take care of these boys, and they need nurturing and love. It keeps me young. Archie won't allow me to do any of the cleaning or laundry, but I do oversee the tasks to make sure it's done properly."

"He's lucky to have you."

"I'll go upstairs and get Henry for you. I'm pretty sure he'd convinced himself you weren't coming."

"I suspected he felt that way. I hope he'll learn to trust me in time."

"I'm glad he called you, Pastor Ollie. You're a good man."

"Please just call me Ollie," I told her.

I pulled my cup of coffee out of the carrier and took a sip. Suddenly finding myself alone in the kitchen gave me too much time to think. I hoped it didn't take Esther long to coax Henry downstairs, and I also hoped Archie wasn't home because running into him on his turf wouldn't go over well.

Luckily, Henry came downstairs within a few minutes, smiling tentatively at me when I stood up and extended my hand to him in greeting. "Please have a seat." I removed his drink from the carrier and set it down in front of the empty seat across from me. "I brought a dozen muffins, none of which I'll be taking home with me."

"Mind you don't ruin your appetite," Esther said from somewhere nearby.

"Yes, Mrs. G," Henry replied then lowered his voice. "No one messes with the woman who enforces the house rules."

"You bet they don't," Esther said boldly. "Reggie, don't mix your dark work pants with your white clothes. You'll end up with light blue underwear and shirts and tie-dyed socks." By supervising the laundry tasks, she meant teaching the residents how to do it properly themselves.

"No one is going to see my underwear and socks, Mrs. G," Reggie said dryly.

"Not with your negative attitude," she admonished affectionately.

"Yes, ma'am."

"See," Henry said, nodding his head in the direction of where the voices were coming from. I must've missed the door to the laundry room because I was too busy wondering what Archie's office and bedroom looked like.

"Okay," I said after another drink. "You had questions about war, cancer, and serial killers."

"Not really," Henry said then shrugged. "I can see it was a silly comparison. I mean, wars are the result of actions and paths people choose, we could discuss whether cancer is genetic, environmental, or both all day long, and serial killers are psychotic and in a class all their own. Being gay isn't a choice, it isn't environmental, it could be genetic, but it isn't the result of a mental disorder."

"We agree one hundred percent," I told him. "Did you spend a lot of time in church growing up?"

"I did," he said, nodding. "I loved the positive messages of love, hope, and helping people in need. I didn't like the fire and brimstone messages though. If you listened to Preacher Daily, you'd think everyone was forging a blazing path to hell except him and his precious family. I feel bad for his son."

I knew just who he was talking about because Preacher Daily and I had gone numerous rounds over the past few years. It seemed we'd be going another round soon. "Your sympathy lies with his son because...?" I let the sentence hang, hoping he'd pick it up.

"His son is as gay as I am. He was my first boyfriend, although a secret one."

"I see." I suspected as much when I met with the volatile preacher at his church, and his son stepped between us to keep the verbal altercation from becoming a physical one. I had no intention of hitting the preacher and would've called the police had he struck me as he'd threatened to do. His son's hands seemed to linger on my biceps longer than was required after his father backed down.

"Geoff is a good guy, but he'll never be free as long as his family is in the picture."

"You've stayed friends?"

"We have, even after I told him I was HIV positive."

"Did you think there was a chance he was positive also?" I asked.

"No," Henry said, shaking his head. "I just needed to hear a friendly voice to silence the hateful ones I'd heard. That's why I decided to call you."

"Geoff gave you my number?" I asked.

"No, I did."

I pivoted in my chair and found Archie leaning in the doorway. He wore gray sweatpants low on his narrow hips, a T-shirt with a unicorn on the front, and nothing on his feet. I'd never found bare feet sexy until then. Archie watched me with an unreadable expression in his nearly iridescent, green eyes.

"Hello, Pastor Ollie," he said coolly.

Chapter Four

Archie

HE WAS MORE BEAUTIFUL THAN ANY MAN HAD A RIGHT TO BE, AND I wasn't referring to his outer beauty. His earnest eyes, warm heart, and yearning to help others made him shine as bright as the sun and just as painful to look at without sunglasses. His lightness was a beacon, pulling me toward him. Fuck, I didn't know how much I'd gotten used to his presence until it was gone. He took my words to heart and had stayed away. I should've been happy, but I was miserable. I missed his smoldering eyes and swarthy looks. He made me feel…cherished, but I didn't realize it until I'd pushed him away. It had been a long time since a man, or anyone for that matter, made me feel so wanted.

The biggest problem was my fantasies of Ollie didn't disappear with him. It seemed like his absence made them grow stronger, and my horny brain got more inventive. My need to see him, and be seen by him, grew to ridiculous heights. I tried inquiring about him without being too obvious, but Milo had little to say about Ollie. I doubted the pastor had told Milo about the way I treated him, so I suspected Milo was doing what he could to protect Ollie from mean ole me. I did learn from the other fellas in their little group they'd formed a bowling team in the Queen City Rogues Bowling League. I wouldn't label any of the men rogues, but I couldn't deny the way Ollie used to look at me was roguish. Of course, later that night, I'd dreamt of Ollie dressed as a pirate who plundered my body and was plundered by me in return.

I was almost desperate enough to form a bowling team of my own just so I'd have an excuse to see him, but the opportunity came to me when sweet Henry unburdened his broken heart to me that morning. Just because I no longer believed didn't mean I wanted to deny others their beliefs. Henry was lost and hurt about so many things—losing his family, friends, and his faith. Faith was a powerful thing and having it ripped away suddenly felt like having a limb severed without warning and left you feeling just as bloody and battered.

Faith didn't have to be all about religion either. There was faith in the universe, our friends and family, not to mention the faith we had in ourselves. Losing one was painful, losing all was catastrophic, and I worried Henry was on the verge of losing all hope and giving up. Ryan's Place worked with several counselors in the city, but I instinctively knew he needed someone spiritual to talk with who might be able to restore a little of his faith. I honestly wasn't thinking of myself and my desire to see Ollie again when I gave Henry his number. I wasn't sure Henry would even call Ollie, let alone invite him here, but there he sat in my kitchen, shining brighter than the sun and looking at me with wide, hungry eyes which roamed my body from head to toe.

He swallowed hard then cleared his throat. "Hello, Archie." Where my voice sounded formal and indifferent, his sounded warm, inviting, and more familiar than it should have. It folded around me like a warm blanket on a chilly winter day. His gaze, so full of longing and need, flickered like flames of lust better and brighter than any fire in a fireplace. Why, oh why, did he, of all people, have this kind of effect on me? I felt drunk at the sight of him because Oliver Knight was more potent than any hot toddy my mammy ever snuck me when my parents weren't looking.

"I didn't mean to interrupt you; I just wanted to pop in and say hello," I said, needing to put some distance between us again.

"This is your home, so I'd hardly say you're intruding," Ollie pointed out.

"All the same, I'll let you guys get back to it. Take care, Ollie."

I meant for that to be it when I returned to my office, but I left the door open while I returned to work which I never did. I could hear Ollie's soft, melodic voice but couldn't pick out the individual words he spoke to Henry. I found his voice both calming and distracting since I should've been putting third-quarter figures together for my accountant instead of straining to hear what Ollie said to Henry. To give the government less reason to scrutinize my non-profit organization, I had someone else do my taxes. It galled me to have to pay someone to do something I was fully qualified to do on my own as a practicing, freelance CPA, but it was the right thing for Ryan's Place. At one point, I heard Henry break down and cry followed by a chair scooting against the tile floor. I pictured Ollie kneeling beside Henry, offering him comfort through his tears while his shattered heart bled.

Jesus. Since when did I become so damn poetic? I sounded like I should be wearing a velvet smoking jacket and puffing on a pipe in between doling out pearls of wisdom cultivated over many decades. I had to fight the urge to creep out of my office and tiptoe down the hall so I could hear what exactly Ollie said to Henry. I mean, I could ask Henry later, but I wanted to be a fly on the wall to watch the way Ollie worked with people.

Esther suddenly filled the open doorway, watching me through knowing eyes. "Wishing and hoping gets you jack shit, Archie."

"I don't know what you're talking about, Mrs. G."

"I know a bullshitter when I see one, and right now, my bullshit meter is off the charts. If you want something in this life, then you go after it. Waiting for life to happen to you is a waste of precious time. Let me tell you," she pointed her long, bony finger at me, "I have no regrets. I never waited for someone to tell me what I could or couldn't do based on my gender. I went to college when people said I couldn't.

I married the man I loved even though everyone told me we were too young and stupid. I had fifty-two beautiful years with my man before God called him home. We didn't have the family we dreamed of for so long, but we had each other, and it was more than enough. Who will you have, Archie? I don't know why you deny yourself opportunities to live life to the fullest, but it reeks of self-punishment. Get over it before you find yourself old and alone like me but without beautiful memories of the man you loved to keep you warm at night."

Esther turned and walked away as fast and as quietly as she arrived, leaving me to stare at the empty doorway in stunned silence. I heard Henry and Ollie's voices getting louder and closer which meant they'd wrapped up their meeting and were heading down the hallway to the front door.

"Thank you so much for meeting with me, Ollie. I can't say the hurt and betrayal are gone, but I do feel so much better."

"I'm happy I could help you, and I hope you won't hesitate to reach out to me again should the need arise." I had needs arising. "My sermon on Sunday will be about honoring the chosen family. I'd love it if you could make it to the service, but I understand if you're not ready yet or have trouble finding transportation. I record my sermons for podcasts in hope to reach LGBTQ+ members all around the world who need reminders they're loved or wish to stay connected to God in a way that's safe and healthy for them." Ollie rattled off his website and how Henry could download his podcasts for free.

When they reached my open door, Ollie jerked to a stop and locked eyes on me. Henry stopped too; his gaze bouncing between us. He said something about heading up to his room, but neither of us acknowledged his remark before he left us alone.

Ollie took a deep breath and released it slowly then he entered my private domain, eyes searching the room for…what? Secrets? Answers to what made me tick? "I didn't realize the address Henry gave me was to Ryan's Place," he said when his gaze met mine once more. "I wouldn't have shown up here without warning if I'd known."

"You wouldn't have shown up here at all," I corrected.

"You're right. I would've asked Henry to meet me somewhere else."

"I hate that you feel unwelcome here," I admitted. "It was never my intent."

"No?" Ollie asked, raising a brow. "You made it perfectly clear you didn't want to see me."

"I know what I said, Ollie." The truth was, I didn't expect him to listen. I mean, I knew he'd stop pursuing me, but I didn't think he'd really disappear altogether. "How have you been?"

He looked shocked I'd asked. "Um, I've stayed busy, but things are going well."

"They're about to get busier from what I hear."

"I'm not sure I know what you mean."

Did he think I meant his dating life? Had he met someone? "Isn't there a bowling league starting tonight?" I prompted.

"Oh. Oh yeah. I've been looking forward to it." He rubbed the back of his neck like he was nervous or something. Maybe he just wasn't sure how to act around me, but who could blame him. "Do you bowl?"

"Oh, hell no," I said emphatically. "I do many things well, but bowling isn't one of them."

"I bet." A slight blush slowly spread across his face, letting me know he wasn't thinking about my bowling skills. I couldn't resist temptation.

"You bet I suck at bowling or that I suck well?"

He shuffled his feet and broke eye contact. "I'd never insult any of your...um...skills."

"Are you any good?" I asked, discreetly adjusting the erection tenting my sweatpants. I was so grateful I had a desk between us.

Ollie's head snapped up, and his dark eyes blazed. "Are we talking about bowling still? Wait! Don't answer because I'm sure this conversation will lead us somewhere you don't want it to go." I was thrilled to know *he* still wanted to go there with me.

"Like a prop closet?" I suggested.

"Or maybe just a closed office." He gestured to the door like Vanna White did the big puzzle board on *Wheel of Fortune*. "Why don't you come and see for yourself how good I am? And yes, in this particular instance, I am talking about my bowling skills. We'll be at Queen City Lanes tonight from eight to eleven."

"Oliver, I don't know. I don't like to leave the house unattended…"

"I can stay," Esther said from the hallway. "I don't mind."

"You stay late on Wednesday nights so I can emcee the drag revue," I pointed out to her.

"Ollie, we're not children who need constant supervision," Reggie said from behind Esther, wearing white powder all down the front of his navy blue T-shirt. I'd overheard Esther giving him lessons on using the washing machine, and it looked like Reggie might've lost the battle in *Man Vs. Machine: Transition Home Edition*.

"What do you have to lose?" Ollie asked innocently. Fuck, I had everything to lose if I couldn't keep my hands off the good pastor.

"Not a damn thing," Esther added before guiding Reggie down the hallway.

"So, will I see you there tonight?"

"I don't know, Ollie. I have so many things I should be doing. I need to place our weekly food order and put third-quarter figures together for my accountant, and—"

"Wash your hair?" Ollie said, offering another excuse I could use. "I promise to be good."

"Define good."

"I'll try not to let on I'm imagining what you look like naked."

"Ollie…" My dick throbbed.

"I'll keep my hands to myself," he promised.

"It's starting to sound like a very dull night."

"Well, there are other parts of me I can share with you if you'd like me to liven up your evening."

"Ollie, shouldn't you be preaching about the sins of the flesh or something?"

"I'm not that kind of pastor."

"What kind of pastor are you then?"

"One who revels in the *pleasures* of the flesh."

"I won't make promises I can't keep," I told Ollie.

"Nor will I."

"I meant I can't say for sure I'll be there."

Ollie smiled serenely. "Think about it. That's all I ask."

"That I promise to do."

"I'll see you later," Oliver said.

"Weren't you just listening, Golden Boy?"

"Yes, but I wasn't referring to the bowling alley, Archie. I was talking about my dreams."

"Oh," I said breathlessly.

Ollie offered a playful wink then left me staring after him with a pounding heart and throbbing cock. One would need to be dealt with before the other would return to normal, but I didn't have time for a quick jerk-off session because I did have more than a dozen pressing things on my to-do list.

"Easy there, big fella," I said, looking down at my crotch. "Good things come to cocks who wait."

It wasn't my first time walking into a bowling alley, but it was the first time I showed up on a league night. I don't know what I was expecting, but it certainly wasn't what I found when I strolled through the alley looking for Ollie's team. There was trash talking going on between the lanes, and each team wore customized shirts with their team name embroidered on the back with a logo and their first names stitched on the front. The color and style of shirts varied from bold and brash to ugly and boring.

Ollie's team was easy to spot due to Andy's enormous height. Their shirts were a silky black button-up with the name Broken Halos embroidered on the back in gold with a crooked halo hanging over the "o" in halo. I had no doubt Ollie came up with the team name and design. I had to admit it was adorable, but not more adorable than the pastor who filled it out so nicely. The silk shirt draped over his shoulders and caressed his pecs. The hem of it ended above the curve of his denim-covered ass. I should've turned around and left as soon as my mouth started watering, except Ollie turned just then and spotted me. The smile spreading across his face was equal parts welcoming and wolfish and too fucking hard to resist.

"Don't get the wrong idea, Golden Boy," I said in greeting. "I'm just here to offer Milo cuddles when he makes a fool of himself."

The remark got a snort out of Ollie, an eye roll from Andy, and knee-slapping laughs out of the Frat Boys, as Milo called them. Milo himself just looked at me with disappointment for a few seconds before he crooked his finger for me to follow him. He only went far enough to get us out of earshot which wasn't hard to do since there was more noise inside this bowling alley than the last Pride parade I attended in NYC.

"What are you doing here?" Milo asked firmly. "Don't give me any bullshit about supporting me and my pitiful bowling because I'm most likely the best bowler in this building."

"Milo, come now," I said, smiling sweetly at him. "I love your confidence, but there are times it's misplaced."

"I guess you'll watch and see won't you," he said cheekily. "Don't fuck Ollie over, Archie. He's missed you like fucking crazy this past month, but he'd eventually get over his attraction to you."

"He's missed me, huh?"

"You have keen vision, so don't pretend you didn't see how he lit up just now."

"I didn't miss it," I admitted, but I had missed him.

"Are you going to pretend you didn't light up inside when you saw him too?"

That was much harder to admit, so I only shook my head slightly. "Why are you so adamant about this?"

"I feel responsible because I introduced you not knowing you'd freak out when you found out he was a pastor."

"I didn't freak out," I protested, but it sounded weak.

"You bolted so fast sparks were coming from your stiletto boots."

"You're so dramatic," I said, rolling my eyes.

"I learned from the best," Milo countered, his eyes softening with fond memories. "I love you, Arch."

"I love you too, Milo."

"I also love Ollie, and I don't want to see confusion or hurt in his eyes when you reject him." Again, he left unsaid.

"I don't think I can give Ollie what he wants from me."

"Have you even asked what he wants from you? I mean beyond the obvious physical attraction." I shook my head. "Then you're making assumptions, and you know what happens when we do that."

"We make asses of ourselves."

"And maybe ruin something beautiful before it has a chance to start," Milo said. He leaned forward and kissed my cheek. "You deserve this, Arch. Take a chance."

Milo returned to the team, leaving me standing there to contemplate what he'd said. He was right even if I didn't want to hear it. I straightened my shoulders and approached the team again. They'd all gathered around Ollie to talk strategy rather than trash talk the team they were competing against that night. They all glanced up at me with varied expressions. I only had eyes for Ollie though.

"First round of sodas is on me. What are you fellas having?"

Chapter Five

Ollie

"Wow, Ollie. I've never seen you bowl like this," Brent said not-so-subtly. "You almost scored as high as Milo. I wonder what the difference could be."

I shrugged casually, feeling everyone's eyes on me, especially the person I knew was responsible for the change. I'd felt Archie's eyes on me every second of the game. I wanted to impress him and make him want me as much as I wanted him. I had channeled Milo's attitude and confidence when I approached the lane each turn and had amazing results. We trounced our knuckle-dragging, Neanderthal opponents. "Just feeling it tonight."

"Yeah, I bet," Adam added then snickered, earning a jab from Tyler.

"So, who wants to get a bite to eat?" Andy asked. "I'm starved."

"You're always hungry," Keeton said. "I don't know where you put it."

"He burns the calories off as quickly as he consumes them," Milo casually said. "It's always been that way. He was as skinny as a beanpole until his senior year of high school. He finally put on some weight and muscle." Milo looked his boyfriend up and down wolfishly. "And just kept adding on the muscle."

A few months ago, seeing the two men together and so in love would've hurt me so damn bad. I'd allowed myself to get too close to Andy and thought I was in love with him. It turned out I loved Andy but was only in love with the idea of him. I had felt an occasional spark of jealousy when he and Milo started seeing each other again. They had a long history, and it was obvious they belonged together. My jealousy had more to do with not finding that kind of love match for myself rather than pining after Andy. It took a while for me to come around to Milo, but he became one of my closest friends. He'd grown even more attentive and protective once Archie started acting weird around me. I didn't like seeing the tension between the two friends, but I was grateful to have Milo as my champion.

"Yeah, I bet he burns off the calories," Adam said, earning a slap in the back of the head from Tyler and an eye roll from Andy.

"What's gotten into you?" Brent asked Adam. "You're acting more juvenile than usual."

"And you're suddenly the voice of maturity and growth?" Adam asked Brent, scoffing at the notion. "I seem to recall—"

"Fellas," Keeton said, interrupting them. "Can we not do this to-night? Let's go grab burgers, fries, and shakes and enjoy our victory instead of bickering like a bunch of little school kids."

We all stared at Keeton in stunned silence. He was usually the one instigating the trouble.

Brent was the first to recover and looped his arm around Keeton and pulled him into him. "You got it, kid."

Keeton squirmed out of his grasp, red-faced but obviously not from anger. "I'm not a kid." I almost expected him to say something like "and you should know," but he didn't.

Keeton and Brent returned their balls, shoes, and gloves to their custom bowling bags and the rest of us followed their leads. I was a little slower than the rest, knowing Archie most likely wasn't joining us, and I wasn't ready to say goodnight, or possibly goodbye, yet.

I felt him approach before I saw him or heard him speak. It

38

showed how attuned I was to him. "Hey, Ollie," he said softly, sounding almost unsure of himself. "What do you say about pizza instead of burgers? I know a hole in the wall kind of place that makes the best pizza outside of New York."

I glanced up and noticed everyone was gone besides the two of us. "It sounds amazing, Archie." I was more excited about having his undivided attention than the food. Well, I assumed we weren't meeting up with some friends.

"Why don't you ride with me rather than both of us trying to find decent parking downtown? I'll bring you back after we eat."

"Sounds fair."

I was so excited to be in a small, closed-in place with him until he put his car in drive and pressed his foot down on the accelerator. He drove like he was on the set of *The Fast and The Furious: Queen City Drift*.

"Are you worried they'll sell out of pizza?" I asked after I managed to unclench my teeth. "Is there a late night special you don't want to miss?"

Archie threw his head back and laughed, pulling my attention to him. I loved his long neck and dreamed of kissing and licking it then sucking his Adam's apple until he was—

Honk! Honk! Honk! "Green means go, asshole!" Archie yelled. I jerked my head back to look out the windshield and saw that the car in front of us was ignoring the green arrow. *Honk! Honk! Honk!* "What the fuck is this guy doing? Texting? Jerking off?"

Suddenly, I saw the passenger's head pop up from where they were stretched across the front seat. I didn't want to make gender assumptions based on the existence of a ponytail, but I had zero doubt about the activities they were engaged in. If I had been confused, the driver wrapping his fist in his or her ponytail and urging them to return their head to his lap would've enlightened me.

"I get he has needs, but this isn't the place." Archie laid on the horn again just as the green arrowed turned yellow. The passenger held up their hand and flipped him off before stretching out over the seat to continue sucking off the driver. By the time the arrow turned red, there was no doubt about their activities and no attempt to keep the head bobbing beneath the seat line.

"I should call the cops and report them," Archie said vehemently.

I wanted to be disgusted but being alone in the dark vehicle with the smell of Archie's cologne or aftershave washing over me made me wish I could lean over and suck him into my mouth. I no longer saw a ponytailed passenger giving head to the driver in front of us. I saw me stretched out over the console, taking his cock deep inside my mouth. I wasn't sure how I knew, but I'd bet big money Archie's cock was uncut and delicious. I imagined Archie's head thrashing against his headrest as I sucked him better than anyone ever had before. His hand would be in my hair, guiding me at the pace he wanted.

A desperate growl pulled me out of my fantasy. "Ollie, don't look at me like that."

I jerked my gaze away from his crotch to look into a gaze that looked as wild and desperate as I felt. Archie briefly closed his eyes then shook his head before returning his attention to the car in front of us. He resumed his honking as had the other cars behind us. There was too much traffic in the other lane to attempt going out and around the cock sucker and cock suckee. Suddenly, a new sound joined the mix, and it was the shrill sound of a police siren. The car in front of us became washed in flashing lights as a cop car approached the intersection.

The passenger jerked to a sitting position and put on their seatbelt, but it was too late. The officer had already seen them. The cop on the passenger side got out of the cruiser and approached the vehicle as the driver appeared to be hauling up his pants. The cop made a short, blunt gesture for the car to turn the corner and meet them in the parking lot of a closed donut shop.

I wondered if my outer appearance betrayed how rattled the experience left me. The thought of sex in a car was something I was normally repulsed by because it was a reminder of the person I used to be. Yet, I somehow knew sex with Archie would never be cold and transactional. We would be together because we both craved each other's touch and the mutual joy we could bring one another. Sex with Archie would never be a means to an end.

"Thank goodness," Archie said. "I am *hungry*." The way he said the word made me wonder if he hungered for the pizza or what I fantasized about doing to him. Whatever the reason, I expected him to continue his crazy, erratic driving and sharp turns, but he slowed it down.

Mamma Maria's was the hole-in-the-wall Archie had described, but it was quaint, clean, and smelled incredible when we walked in. Even better, we were the only ones inside that late at night.

"Are you sure they're still open?" I asked.

"I'm positive," he said with a quirked smile then started walking to a corner table in the back of the restaurant even though the sign asked patrons to wait to be seated.

"What's so funny?" I asked, rushing to catch up to him.

"Not funny, Ollie." Archie shook his head like he wasn't going to say anything else, but he surprised me once we were seated across from each other with nowhere to look but in one another's eyes. "Are you aware you made this needy little groan when you walked through the door?" I shook my head and felt a hot flush creeping up my neck. "I didn't think so. You either didn't realize how hungry you were until you walked in or you've never smelled good pizza."

"Probably both."

"You want it so bad you're practically salivating," Archie told me. The dark look in his eyes said he wasn't talking about pizza any longer.

"I do." And neither was I.

"It doesn't stop you from thinking about others first, no matter how hungry you are." His statement easily applied to both of my hungers. I didn't expect the restaurant employees to stick around be-yond closing time to feed me. As for Archie, hell yes, I wanted him, but not at the risk of his happiness and not if he would resent me in the morning. "Trust me, Ollie. We're welcome here."

"How can you be so certain? I'm not even sure they know we're here?"

"They know." I started to ask how he knew, but a short, round woman with the sweetest smile and Archie's green eyes came out of the kitchen and headed toward our table. She looked familiar to me, but I couldn't place from where I recognized her. I blamed Archie's driving and his sexiness for my inability to think. "A mother always knows."

"My baby," she said when she arrived at our table.

Archie rose to his feet swiftly and hugged the woman. "Hi, Mamma."

"Who's this handsome man you brought to meet Mamma?"

"Mamma," Archie said then blushed. "I didn't bring him here to meet Mamma; I brought him here to feed him. He's never had your pizza before, and we both know that's a crime."

"Punishable by death," she said dramatically when he finally released his grip on her. "What is your name, beautiful boy? I'm Maria White, but most people call me Mamma or Mamma Maria."

I slid out of the booth and stood before her, desperate to make a good impression, although I didn't know why. Well, I knew why but knew better than to hope anything would come of this night. "Oliver Knight," I said warmly, extending my hand.

"I've heard of you," she said, hugging me instead of shaking my hand, which meant my hand got pinned awkwardly between us. I was just grateful I hadn't grabbed her boob by accident. "You're the pastor who organizes the basketball leagues for troubled youth each year. Those kids love you."

"That's me," I said, happy she'd heard good things about me. "I'm the pastor at Grace Fellowship Church."

"I didn't know you and my son were friends." She whipped her head around and pinned Archie with a no-nonsense look. "Why didn't you tell me?" Archie opened his mouth to answer, but no words came out.

"It's a new development, Mrs. White. We have mutual friends who introduced us."

"Please call me Mamma or Maria," she reminded me then looked at Archie. "Which friends?" she asked her son. "I'd like to treat them to a free pizza or calzone."

I moaned a little when she mentioned the calzone. "Why are you starving your friends?" she asked, gesturing to me. "Sit, sit," she instructed us. "My boy loves a calzone too. Is that what you'd like?"

"It sounds delightful, but I shouldn't eat an entire one by myself. Do you want to share one with me?" I asked Archie.

"I'm fine with sharing," he replied. "I usually get sausage and green peppers in mine."

"Sound delicious to me."

"One calzone and two side salads with creamy Parmesan dressing and breadsticks coming right up," she said on her way back to the kitchen.

"She must not have understood you wanted to share the calzone because you aren't very hungry." He shook his head and smiled wryly. "Subtlety isn't Mamma's specialty."

"She's perfect the way she is," I told him then leaned forward and dropped my voice. "I'm very hungry, Archie. I'm starving."

"Ollie, please…" His words died, and in his eyes, I saw he didn't want me to stop. He might tomorrow though, and I couldn't risk feeling the sting of his rejection again, so I had to do a better job of pretending I didn't want more than he could give.

"Relax, Archie," I said softly. "I know your stance. I was talking about food. I wanted to split the calzone with you because I don't need anything too heavy on my stomach before I go to bed."

Maria returned to our table with a large glass of ice-cold milk she set down in front of Archie. "I forgot to ask what you'll be drinking."

"That glass of milk looks perfect."

"Great." Maria slid Archie's glass across the table to me, eliciting a shocked gasp from her son. "Oh, you stop. I'll be right back with the salads, breadsticks, and your glass of milk."

"Thanks, Mamma." There was a softness in his eyes and a reverence in his tone when he talked to his mother. It hit me low in the gut. There was nothing more beautiful to me than a person who loved and cherished their family.

When Archie returned his gaze to mine, I had to look away. I didn't want him to see the naked desire I felt to belong to someone. It wouldn't end well for whatever was blossoming between us.

"I gotta say, Ollie. I'm dying to know what makes you tick."

"What do you mean?" I was confused because I was pretty much an open book.

"I respect your love for God and your desire to help people. Hell, I'm grateful Henry could call on you today."

"Henry can call on me any day," I told him. Archie narrowed his eyes as if he misunderstood my words. "Not in a romantic way."

"But you have romantic cravings?" What the hell did he think our fooling around in the prop closet was all about?

"Romantic and sexual," I replied because they weren't the same thing. "Just not for Henry. Him, I want to help spiritually."

"But with me…" he said, steering me into a confession I wasn't ready to give him.

"I want what you're willing to give me, Archie." I offered a soft, friendly smile. "If all we can ever be is friends, it will be enough for me. The truth is, I've been disappointed by men who didn't want the same things as me or couldn't see past my clergy collar. Your reticence isn't new." It just hurt more, but that was my problem, not his.

"Ollie…"

Maria had the worst timing, or the most impeccable timing depending on what Archie said next. "Here you go, boys," she said, setting down our salads and a basket of breadsticks to share along with his glass of milk.

"Thanks, Mamma," we both said at the same time, earning a sappy smile from her. I thought she might be getting the wrong idea about us. Then I knew it was the case when she said, "Too bad you guys didn't order a plate of spaghetti to share like *Lady and the Tramp.*"

"Mamma," Archie said in a low tone, pleading for her to stop talking and give us privacy.

"Oh, all right," she said, waving her hand in the air. "I can tell you don't want me telling Ollie it's your favorite Disney movie." She smiled mischievously then added, "He had a hard time figuring out if he wanted to be the lady or the tramp growing up."

I nearly choked on my drink of milk. Maria pounded on my back then rubbed it in small circles. "I'm all better now," I told her.

"I'll leave you boys alone. Your calzone will be out in just a few minutes."

"Where were we?" Archie asked when we were alone once more.

"You'd just said 'Ollie' with this sad voice and dramatic pause. I think you were about to deliver some bad news."

Archie looked down at the table for a few seconds as if he was trying to recall what he was about to say, or maybe choose his words better. Whatever the reason, he was more composed when his green gaze met mine again. "Ollie…" Same serious tone, same dramatic pause.

Oh boy.

Chapter Six

Archie

I F EYES WERE THE WINDOWS TO OUR SOULS, I WISHED LIKE HELL OLLIE would lower the shades because seeing him brace himself for my rejection was painful. I don't mean a dull ache either; I'm talking my gut burned and twisted like I'd swallowed battery acid. As flattered as I was by Ollie's attraction to me, I could tell his pain went much deeper and existed a lot longer than I've known him. So, even though I was aware I didn't shoulder the burden of his despair alone, it did nothing to ease the acid burning me alive from the inside out.

"Here we go, boys," Mamma said, busting her way through the swinging door with a smile for me that said, "don't fuck this up."

I should never have brought Ollie here, but it just felt right until my mom mistook my actions as bringing home a boy to get her approval. Damn, I'm pretty sure we both would have come out of the evening feeling better if I'd just found a secluded parking lot for him to blow me while I jerked him off. We both got so worked up after watching the silhouette of the guy getting worked over by his lover. Some might say a passionate exchange would've confused Ollie more than I already had but bringing him home to Mamma wasn't any clearer. First, I gave his number to Henry, then, I show up at the bowling alley to watch him bowl. He might not have been my only friend on the team, but he was the one I couldn't look away from.

Everyone knew it, including him. I could've left and told him I'd see him later, but I invited him for pizza at my mother's restaurant instead. Talk about giving a man mixed signals.

"Is there anything else I can get you?" Mamma asked, pulling my eyes away from Ollie's somber ones and up to hers which were identical to mine in color and shape and all-knowing. I didn't see recrimination in her eyes; I saw encouragement to take a fucking chance again.

"I'm good, Mamma. How about you, Ollie?" I softly asked when I looked back at him.

He shook his head. Mamma had never been one to withhold affection, and she wasn't about to start then, even if Ollie was a virtual stranger to her. She gently cupped his chin and dropped a kiss on top of his head. "You let me know if that changes, love."

Ollie's expression changed from sorrowful to content at the gentle, brief touch. It moved me more than any words he could speak, and I was grateful he hadn't pulled the shades down over his windows after all. It turned out I wanted to know his story. Mamma removed her hand and returned to the kitchen, leaving us alone once more. Ollie blinked and the yearning I saw moments before was gone, and he was back to bracing himself for bad news.

"Do you mind if we eat first?" He looked down at the calzone between us. "I don't know. There looks to be at least two thousand calories there, so maybe you should drop the hammer and kill my appetite."

I snorted. "I'm not dropping the hammer on you, Ollie."

"You've had a change of heart then," he said stubbornly. "I'm good at reading people, and your expression said you were about to let me down easy."

"Wrong," I said just as stubbornly. "It was more of like I didn't know how to proceed because I'm not sure I can be just your friend, and a relationship isn't something I want."

"With me?"

I wanted to reach across the table and hold both of his hands, but I made tight fists beneath the table to keep from doing it. "With anyone." He released a long sigh and looked slightly mollified by my answer. "I want to try being friends with you, Ollie. You bring something into my life that I crave." A dark eyebrow shot up in silent question. "You give me lightness, Golden Boy. I didn't know how much darkness and negativity had permeated my soul until you showed up and lit up my world."

"I want to light up your world." He blushed a bright pink which I found so fucking adorable. "I didn't mean that to come out sounding suggestive."

"Anything you say through those gorgeous lips is going to sound suggestive."

Ollie ran his fingers over his lips, making me want to do the same. "You think my lips are gorgeous?" God, why did he have to sound so uncertain? He was so much easier to resist when he behaved boldly and shamelessly.

"I wouldn't have said so if I didn't think it," I replied. "If we're going to be friends, you need to accept I will not say things I don't mean. I won't blow sunshine up your ass to make you feel better. If you ask me if your ass looks big in something you're wearing, I will give you an honest answer." After I fantasize about stripping him naked first.

"Do these jeans make my butt look big?" And just like that, I saw myself kneeling in front of Ollie stripping the denim down his lean legs.

"No, they don't." My voice sounded raw and strained.

"Good to know." Ollie took a big gulp of milk. "I appreciate your honesty and candor. Too many people are afraid to be themselves in my presence." He didn't give me a pointed look that suggested I was one of them, even though it was true. I wanted to think we were starting fresh.

"Let's eat this beast of a calzone so I can take my friend back to his car since it's getting late and he has many souls to save."

Ollie shot me a wry smile then we tucked into our calzone, both of us moaning with the first bite of savory sauce, melted cheese, sausage, and peppers. Ollie licked sauce and cheese from the corner of his lips then went back in for another bite.

"Amazing, isn't it?" I asked.

Ollie looked up just as I licked my lips. He paused mid-chew as lust danced in his eyes and turned his cheeks red. He blinked a few times then continued his chewing. "It's the best I've ever had."

I had so many comebacks but kept them to myself and resumed eating. The calzone was so big we couldn't eat it all. Mamma boxed it up so Ollie could take it home with him along with the breadsticks we didn't touch. He tried to pay for our dinner, but she wouldn't hear of it. Instead, she hugged him tight and told him to stop in and see her anytime.

"I live upstairs if you happen to show up when I'm not around. I'd love to get to know you better." I wanted to tell her she was barking up the wrong tree but saw the stubborn set to her jaw when I leaned in to kiss her cheek goodbye. She would have to learn for herself Ollie wasn't meant to be mine in the way she wanted.

After scaring him to death with my driving skills earlier, I took it much slower to prove I did know how to keep all four tires on the ground. There were many cars still in the parking lot when we returned to the bowling alley, so the opening night of the bowling league must've run later than I imagined. I pulled to a stop behind Ollie's sensible dark sedan and pasted a friendly smile on my face. I hoped it masked how badly I wanted to lean forward and kiss his lips once more. Were they as soft as I remembered? Would his breath hitch sexily in his throat?

"Thanks, Archie. I had a fun time."

"Don't be a stranger, Ollie. I've missed seeing you around."

He smiled crookedly when he heard the sincerity in my voice. "I've missed you too, Arch."

Ollie got out of the car and closed the door, but instead of driving off, I put my car in park and followed him. He spun around when he heard my car door shut. "Did you forget—"

"Yeah, I did." I pulled him into my arms and hugged him tightly. "Friends hug when they say goodbye." Friends didn't get an erection, but maybe he wouldn't notice mine straining against my jeans. I knew it wasn't the case when I felt him harden in response. I held him tight enough to feel a delicious shiver work its way through him, and my body reacted in kind. "Ollie," I whispered, unable to keep the want and need from my voice. He tried to pull back, but I kept a strong grip. I couldn't let him look into my eyes until I could mask all the things he made me feel other than friendship. "Don't move yet."

"I'm not going anywhere, Arch."

I ran my nose along the side of his neck, hoping my brain would remember the way he smelled. His scent was both familiar and foreign to me, a mixture of sexy and clean. It was like he'd tried to cover up his earthy sexiness with soap too pure to get the job done. Ollie's hands fisted into my shirt as he traced his nose along my neck, sending jolts of lust and making my flesh pebble in his wake. We weren't off to a great start at keeping things in the friend zone.

"Friends sniff each other's necks," Ollie said, reading my mind. "Be glad we're not pretending to be dogs. I'd be sniffing something else."

I couldn't keep from groaning. Smelling wasn't the activity I imagined when I thought of Ollie's face pressed between my ass cheeks. I could almost feel the wet press of his tongue teasing my puckered hole.

I pulled back then and looked into his eyes. "Is that what we're doing, Ollie? Are we pretending to be friends?"

"I think we're grappling with feelings much stronger than either of us are willing to accept right now and trying to find a way to be in each other's lives that doesn't feel threatening. I want to be a safe place for you to land, Archie, not make your life more complicated. If this is too much for you—" I cut his words off with a chaste kiss on his lush mouth.

"Friends kiss sometimes," I whispered while fighting the urge to do things that would forever obliterate the friend zone for us.

"What other things do friends do together?" Ollie asked breathily.

I opened my mouth to respond we could do all the things together, but a blaring horn saved me, and before I could turn around, it was honking again. *Honk. Honk. Honk.* I whipped my head around and couldn't believe my eyes. "It can't be." It was the same boxy, silver car with rusted-out wheel fenders.

"Even if you don't believe in God, you must believe in Karma," Ollie said as we both stared at the same son of a bitch that sat through a green light so he could get a blow job. "I guess he doesn't like being blocked any more than we did."

"Get in your car, Golden Boy. I'll take care of this."

"And leave you to take him on by yourself?"

About that time, the passenger window rolled down, and the driver leaned over as far as he could. "Move your stupid ass." *Honk. Honk. Honk.*

"What happened to your girlfriend?" I asked, guessing about the gender. "Did she go home to gargle the nasty taste of you out of her mouth?" Ollie snorted beside me. The driver's eyes widened. "That's right, asshole. I was one of the cars stuck behind you at the intersection. I have a message for you, little boy. Real men can multitask. We fornicate *while* driving. Now you stay right where you are and shut the fuck up while I say goodnight to my fella." *My fella? Oh fuck.*

The driver returned to his seat and rolled up his window. I returned all my focus to Ollie and saw that his lips trembled with laughter. "You think his grandma knows what he gets up to in her Oldsmobile?" he asked.

"Probably not."

"You going to show him how real men act?" Ollie challenged.

I cupped his face with both hands and slowly closed the gap between us. "I feel like we need to teach him a lesson." I took my time pressing my mouth against Ollie's pliant and eager lips. I left my eyes open for a few heartbeats, memorizing the content look on his face, the adorable freckle beneath his right eye, and how long his fan of eyelashes looked. When it got to be too much, I closed my eyes and focused on the kiss so I could teach the punk a lesson. Yeah, right. What happened to being honest? Ollie opened his mouth to breathe, and I licked the underside of his upper lip before sliding my tongue seductively against his. I felt Ollie's pulse racing beneath my thumbs, and his hands tugged on my shirt like he couldn't decide if our kiss was too much or not enough. This was nothing like the frantic kiss in the prop closet; it was hotter and even more devastating.

Ollie pulled away first then stared up into my eyes. "I think you taught the young man a valuable lesson tonight, Archie."

All I did was make myself ache with wanting Oliver Knight, but I nodded my head as I agreed. "You won't be a stranger, will you?"

"After that kiss?" he asked, eyes twinkling with pure mischief.

"Ollie," I said with a sigh.

"I'm teasing, Arch. I'll see you soon."

He gave me a quick kiss then turned and got in his car. *Honk. Honk.* I flipped the driver off as I rounded the hood of my car and pulled open the driver's door. I figuratively kicked my ass all the way across town because there was no way in hell I could go long without tasting Ollie again. I wanted to see him smile, hear his laugh, and most of all I wanted him to start talking dirty to me again. I was certain he felt the same pull I did and hoped he would show up at Queen City Divas, but my heart felt crushed when the night came and went with no signs of Ollie. I expected he would text me at some point because it's what friends did, but two more days passed without a peep from him.

I was driving myself crazy wondering if he'd met someone else, someone who was willing to give Ollie the happily ever after he deserved. My mom didn't bring him up when she called me Friday morning to invite me to bingo that night, but I knew she'd pepper me with questions if I agreed, so I told her I already had plans. "With

Ollie?" she'd asked hopefully, and I had to let her down easy.

"There's nothing between Ollie and me, Mamma." There could've been if I'd only met him halfway.

"I'm sorry, Archie," she said sympathetically. "You know what will cheer you up?"

"Chocolate cheesecake with fresh strawberries and real whipped cream?"

"Bingo night with Mamma. Please come with me."

How could I resist? "What time should I pick you up?"

"Hell no," she said, and I imagined she was shaking her head vigorously. "I'm not riding anywhere with you. I'll meet you at the seniors center at seven o'clock."

I laughed because it reminded me of Ollie's reaction to my driving. "I'll be there, Mamma."

After I hung up, I recalled the happiness Ollie expressed when my mother showed him maternal affection. I wondered if it was something he lacked in life and was responsible for his sorrow. Before I could talk myself out of it, I googled Ollie's name. I looked at the images the search brought up and tried my best to ignore the way my heart raced at seeing his smiling face. I nearly touched the screen the same way I caressed his face just a few days before. It was probably a really big sin to pop wood in my office while staring at Ollie wearing his clergymen's dark clothes and stark white collar, but I couldn't seem to work up a damn or talk my dick down. Both man and beast missed Ollie something fierce.

I returned to the main Google page and clicked on the link to his church's website. His smiling face appeared in a small picture on the upper right corner of the screen. Beneath the photo was a link to his bio. I knew clicking on the link would tell me a lot about Ollie, but I realized I didn't want to find out from any source other than his lips.

I closed my browser and returned to my lengthy to-do list until it was time to get cleaned up and meet my mother at the senior center where she occasionally played bingo. At first, I thought I'd just throw on a T-shirt and a pair of jeans but decided to wear my favorite lacy shirt that Ollie seemed to love so much. Once I had it on, my face looked too pale in my reflection in the mirror, making the circles beneath my eyes stand out more. I put a little foundation and concealer on my face to cover up my nights of sleeplessness and just kept going until I was full-on glam.

"Feeling it or faking it?" Mom asked when I walked up to her outside the senior center.

"Both," I said honestly. "Ready to whip some bingo ass?"

"I'm always ready to whip some ass."

When we walked into the auditorium, my breath snagged in my throat, and I came to an abrupt halt.

"Isn't that Ollie behind the podium?" my mother asked from beside me. "It must be his turn to volunteer for bingo night."

"His turn?"

"The local clergy take turns."

"He's been here before?" I asked.

"Of course."

"You said you recognized him from some youth basketball thing," I said accusingly, feeling the charge in the atmosphere the instant Ollie realized I was in the room.

"I only remembered yesterday that I also knew him from bingo nights. I probably don't attend frequently enough for him to recognize me." Her innocent act didn't fool me, but it was hard to be pissed when I looked up into the most beautiful, soulful eyes I had ever seen. Then I noticed the dark circles beneath his eyes; they matched the ones hiding beneath my makeup. My heart squeezed in my chest. Was I the reason he wasn't sleeping? I mean, part of me said "good" because he was the reason I tossed and turned and couldn't sleep worth a damn, but the biggest part of me wanted to kiss away those shadows of discontent and make him feel better. For once, my physical attraction took a back seat to the emotional connection I felt with Ollie when I crossed the room to speak to him.

Chapter Seven

Ollie

CALLING BINGO NUMBERS ON A FRIDAY EVENING WASN'T MY IDEA OF a good time. I had to really psyche myself up for the abuse the elderly players would lob my way if I didn't do things just right. They were particular about the speech tempo, volume, and cadence of calling numbers. Too fast and they got pissed. Too slow and they got pissed. Too quiet and they got pissed. Too loud and they got pissed. These people were serious about their bingo, and I learned the hard way injecting humor wasn't part of my duties.

The sleepless nights I'd had since parting ways with Archie didn't improve my mood. I'd never met anyone who twisted and knotted my insides the way Archie did. We parted on good terms on Tuesday night, and I knew he would've been fine if I showed up at Queen City Divas on Wednesday or called or texted during the week, but I didn't do any of those things. Why? Archie had taken the first step by showing up at bowling night then took it another step further when he invited me to his mom's pizza joint. Therein lay the crux of the issue. Archie took those steps, but they weren't convincing. It reminded me of the tentative steps babies took when they first learned to walk. Archie acted as if he wanted to take a chance but looked like he was afraid of the fall. I wasn't sure how I could convince him he was safe with me, or even if I should. Why was it up to me to prove anything?

Why shouldn't I demand Archie prove he's not a flake, as his hot and cold behavior sometimes indicated?

Those were just some of the thoughts and questions cycling through my turbulent mind, but not all. Memories of the kisses we shared and images of the things we could have were included in the mix, so I was at a constant state of confusion and arousal. I felt like I was at my wits end and ready to snap beneath the slightest pressure. That's when Archie walked into the community room at the senior center. I felt his presence before I saw him with my own eyes. Our gazes met, and I was unable to look away from his splendor. I saw the moment when his surprise turned to joy before it faded into... What did his frown mean? Was he upset to see me or was it concern causing his brow to furrow? I knew I was about to find out when Archie left his mom's side to briskly walk across the room.

"Ollie, I didn't expect to see you here," Archie said in a neutral tone.

I just stared at him, unable to think or even blink, because he was the most beautiful being I'd ever seen. Whatever he'd done with his makeup made his eyes look bigger, greener, and shinier. I'd never seen eyelashes that long on another person. And his lips... The gloss made them look plumper, and I was dying to know if the shiny substance had a taste. If so, what would the pink gloss taste like? Strawberry? Melon? Cotton candy? How would those luscious lips feel working up and down my cock?

"Um," I finally managed to say in an embarrassing squeak. The lips I couldn't stop staring at spread into a slow smile which finally made me look into Archie's eyes again. I wanted to see if they looked as inviting as his lips. His green gaze expressed the hesitance I was accustomed to seeing from him, but I also saw joy. I didn't know how someone could look both unhappy and happy at the same time, but he somehow pulled it off. Archie raised one perfectly shaped brow and waited for me to say something else. What did he want? An apology? "Are you unhappy to see me?"

"Of course not. What we have here is a failure to communicate." My left eyebrow lifted at the *Cool Hand Luke* reference. Apparently, Archie quoted movie lines when he was angry or nervous. I thought it was adorable. "I thought our parting kiss indicated we were in a good place. I thought you said you'd see me soon. Oh, wow," he said then briefly covered his mouth to hide a smirk. "That sounded really needy and desperate."

To me, it was music to my ears. He apparently had missed me a little to react in such a way. "You sound like you're still trying to figure out what this thing is between us," I said.

"And you're not?" Archie countered.

I shook my head. "I know exactly what I want."

A delicious shiver worked its way through Archie's body. "You have a funny way of showing it."

"I'm here now, and it's only been a few days."

"Us being in the same room is a coincidence, unless you and my mom are working together as a team." I looked over his shoulder and saw his mom smiling broadly as she waved at me.

"I'm not a big believer in coincidence."

"You think us being here on the same night is fate?"

"I've been calling bingo numbers on Friday nights every six weeks for the past three years, and I've never seen you here before tonight. I did recognize your mother but couldn't remember where I'd seen her."

"Mamma doesn't play regularly, and I don't always come with her," Archie explained. "I'm probably only here once or twice a year."

It was obvious Archie needed our run-in to be a mere coincidence, and who was I to try and persuade him otherwise? To do so might set us back to the way things were before our truce.

"Regardless of the how or why, I am glad to see you. I've missed you, Archie."

"You do look rough," Archie said, raking narrowed eyes over my face. "Are you sleeping?"

"Some."

"Eating?"

"Some."

"Are you...." He let his words trail off, but I knew what his ornery glance meant. He wanted to know if I took my dick in my hand while thinking about him.

"I've done a lot of that."

"Ollie," Archie moaned softly.

"You started it."

"Excuse me," Edith Hastings said. "We were supposed to start bingo a minute ago."

"There's my cue," I told Archie, wishing I could pull him into my arms and taste his ornery smile. "Can we talk after bingo is over?" I wanted to reach out and touch him, but I knew it would lead to other things.

"That would be great."

"Any time now, Ollie," Agnes Milgrove said.

Archie winked before he left me alone to deal with the mob of angry seniors. He rejoined his mom, and they took their seats at a table in the back. Maria handed him two bingo cards and an ink dauber before she set several cards in front of herself. I waited to see if she would pull out a lucky charm or something, but she just looked up and offered me an encouraging smile once her cards were situated as she liked them.

Someone cleared their throat impatiently, pulling my attention away from the Whites and onto my duties. I quickly approached the podium and switched on the microphone. "Testing. Testing."

"We can hear you just fine," Mr. Barnsworth said from the table on the far-left side of the room. "Not sure about Mrs. Pedigrew though." The woman in question held up her middle finger in his direction, making Mr. Barnsworth's friends laugh.

"My name is Oliver Knight, and I'd like to welcome you to poker night."

I heard little Maura Hammil snicker before she muttered, "Smart-ass."

"For tonight's game, jokers are wild."

"Cut the bull and get to bingo," Doris Donovan yelled from the middle of the room. "We're old, Ollie. We might not make it through the night, so let us have our fun."

"There's the positive spirit we all love so much, Doris," Hank Adamson grumbled. "No wonder you never remarried." I figured it had more to do with the fact she carried a portion of her deceased husband's ashes in an antique Goody's Headache Powder tin everywhere she went. That definitely didn't invite a fella to pull up a chair and strike up a conversation.

"All right," I said, holding up my hand. "It was a poor joke on my part. I'm sorry. Let's just get started." I made the mistake of glancing in Archie's direction and caught the huge grin on his face. He was having a great time at my expense, and it made me want to retaliate. Those plans would need to wait, of course, because there were over a hundred pissy senior citizens keeping an eye on my every move. Instead of making a crude gesture about what I wanted to do to him, or have done to myself, I flipped on the switch, sending the bingo balls bouncing around the machine like the ones they use to pick lottery numbers. The balls were captured and sucked into the shoot where I'd pull them out one at a time and set them aside until it was time to reload the beast.

"Our first number is B-12 which is both an excellent daily vitamin and a great way to kick off our night."

"Shut up and call the numbers, Ollie," a grouchy, masculine voice said from the back of the room.

"You didn't tell us the prize we're playing for, Ollie," Mrs. Bickel yelled. "Don't tease us and say it's for an Alaskan cruise like the last time. You might be handsome, but you're not a bit funny. I want cash or gift cards, and I don't want to waste bingo cards on something like a crockpot."

"Yeah, Ollie. Pull yourself together, man," someone yelled from the back, but I couldn't tear my eyes away from a laughing Archie to look and see who. "What's wrong with you tonight? You're goofier than usual." I could feel an embarrassed flush creeping up my neck as the object of my distraction rose slowly to his feet and gracefully walked to the podium. The only sound in the place was the whirling of the bingo balls in the machine as all eyes in the room watched Archie approach me behind the podium.

He leaned close until his lips nearly touched my ear then covered the microphone with his hand for extra assurance the seniors wouldn't hear what he had to say. "You're dying out here tonight, Ollie. I've never heard you give a sermon or address your NA group, but I imagined you'd be smoother, more polished. It seems like you're distracted tonight."

I swallowed hard and turned my head to look into his turbulent eyes. "Very," I whispered, grateful the podium hid my growing erection.

"Let me help you with your…um," Archie inhaled slowly as if he could smell how badly I wanted him, "distraction." I nodded, not sure what the hell I was even agreeing to. Archie lowered his hand from the microphone and straightened away from me, taking the smell of vanilla and citrus with him. I expected him to return to his seat, but instead, he picked up the top envelope in the box of prizes. Then he nudged me out of the way just enough for him to have access to the microphone. "The first prize is a handmade quilt donated by Mrs. Fletcher."

I heard some grumbles from around the room and saw Mrs. Fletcher's cheeks turn pink with embarrassment. The ladies seemed much happier, and I couldn't blame them. Mrs. Fletcher had given me one of her quilts for Christmas the previous year, and I loved it.

"Someone will be very lucky to own one of your quilts," I said to the shy but gifted woman.

"B-12 was the first number," Archie reminded them then shot me a playful wink as he placed his hand at the small of my back. "What's the next number?"

I tore my gaze away from his and pulled out the next number in the shoot at the same time as Archie slid his hand lower to cup my right ass cheek. Archie's body was angled so we were both hidden behind the podium. He was free to tease and taunt me without anyone seeing us. I don't know how, but I managed not to react in front of the crowd.

"N-40," I said into the microphone. I was proud my voice hadn't given away that Archie was trailing a long finger over the crack of my ass, making me want to feel it again when there were no clothes between us.

"Bingo!" Mrs. Donhausen yelled. Her dementia had worsened over the past six months, and she no longer played, but her daughter still brought her on good nights to make her feel like her old self.

"Congratulations, Mrs. D," I said, making the woman clap happily. The rest of the group was used to her calling bingo and the announcer pretending she won. "G-59." I shifted my legs ever so slightly apart, and Archie slid his hand lower, teasing my taint through my pants while he appeared to innocently watch over the crowd to make sure everyone had time to stamp their bingo cards with their daubers. "O-69." The number made him purr, and I suddenly saw us in the sixty-nine position in the center of my bed.

Archie's torment went on through the night. He brushed the back of his hand over my aching cock, trailed a finger over my thigh, dug his fingers in the small of my back in the same way I imagined he would when I fucked him. *When*, not if. All of this was accomplished while he kept his erection pressed against my hip, letting me know he was just as turned on as I was. When I announced it was the last game, Arch put some distance between us and removed his roaming hand from my body so we could get ourselves under control before we had to walk out from behind the podium.

"Good thing there wasn't a fire drill," I whispered as I followed him off the makeshift stage to where his mother waited for us while everyone else shuffled for the door.

"Don't say 'drill,' Ollie. You're giving me ideas." I was going to make him pay so bad at my first opportunity.

"Guess it just wasn't my night, boys," Maria said when we joined her. "At least others had a lucky night or are about to."

"Mom!" Archie said in a horrified voice.

"Archie, it's good to know where your mind is right now. I was talking about the ladies who said they were headed to Graeters to use up their gift certificates for ice cream. Raspberry and chip does sound delicious. I think I'll join the group heading over there." She looked at me then and offered me a smile as warm as the quilt Mrs. F. donated to bingo night. "It was great to see you again, Ollie."

"You too," I said, accepting the hug she offered.

"Be careful," Maria said then followed it up with "driving home" in case he was confused about her meaning.

"You too, Mamma," Archie said, hugging his mom. "Watch out for the brain freeze."

"Call me tomorrow, or come see me," she said over her shoulder as she headed for the door.

"So," I said once we were alone. "What was—"

My words were cut off when Archie firmly gripped my head and slanted his lips over mind for a desperate kiss, making me instantly hard again. I was shocked at first, but then I slid my fingers beneath the lace shirt he wore, caressing soft skin over hard muscles. I ached to touch him like this when there was no chance for interruption. I wanted to mark his fair skin, claim him, and possess him in ways I'd never done before. The intensity of it was frightening and made me pull back before I could do something stupid.

"What are we doing, Arch?" I asked, breathing as hard as if I'd run a mile. "What do you want from me?"

"Right now?"

I needed to know what he wanted beyond tonight before I was

willing to let my guard down fully. I could see he wasn't ready to have that discussion, so I'd settle for what he was willing to give me. "Yeah, right now."

"I want a quiet place where we can share a meal that doesn't include my mother interrupting us. I want us to talk so I can get to know you better, and I want more kisses."

"Dinner, talking, and kissing?" I asked, making sure I knew exactly what he was willing to offer me.

"It sounds like junior high, doesn't it?" Archie asked, sounding embarrassed.

"It sounds amazing, Arch. I know just the place we can eat and talk without anyone bugging us. The food is pretty basic but tasty."

Archie lifted a brow in question. "How private are we talking?"

"Come home with me, Arch. I don't want to share your attention with anyone else. I can assure you of two things: I make the best grilled cheese sandwich you'll ever have, and my intentions are honorable. You said you want to eat, talk, and kiss. That's all I'm offering."

"You think either of us can behave ourselves with a bed nearby?"

"We won't know unless we try."

I saw the moment he decided to accept my offer, and I vowed to keep my word, no matter how hard he made me or how much he chipped away at my resolve. I wouldn't strip Archie White down and love him the way he was made to be loved until I no longer saw hesitation in his gorgeous, green eyes.

"Do you also have tomato soup?" he challenged.

"As if you could have one without the other," I replied. "Follow me."

I didn't wait for him to respond verbally. I'd said all I was willing to right then. I needed to use my actions to communicate and demonstrate my intentions to Archie. I glanced over my shoulder to see if he was following me and saw he hadn't budged from the spot where I left him. I would've been nervous had he not been smiling like the Cheshire cat.

Chapter Eight

Archie

MY HEART RACED THE ENTIRE TIME I FOLLOWED OLLIE BACK TO his place. At one point, I allowed myself to dream that "kissing" included his dick in my mouth. The image was so vivid I nearly rear-ended his car at a red light which made me think about a different kind of collision involving rear ends. "We agreed to kiss," I said out loud to myself. "That means mouth-on-mouth action only." I nodded in an attempt to convince myself even though I knew damn well I'd cave if Ollie made the first move toward something other than mouth-to-mouth action.

I expected Ollie to live somewhere inside the city limits, but I followed him north to a more rural setting where cornfields grew on either side of the country road. I bet it was a lovely drive during the day, but at night, it felt creepy as fuck and as foreign to me as if we had magically transported to another land. I was a city boy through and through; the only jungles I roamed were ones made of concrete.

Ollie slowed down to take a sharp curve to the left, so I did the same. Once we came out of the curve, the fields gave way to trees, and the once straight road wove its way up a curvy hill, reminding me of a roller coaster ride. Ollie flipped on his turn signal at the top of the hill, and that's when I saw the driveway to the small, country church. It looked like it was built 200 years ago but had been lovingly maintained. The sign in front of the church was a new addition. It wasn't one of those tacky ones where you could replace the letters daily or weekly, Ollie permanently and boldly identified Grace Fellowship Church as a place of worship for the LGBTQ+ community in rainbow letters. Ollie didn't need glitter or unicorns to get his point across.

I followed Ollie down the gravel lane past the church to a small house sitting nestled in the woods. It was close enough for him to walk to work, but the trees surrounding the home afforded him privacy and allowed him to separate his work and his private life. The only downside to me living at Ryan's Place was never fully getting away from my work and responsibilities. I was working on getting out more and reclaiming a life for myself. The man who exited his car and waited for me to do the same was a big reason for the change. At some point, I would need to admit meeting Ollie was the biggest reason I'd started emceeing the weekly fundraising events.

"Nothing below the neck," I reminded myself as I turned off my car and got out to meet Ollie.

"I probably should've warned you just how far you had to follow me," Ollie said sheepishly.

I would follow you anywhere. The thought came swiftly and out of nowhere as if some invisible narrator was telling my story instead of me. I didn't know Ollie enough to know if I'd follow him anywhere. I hadn't allowed myself to believe in that kind of blind faith in more than a decade, so the urge to get back in the car and drive to safety was overwhelming.

Ollie, sensing my nervousness, said, "Nothing will creep out of the woods and bite you, Arch. You're safe here with me." His white teeth gleamed in the moonlight, and I felt a whole lot like Little Red Riding Hood looking into the eyes of a wolf in pastor's clothing.

"My, what kissable lips you have," I breathily said once I stood in front of him. Ollie's laughter bounced off the swaying trees and carried in the wind, breaking the tension gripping my body. My car headlights were programmed by the manufacturer to turn off automatically after a few minutes, allowing a person to get inside their home or wherever they went after dark. In this case, I'd only had enough time to reach Archie before they shut off. Our only light source was the moon which bathed Ollie its splendor, making him look angelic and pure until our gazed met and held. His dark eyes promised me devilish delights that were otherworldly and earth-shattering while his smile promised serenity and peace. I found I wanted all of those things, and I could have them if I would only take a chance.

Ollie extended his hand like an olive branch, and I reached out to accept it, knowing I'd regret it for the rest of my life if I didn't try. *Okay, Ollie, you win.* I couldn't blame a faceless narrator this time because I knew the words came from my soul. Ollie gently squeezed my fingers between his and guided me to the front of his house. I wished the walk was longer when he released my hand to unlock the door, but he reached for me as soon as he opened it. Did he think I was on the verge of bolting? I wasn't.

Ollie flipped on a switch, and a lamp came on in the corner of the room, casting a soft glow around the living room instead of garish, overhead lighting most people used in their homes. The charcoal gray recliner looked well-worn, comfortable, and almost large enough for both of us. *Down, boy,* I said to my dick. A sofa in a fabric matching the recliner, a coffee table, and two matching end tables made up the rest of the furniture in the room. A large picture window overlooking the front yard took up most of the front wall, two other walls were painted in a warm, medium bluish-gray color, and the fourth wall was covered in floor-to-ceiling bookshelves. My favorite feature in the room was the stone fireplace and roughly hewn mantle made from old timber. It was aged, warm, and inviting, contrasting with the flat screen television hanging above it. An ivory area rug with a modern pattern of blue, gray, and black covered the hardwood floors which looked to be original to the house. They'd been lovingly cared for just as the church appeared to be.

"It's not much, but I love it," Ollie softly said, sounding like he might be embarrassed.

"It's a beautiful space," I assured him. My eyes caught on the artwork hanging on the wall. I released his hand to inspect them closer. There were four framed sketches of the church showing how it looked in all four seasons. The artist had such incredible skill, and I felt like I was looking at black-and-white photos of the building instead of drawings. The shading and detail were some of the best work I'd ever seen, and although I was no expert, I recognized talent when I saw it.

"Don't stare too close or you'll see the imperfections."

I snapped my head around and was shocked to see Ollie had joined me. I was so enraptured with the drawings and hadn't heard him approach me. "Ollie, did you draw these?" He nodded, and I turned to look back at the art on the wall. I noticed the small signature at the bottom. Oliver Knight. Well, it was a big "O" then squiggles followed by a big "K" and more squiggles. "I'm speechless, Ollie. These are so fucking beautiful." Then I gasped when I realized I'd dropped the f-bomb in a pastor's house. "Sorry."

Ollie laughed. "I've said that word myself a time or two. You don't have to hold back your thoughts and feelings around me, Arch. You don't need to put on an act or be anything other than yourself. I like you just the way you are."

"You don't really know me, Ollie."

"I know you where it counts," he countered. "The rest is just hot fudge on a brownie sundae." Why did everything he say sound so damn sexual? "Hungry?"

"Starving."

Ollie took my hand once more and led me down a short hallway with two doors on either side. I saw a neatly made bed through the open door on the right and a small, tidy bathroom on the left. The kitchen was bigger than I expected it to be, but then again, the space acted as both the kitchen and dining room. A large, round table made from a dark, knotty wood took up the far-right corner of the room and was surrounded by six chairs. One wall of the dining room was painted a deep red and acted as a backdrop for more of his drawings. The rest of the kitchen was painted a warm beige color. The counter-tops and cabinets were white, sterile, and would've looked utilitarian if not for the bright pops of color from the red canisters, coffee pot, and stand mixer. The appliances were new, state of the art, and polished stainless steel. They belonged to someone who enjoyed their time in the kitchen.

Ollie squeezed my hand before he released it. "Make yourself comfortable while I whip us up something to eat."

I headed straight for the art. In his kitchen, he'd hung sketches of the wildlife I suspected inhabited the woods surrounding his house. Squirrels hoarding nuts, bunnies eating leaves, and birds flying, bathing in a fountain, or nesting all decorated his walls.

"You're a gifted artist," I said, breaking the silence. Ollie didn't respond right away, so I looked over my shoulder and found him staring at me like he couldn't believe I was standing in his kitchen nook. That made two of us. Clearing my throat seemed to break his trance.

"Did you ask me something?" he asked.

"Um, no. I was complimenting your artistic skills."

"Oh," he said, turning away quickly and crossing the room to open the refrigerator. "It's just a fun hobby."

"Paint by numbers is a fun hobby," I said wryly. "This is…extraordinary. Please don't dismiss it."

Ollie turned his head sharply to look at me once again. "I'm not dismissing it, Arch. I just don't see my work in the same way you do."

I looked back at the drawings and noticed the finer details that made each one seem so damn lifelike while Ollie rustled around with ingredients for our late dinner. "You want some help?" I offered.

"No way," he replied. "I don't want you learning my secrets."

"Secrets for grilled cheese?" I looked over my shoulder and

Broken Halos

noticed he'd pulled butter and a block of cheese out of the refrigerator, not a package of Kraft Singles like I used in my sandwiches. "I'll let you keep your secrets…for now." The last two words sounded like I had diabolical plans for him.

I sat at the table and watched Ollie move comfortably and efficiently like he'd made this soup and sandwich combo many times and could even do it in his sleep. "What made you decided to become a pastor?" I asked.

"Jumping in with the tough questions?" Ollie asked in good humor. "I like this about you, Archie. No games."

"I'm surprised you feel this way after I ran so hot and cold with you over these past few months."

Ollie's hands stilled, and he looked over his shoulder at me. "I didn't see it that way, Arch."

"How did you see it then?" I asked, leaning forward to prop my elbow on his table and resting my chin on it.

"I knew your battle was an internal one and not purposely directed at me. I made you feel something you didn't like, or perhaps didn't want, and you weren't sure how to react. Well, the first night was a kneejerk reaction to my vocation, but after that, I saw your struggle wasn't meant to hurt me."

I sucked in a sharp breath. "I never meant to hurt you."

"I know, Arch. I've been on the receiving end of people who deliberately set out to hurt me, and there is a difference."

"I don't see how," I said, shaking my head. "Hurt is hurt."

"No, it's not," Ollie said. "I've learned over the years there are many levels of hurt, and they're not the same. Our initial reactions to the plateaus of hurt are similar, but after time, emotional distance, and introspection, we can see the differences. It changes the way we process others' actions and allows us to see things more objectively."

"Give me an example, Golden Boy," I said, completely enthralled by his line of thinking.

"For example, someone saying something off the cuff that upsets

69

you versus someone deliberately being hurtful."

"How are those types of hurt any different?" I questioned. "Someone telling me my ass looks big in my jeans is going to hurt my feelings whether it's done deliberately or not."

"It's in the delivery," Ollie said. "In the first scenario, someone might not come out and say your ass looks big in the jeans. They might've remarked about the cut or the fit which you assumed was meant to say you looked bad. The second scenario is a person coming out and saying your ass looks big in those jeans. Do you see the difference?"

I had to think about what he was saying, and I could see he had a point. The initial reaction to the comments would be similar because both hurt my feelings, but after time and contemplation, I could point out that the first person didn't intend to cause hurt feelings. Unless they like to engage in passive-aggressive behavior, but that's not what we were talking about here. The second person intended to be mean and hurt my feelings.

"I've never really thought about it until you broke it down for me, but yeah, I do."

"It took some time, but I eventually recognized the reasons you ran from me were also responsible for the wall you built between us. I also hoped after some time passed you'd see there was no reason for you to fear me."

I scoffed a little at that one. "I wasn't afraid of you, Ollie."

"Perhaps not physically." *Touché.* "That's why I kept coming back until you asked me not to." *Ouch.*

"Okay, it wasn't my finest hour," I admitted. "I'm ashamed for the way I acted that night on the stage and later in the prop room."

Ollie set down whatever he'd had in his hands and turned to face me fully. "Why were you ashamed? Was it because of the way you wanted me or the way you reacted to my attention?"

"Both," I said softly. "I didn't want the attraction I felt toward you, and I hated the crass way I treated you."

70

"Interesting," Ollie said then turned back to assembling sandwiches.

"Which part?"

"Both."

"Are you going to expand on that?" I asked.

"Are you?"

"I already did, Ollie."

I saw his shoulders shake with laughter before I heard the giggle bubbling from him. "This is some date we're on."

"Date?"

Ollie turned away from the counter and opened the drawer at the bottom of the stove. He held up an ancient-looking cast iron skillet. "If I'm busting out my good cookware then it's a date." He set the heavy skillet on the stove and turned on a burner. "I just find it interesting, amazing really, that we're talking this way in my kitchen while I cook us food." Ollie dropped butter in the skillet and pushed it around with the spatula until it melted. "I like it."

"Are you ready to tell me why you chose to become a pastor?"

"Are you ready to tell me why it turned you off so much?" Ollie countered.

"It wasn't your vocation alone which sent me running; it was the reservations I assumed you'd have about me."

"Because of my faith?" Ollie asked while putting the assembled sandwiches in the hot skillet. "You thought I'd disapprove that you were a former drag queen?"

"And how I like to wear makeup on occasion," I said, pointing to my face. "Even if you were as open-minded as your lusty gaze indicated, I assumed you would only be interested in clandestine fucks to get your jollies off. I never expected you'd want to be seen with me in public."

I almost regretted the words because I didn't want Ollie to look at me with pity. He said nothing while he emptied the can of tomato soup into the saucepan and added milk and a dollop of butter. Ollie whisked the ingredients together in the pan while turning on the burner beneath it. He still didn't say anything until he checked the bottom of the sandwiches to make sure they weren't burned. When he finally looked at me, I didn't see the dreaded pity; I saw anger.

"Those cowards weren't worthy of your time, Arch."

"Golden Boy, you don't have to say that. I won't lie and say it's water under the bridge, because I obviously still carry a chip on my shoulder, but these are my issues to work through."

Ollie shook his head before he turned back to the stove and expertly turned over the sandwiches and stirred the soup. "I'm afraid to tell you the reason I became a pastor. It might change the way you feel about me."

His statement caught me off guard. "That's not possible, Golden Boy." I stopped Ollie when he opened his mouth to respond. "Tell me after we finish eating. Your recliner looks comfy and big enough for both of us."

Ollie nodded then continued toasting our sandwiches while I breathed in the delicious smell of bread, butter, and melting cheese. My mouth was watering by the time he carried our plates and bowls to the table. I knew without a doubt it would be the best grilled cheese sandwich I'd ever had, not just because of the ingredients Ollie used, but because he made it for me.

I was happy to see confidence in his culinary skills replace the insecurity I'd seen moments earlier. The confidence turned to something darker and sexier when I brought the sandwich to my mouth and took a bite. The moan escaping my mouth was pornographic and indecent.

"Perfect," I mumbled around a mouthful of heaven.

Chapter Nine

Ollie

ARCHIE'S PRAISE AND MOAN OF PLEASURE SENT HAPPINESS HUMMING through my body like a current of low-voltage electricity. "I've never seen anyone put butter in tomato soup before," Archie said after dipping his sandwich in the soup before taking a second bite. "Mmmm. How'd you know to do that?"

"It's a trick I learned from a remarkable woman," I told him. "I'm so used to putting it in there, I didn't think to ask if you minded." I tore off a chunk of my sandwich and dunked it in my soup. "It is good though, isn't it?"

"Delicious. It makes me want to learn all your other cooking secrets."

"I don't have very many," I assured him.

"This grilled cheese is one of the gourmet kind they charge twelve dollars for in New York City, but yours is much better. You could get at least fifteen for it," Archie said after his third bite. "Throw some garnish on the soup, and you could get at least five dollars for it. Maybe more."

"People pay twenty dollars for grilled cheese and tomato soup?" I asked, sounding incredulous.

"*Gourmet* grilled cheese and tomato soup." Archie took another bite, and his eyes nearly rolled back in his head. "What kind of cheese did you put in this thing? I can tell it's not American or Velveeta."

"*Velveeta*? That's not real cheese, Archie."

"Since when? It's great in macaroni and cheese and makes excellent nachos."

"I can see I need to make you real baked macaroni and cheese so you can tell the difference between real and imitation."

"I'll let you prove it to me," he said eagerly. "School me, Golden Boy."

His use of the silly nickname stifled a little of the joy I felt when he made a fuss about my cooking. He wouldn't think I was so golden when he learned the truth of my past. Archie could've learned a lot about me if he'd read my bio on my website. He either didn't know the site existed or wanted a first-person account from me.

"You're not eating," Archie said, nodding to my sandwich and soup. "I hope it isn't from the question I asked you, Ollie. You don't have to answer anything that makes you uncomfortable. Especially on a first date as you pointed out."

"I'm not hungry," I told him. "I had a decent dinner before I went to bingo. Would you like my sandwich?"

"I can't take food out of your mouth, Ollie."

"You're not," I replied, sliding my plate across the table to him. His eyes said he wanted to devour the sandwich, but the slight frown on his lips expressed concern I was only being nice. "I'm offering it, and I'd rather you eat it than throw it away."

Archie gasped like he couldn't believe I'd do such a thing. *If he only knew the things I'd done.* I realized I wanted Archie to know the truth. If he was going to pull away from me in disgust, I needed him to do it before our relationship grew deeper.

"You need to know who I really am so you will stop putting me on a pedestal. I'm a man—born of flesh and blood and baptized by fire. I bleed when I'm cut, and I have scars no man can see. There is nothing pure, golden, or saintly about me. We are equals in all things, Arch."

"Ollie—"

"Eat your soup and sandwich, Arch," I said, cutting him off. "Talking and kissing await us." *I hoped.*

"Nothing you say will disappoint me," Archie boldly said, covering my hand on the table. He couldn't possibly know that, but I appreciated his effort.

I ate a few more bites of soup while he ate my sandwich and finished his bowl of soup. "Would you like more?" I asked, partly hoping he'd say yes so I could delay our discussion and partly hoping he'd say no so we could get it over with.

"I couldn't handle another bite. To the recliner, Golden Boy." He didn't say Bat Cave or call me Robin, but it had that same feel.

"Do you always speak in movie lines?" I asked, stalling for time.

"Only with people I like," Archie said. "I'll still like you after our little chat, so get the ridiculous notion that I won't out of your head right now." He wasn't fooled by my tactics.

I led Archie to the dimly lit living room, and we discovered the recliner was definitely big enough for us both. We lay facing one another beneath the quilt Archie pulled off the back of it.

"Mrs. Fletcher from bingo made this for me for Christmas."

"She's very talented." I nodded. "Ollie, I know you run an NA chapter which means you have a history with drugs, alcohol, or both." Archie's green eyes were relaxed and sincere with none of the hesitancy I was used to seeing. "I'm not disgusted or disappointed to know this about you."

"What if I told you I spent six months in jail?"

Archie's eyes widened then a crooked smile spread across his face. "Okay, you got me there. How long ago?"

"I was arrested the day after I turned eighteen, so fourteen years ago."

"So, you're thirty-two," Archie said. "You look younger."

"How old are you?" I asked. I knew he was older than Milo, but not by how much.

"Thirty-five."

"You look ten years younger," I said in awe.

"Good genetics, and I take excellent care of my skin." Archie inched closer and slipped his hand around to rest on the small of my back. "What did young Oliver Knight do to end up in jail?"

"I broke into homes of the super-rich, stole their things then pawned them to buy food for runaway kids. I didn't want them to turn out like me."

"Turn out like you how, Ollie?" The fingers from his free hand ghosted over my chin.

"A drug addict and prostitute."

The fingers on my chin stilled, and Archie closed his eyes, but not before I saw the pained expression. When he reopened them, all I saw was compassion and understanding. "Your story is way too common for our people. Abandoned and tossed on the street with no place to go. Is that what happened to you, Ollie?"

I could only nod.

"You think I'm disgusted by you? Did you think I'd judge you for doing whatever it took to get by?" Archie dug his fingers in my skin and pressed a kiss to my forehead. "It makes me respect you more. Look at who you've become, Ollie. Look at all the people you help. I don't look at you and see a disgusting man; I see a man I'm proud to know. I'm dying to know the journey you took to reach this moment in your life, but I think we've done enough talking tonight."

"We have?" I asked.

Archie nodded. "Don't you think we've taken big steps tonight? We both opened up to each other. I think it calls for a kiss."

I closed my eyes and said a quick prayer of thanks Archie still found me kissable. Archie rubbed the tip of his nose along mine ever so softly, making a sappy sigh escape my mouth. "Just kissing, right?" I asked, reminding myself more than warning him off.

"For tonight." Archie kissed the tip of my nose. "Nothing below the neck." As if his words were a command, I tilted my head back and exposed my neck to him. Archie lowered his head and sucked the tender flesh in the dip above my clavicle then licked a path up to my ear. "You taste better than I imagined."

"You've been imagining what I taste like?"

"Wasn't that your intent when you sent the racy text messages?" Archie asked, his breath ghosting hotly over my flesh and making goose bumps pebble on my skin. "You had to know they'd make me hard and aching for you."

"Would you believe me if I told you I don't normally send those types of texts?"

Archie lifted his head and looked into my eyes. "Really? You're so good at it."

"I acted on pure instinct. I recognized you wanted to brush me aside, and I wasn't willing to go without a fight. Maybe, on some level, I wanted to show you I am a man with needs just like all others."

"Being a pastor doesn't change how you see sex?" Archie asked, hesitation returning to his eyes. "You don't think it's a sin to have sex out of wedlock?"

"My love of God doesn't make my needs as a man go away. I still get blue balls and ache if I don't let off some steam, but I usually take care of business myself. As much as I enjoy sex, I want it to mean more than just a physical exchange with a random guy."

"Is it because it reminds you of your days on the street when there was no emotional connection? Just a transaction to survive?" Archie brushed the back of his hand over my cheek.

"I think it has a lot to do with it," I admitted. "It took a long time and a lot of therapy before I could see sex as something healthy and good. Yes, my physical needs are sometimes at war with my theological beliefs, but I try to make decisions that are good for everyone involved. I need to be able to look at my reflection in the mirror and know I'm the best person I can be and the decisions I made didn't bring harm to anyone. That's my contract with God which is what Christianity really is—one's personal relationship with God."

"Two consenting adults enjoying one another's bodies isn't harming a single soul," Archie said.

I nodded, but added, "There's obviously more to it than being consenting adults. Adulterers and people in a position of power may gain someone's consent before a sexual act, but it doesn't make their actions right."

"Of course," Archie agreed then smiled. "Our conversation has steered into deep waters again."

"I'm sorry."

"Don't be," Archie said before lightly kissing my lips. "There's no way for this to work between us without airing these things out."

"And you want this to work out?" I asked hopefully.

Archie rubbed his nose against mine again. "I want to try."

"Me too. This feels right to me."

Archie slanted his head and pressed his lips to mine, gentle pecks at first before his tongue traced the seam between my lips. I automatically parted them, eager to feel his tongue inside my mouth again. Archie was gentle at first, teasing the tip of my tongue with his own before sucking mine into his mouth, making my dick throb and pulling a desperate groan from my chest. I slid my hand under his lacy shirt to feel the silky smooth skin underneath. I trailed my fingers over the hard planes of Archie's abdomen, reveling in the way the muscles quivered under his skin.

He released my tongue and looked at me with hungry eyes. "I thought we were just kissing."

"My fingertips are kissing your soft skin," I countered.

"Well, my fingertips want to get in on the action too," Archie said, reaching for the buttons on my shirt. "You wear the softest flannel shirts, and they invite a man to rub his face against them. God, how am I going to resist kissing every inch of you I reveal?" he asked after he freed two buttons from their prison. "But a deal is a deal."

"Maybe we renegotiate," I suggested. I wanted Archie's lips working a path down my chest.

"Uh-uh. I don't want you to have any regrets." As if. The only way it would happen is if… Oh! I stiffened when I realized he still wasn't comfortable with our situation. Heat and hunger had overshadowed his hesitation, but it was still there hiding in the wings. Archie freaking out and rejecting me after sex would be something I might not overcome. "Don't pull away from me," Archie urged, tightening his grip on my flannel.

"I'm still right here, Arch."

"I felt you mentally checking out just now. Why?"

"I realized we're not in the same place," I admitted. "I'm ready to rush headlong into this, but you're not." I slid my hand up to cover his heart. I loved seeing the contrast between my darker skin and Archie's fair skin beneath the lace. "What do you need from me, Arch?"

"Honesty and time. Life has taught me to be cautious. Unlike you, I'm okay with random hookups because I've been convinced it's all I'll ever have. In your eyes, I see the promise of more, and I need time to believe it's real—that you're real."

"I can give you time, Arch." And I would, no matter how desperate I was to know him in every possible way.

I wrapped my hand around his neck and pulled him back to me, lifting my head to meet him halfway. Our kiss wasn't slow and tentative; it was hungry, wet, and filled with promise. Kissing Archie didn't just involve our mouths; it was a full-body experience. My nerve endings fired to life, emitting messages of want and need and lust until I ached for him from the tips of my toes to the roots of my hair. By this time, Archie had my shirt completely undone, pushing it open and touching me everywhere with his greedy hands. I was overcome with the need to at least feel his bare chest against mine.

The buttons on his shirt were much smaller than mine, and laughter reverberated in Archie's chest when I struggled to get them open with my clumsy fingers. He reached between our bodies to undo them himself, but I pushed his hands away, swallowing his laughter. I would persevere. Archie's laughter turned to guttural moans when I finally spread his shirt open and aligned our bodies so they pressed to-gether from head to toe. Archie kissed me harder and gripped my ass, rolling and pulling me on top to straddle his hips in the recliner, press-ing my raging hard-on tighter against his and urging me to rut against him. The friction sent shivers of pleasure racing down my spine.

I slid my hands in his hair, fisting the silky strands in my fingers while we kissed hungrily, desperately. I broke our kiss so I could look into his eyes. "Archie," I whispered when I saw how far gone he was too. It would've been easy to convince him to go into my bedroom with me, but the time wasn't right. That didn't mean I couldn't make him feel good and give him something fond to think about while we worked up to the point where I'd have him naked beneath me in my bed. I rocked my hips forward and back, months of need and lust spurring me on faster and harder.

"More," Archie said, sounding as desperate as I felt. His body bowed beneath mine. He was close. I could feel it—smell it.

"Come for me, Arch. Show me how much I turn you on."

He arched his neck and gritted his teeth. I leaned forward and sank my teeth in the tender part where his neck met his shoulder. Archie's breath hitched then held for a few heartbeats before he re-leased it on a grunt as he came, soaking the front of his jeans. "Ollie!" he cried out.

I came too, long and hard, while rutting against him. Archie cap-tured my cries with his lips and held me tight in his arms once I col-lapsed on top of him. He ran his hands up and down my back, learn-ing the curve of my spine while I fought to catch my breath.

"I haven't done that in a long time," Archie whispered.

I raised up and looked into his sated eyes. "What? Come?"

"Not in my pants," Archie said with a wry smile. "This takes me back to my junior high days."

I snorted. "Got an early start, huh?"

"You didn't?"

I shook my head, hoping he'd let it go. I wasn't ready to talk about my first sexual experience and the consequences I endured afterward. Archie must've sensed it was a touchy subject because he quickly kissed me to pull me back to him.

"Stay right here with me, Ollie." He ran his hand through my hair, and I leaned into his palm.

Getting hot enough to come in your jeans sounds sexy until your underwear starts sticking to you. "Would you like to take a shower and borrow some of my clothes?"

"Throwing me out already?" Archie asked wryly.

"Of course not," I replied, tweaking a hardened nipple. "You're welcome to stay here tonight since you're in an unfamiliar location and it's almost midnight. We can throw our sticky clothes in the washing machine, and I'll let you borrow a pair of my sweats to wear to bed."

Archie tilted his head to the side as he considered my idea. "I really don't want to run into the spooky corn children on my drive back home, and it is getting late. If it's not too much of an imposition, I'd like to stay."

"It's not an imposition."

"There's just one problem, Ollie." His expression and tone turned grave. Did he turn into a pumpkin after midnight?

"What's that?" I asked.

"I sleep naked."

Chapter Ten

Archie

"FOR SHAME, FOR SHAME," REGGIE TEASED. HE JUST HAPPENED to be coming down the staircase when I sauntered through the front door Saturday afternoon. Reggie took one look at my borrowed sweats and T-shirt and knew I hadn't just returned from running errands. I never left the house wearing anything so casual unless it was to work out at the gym or yoga studio. Besides Henry, Reggie was our newest member of the household, but it didn't take living here long to know weekends were my leisure time. I took my rest, relax, and recharging very seriously.

"Is this what the face of shame looks like to you, Reg?" I asked, pointing to my Cheshire grin. Before he could answer me, I walked the hallway like it was my personal catwalk and I was the Queen of Queers. Oh, yes, baby. Sometimes diva wasn't a big enough label to describe the way a person felt inside.

"Work it," Reggie called after me.

I reached my bedroom door, executed a sassy turn, and placed a hand on my cocked hip. "Baby, I own it." Reggie's laughter echoed down the hallway as I shut the door, sealing myself inside my personal haven.

Outwardly, I often chose to wear bold colors or patterns, and I liked to create new dramatic looks with makeup. Inside my room, I needed a space that was a peaceful oasis. I chose warm earth tones for my furnishings but added pops of warm colors like jade, amethyst, and teal in accent pieces like my bedside lamps and the throw pillows on the chaise in the corner and on top of my chocolate brown comforter. It was when I looked at my perfectly made bed with tidy pillows that it sank in I had spent the night away from home. The world didn't end, the house didn't burn to the ground, and as I told Reggie, I didn't feel an ounce of shame for staying the night at Ollie's house. Maybe it had more to do with the person who slept across the bed from me, and his sultry, warm eyes which invited me to scoot closer and stay longer. Eyes the same warm, chocolate brown as my comforter.

I looked around my space and wondered what Ollie would think about it. Would he find it a warm and inviting space as I did, or would he think the crystals hanging from the lampshade and my gilded, glamorous vanity was too much? Would he be turned off by the drawers inside the chestnut wardrobe that held lacy panties, bras, garters, and stockings? Would he want me only to wear those things for him in private as the others had, or would he like knowing I was wearing something lacy and delicate beneath my clothes? Ollie said he liked me just the way I was, but what if I showed up at his church and the strap of a bra or negligée peeped out from beneath my dress shirt? It was one thing to say you were okay with it, but another to embrace it publicly.

The mere thought of Ollie pulling away from me dimmed the joy I felt from waking up in his bed. Ollie's eyes looked at me with adoration, and I couldn't bear the thought he might look upon me with shame, disappointment, or disgust. I could handle that kind of rejection from the others before Ollie but not him. He was supposed to be different, someone I could trust. It was better to cut this off before—I wouldn't allow myself to finish the thought. There was no way I was going to sabotage things with Ollie before they even really started. I'd tried pushing him away and made myself miserable in the process. I was determined to take a chance with him and let myself hope Ollie was as real as he said he was.

My cell phone rang in the pocket of the borrowed sweats. I'd hoped it was Ollie and groaned a little when I saw it was my mom. I knew she wanted to pump me for information about what happened after she left, but I wasn't ready to talk about the special moments I'd shared with Ollie. How did a thirty-five-year-old man explain dry humping Ollie felt better than the penetrative sex I've had the past few years? Wait. Why would this thirty-five-year-old man think he needed to be that explicit during a conversation with his mom?

"Hello, Mamma," I said into the phone.

"I want him, Archie."

"Who?" I asked, playing dumb.

"Ollie. Who else, knucklehead?"

"Mamma," I said slowly and softly, "I don't know how to break this to you. Maybe it's best if I just rip the Band-Aid off." I paused for dramatic effect. "Mamma, Ollie isn't into you. Please don't take it personally."

"Don't be a smart-ass, Archie," Mamma said, unable to keep the humor out of her voice. "I thought you were going to tell me you ran him off already."

"Mamma, I don't run guys off. They run on their own."

"Now you have a guy who wants to stay, and you're wanting to push him away before he can change his mind and hurt you like all the others did." She wasn't wrong. Hadn't I just battled my instinct to push him away? "None of them were worthy of you. Quite frankly, it was pretty silly of them to expect you to leave your alter ego in the dressing rooms of Queen City Divas when you finished performing. Lady Bea Trix wasn't an act, Bea is part of who you are. Ollie won't be turned off by your alter ego nor will he be embarrassed by it."

"How do you know?"

Mamma let out a long-suffering sigh like she was preparing herself to address the village idiot once more. "I have eyes in my head,

84

Archie. I was in the same room with you guys last night, not that either of you remembered you were standing up in front of a room full of senior citizens."

"Senior citizens and you," I countered.

"Sweetheart, I am technically a senior citizen. I have an AARP card to prove it. Don't try to distract me with sarcasm or sweetness. I'm on a roll this morning."

"You don't want me to interrupt you because you'll forget what you were going to say."

"This is also true," Mamma agreed. "Listen, I saw the way his eyes lit up when he saw you, and I saw the way you reacted to him."

"How was that?"

"Baby, he has a magnetic force field pulling you toward him. I think you were aware you crossed the room to speak to him the first time but not the second. You saw he was stumbling and went to him like it was second nature, and the two of you together are…" Her words faded, and I pictured her fanning her face with her hand. "Gorgeous. Sexy. Right."

"Mom, we've all seen what happens when the moth gets too close to the flame."

"You're no moth, so stop insulting yourself. My son is a beautiful, majestic butterfly and Ollie is an exquisite flower where you can safely land. I know you've dated some real losers in the past, but Ollie isn't one of them. Please tell me you can at least see that much."

"For a minute, I worried you were going to ask if I've been sipping Ollie's nectar."

"Please," she said, using the same voice one uses to say *duh*, "that's a foregone conclusion. If it hasn't happened already, then it will soon."

I thought of how badly I wanted truly to make him mine when I rolled him beneath me in the center of his bed, but we had things to prove to one another which didn't involve sex. So, we settled for more making out and more rutting, only naked the second time around.

My sticky release mixed with Ollie's when we finally came. I could've lingered in his little house for the rest of the day, but he had things to do before the big gala event at Queen City Divas. Ollie didn't subscribe to lazy Saturdays like I did. Yet.

I borrowed his kitchen to prepare a nice breakfast while he worked in his small office upstairs. Afterward, we kissed and made out in his oversized recliner some more, neither of us wanting to part ways.

"Earth to Archie," my mom said in a singsong voice. "Are you still there?"

"I'm here," I said. "I, um—just checked out for a minute."

"I bet you did."

"Mamma," I said in a warning tone. "Look, I'm not going to deny I'm attracted to Ollie or that I want him to be different than the others. I'm just saying it's going to take time, and I don't want you to get your hopes up."

"Let me worry about me, Arch. Anyway, while you were daydreaming about Ollie, I asked you if you'd like to go with us to attend his church in the morning."

"Us? Who is us?"

"Esther, me, and the newest resident at Ryan's Place. I think Esther said his name is Harry."

"His name is Henry." I sat on the edge of my bed and stared at the water color painting of Grace Kelly on the opposite wall. "I'm not surprised he wants to attend Ollie's church. They had an instant connection after I introduced them. Henry needs someone like Ollie in his life after the way his mother and church treated him."

"Henry is also very lucky to have you, my love. I am so proud of you."

This was a point of contention between us. I didn't like her making a fuss about me doing something anyone with compassion and resources should do. Mamma liked to remind me should and would aren't the same thing, which I knew, of course. Instead of my usual deflection, I said, "Thank you, Mamma."

"That's more like it," she said approvingly. "So, back to my question. Would you like to go to church with us tomorrow morning?"

I couldn't remember the last time I'd gone to church, well, mass since my mom was raised as a Catholic. She left the church when she was treated like a scarlet woman after leaving her abusive husband, my sperm donor. Apparently, a woman fleeing for her life was somehow more shocking and sinful than her husband beating her. She probably had it coming, right? Hypocritical assholes. I couldn't say all priests acted as cruelly as hers did when she sought help from him, but it was hard to rinse the bitter taste out of my mouth anytime religion was brought up. I thought my mom felt the same way, but I could hear the excitement in her voice. Had she missed attending services all this time, and I didn't know it? Or was she excited to see one of Ollie's sermons.

"Mamma, if this is part of a matchmaking scheme—"

"It's not," she said abruptly. "I'm going regardless of if you join me."

"Can I think about it and let you know in the morning?"

"Absolutely," she said. "I'll be there at nine to pick up Henry, and you can join us if you wish. Have fun tonight at Queen City Divas."

"I will."

"Will Ollie be there too?"

"He will," I told her. "We've got a special gala going on, and Milo is performing."

"How is Milo?" Mamma asked.

"In love."

"Maybe it's in the air."

I snorted. "I don't think love is contagious."

"No, but seeing others find happy, healthy relationships gives us hope and opens our eyes to opportunities."

Us. It reminded me that my mom had never experienced the epic love she hoped I'd find. She thought she was too old to find her happily ever after, but I didn't think so. My mom was vibrant, beautiful, and warm. She knew how to make people feel welcomed and loved. It reminded me of the way Ollie reacted to her kindness when they met, and the thought led me to images of a young, homeless Ollie doing whatever it took to get by. My heart squeezed painfully in my chest, and I struggled to reconcile that image of Ollie with the smiling, healthy, and happy adult version of him.

"That's right," I said to my mom. "There's hope for both of us."

This was where she normally argued with me just like I did when she made a fuss over my running Ryan's Place. Instead, she said, "Thank you, Archie."

"That's more like it," I said, repeating her words to me.

"I'm sure you have many things to do before you get ready for the show tonight. I'll see you tomorrow morning even if you don't come with us. I love you, Son."

"I love you too, Mamma."

After we disconnected, I sprawled in the center of my bed and watched *Rear Window*, admiring Grace Kelly's beauty and gracefulness. It was one of my favorite movies, and I knew every word by heart. Those black-and-white movies felt like old friends, and I often turned to them for comfort when I was stressed or my mind felt chaotic. I wouldn't say being with Ollie was stressful, but my brain was busy trying to process all the things I learned about him and how it made me want to know more. It was safer to get lost in my favorite movie than allow my brain to spin and possibly create issues where there were none.

It was while watching my favorite actress that I got the idea to dust off Lady Bea Trix's wardrobe and have a little fun. I stopped performing drag when Ryan fell ill, and afterward, creating a legacy from the home he left to me became my focus. There were times I missed transforming into a sexy, sultry queen who wore satin and lace. Milo had been after me to at least dress as Bea when I emceed the charity events each week, but I was hesitant to do it. I felt like I'd lost the connection to Bea and worried it would be too hard to get her back. I'd never know unless I tried. And, if it also tested Ollie's commitment to liking all the sides of me, it was a bonus.

"Check you out," Milo said when he arrived at QCD to get ready for the night. I was already dressed in an off-the-shoulder, full-length pink satin dress with a slit up to mid-thigh and touching up my lipstick when he walked into the shared dressing room with a garment bag folded over his arm. "What's the special occasion? I've asked you to invite Bea to the party since you returned to emcee the weekly events, but you've declined each time."

I shrugged casually, but even I could see how tight my expression was. "I just thought it was time." I was bracing myself for Ollie's rejection with every layer of lace, satin, and makeup I put on.

"Time to test Ollie?"

"No." I'd be damned if I admitted it to anyone. I clasped a string of pearls around my neck then started putting on the snug, satin gloves that would end at mid-bicep.

"Uh-huh," Milo said, not buying it. "I don't blame you for being cautious with your heart, but I'm warning you now I'm looking forward to saying 'I told you so.'"

"You're starting to sound like Mamma."

"Maria is a wise woman, so I'll take it as a compliment."

"Lady Bea, the show starts in five minutes," Tony, the stage manager, yelled through the closed door. "Are you ready?"

"Be right there, Tony." Then I focused on Milo once more and found him smiling indulgently at me, and I had to fight the urge to roll my eyes. "Break a nail, Peach," I said to him before leaving the room.

I channeled my inner Hollywood starlet and put an extra sway into my hips when I walked onto the stage. "Hello, boys," I said in a breathy voice. "Miss me?" Whistles, catcalls, and howling abounded as I made my way toward the front of the stage, but I only cared about one man's reaction. I knew exactly where I'd find him too—sitting front and center. The spotlight followed me as I sassily walked, hips rocking from side to side. The dress, clothes, and wig made me feel powerful and sexy. When I reached the end of the stage, I stuck my left leg out, showcasing the white stockings ending at mid-thigh. More whistles and catcalls, but those weren't what made me shimmy my shoulders in delight; it was the desire and adoration rolling off Ollie as his eyes raked over me from head to toe. No, seeing me in drag for the first time didn't disgust him one bit.

I introduced the first act, Lady Vava Voom, then went backstage to watch the performance and wait to introduce the next act. The air around me felt charged suddenly, and I could almost hear the crackle of electricity. My hair stood up all over my body, and my skin tingled like it did when Ollie touched me. I turned and found him standing directly behind me. He wore a dark, feverish look in his eyes which promised he wanted to do delicious things to my body.

"Golden Boy, please don't give me an erection while my dick is tucked and taped. It's the most unpleasant experience."

Ollie's lips turned up in a crooked smile. "I just need to know one thing for now then I can go back out there and behave for the rest of the night."

"What's that?"

Ollie cupped the back of my neck and kissed me. He only let his lips linger for a few seconds before he pulled back and licked his lips. "Mmmm. Cherry."

Chapter Eleven

Ollie

I TOOK TWO STEPS SLOWLY BACKWARD, WIGGLING MY FINGERS. "I'LL SEE you in a few hours, Trix." Archie looked stunned, aroused, and a little bit confused as if maybe he wasn't sure if he wanted me to leave or stay. I made the decision for him because I knew he needed space to accept the growing feelings between us and time to believe it was real. I would give him both as long as I had hope in my heart something amazing could develop between us.

"How's Archie?" Brent asked when I returned to the table.

"He's back too quickly for anything good to have happened. Glassy eyes, glossy lips," Adam said, his eyes searching my face, "I'd say he stole a kiss."

"Excellent deduction, Watson," Tyler said in a proper British accent. "Now, the real question is: Did Ollie return to the table of his own accord, or did his heart's desire give him a gentle shove?"

"Leave him alone, guys," Keeton said, rolling his eyes. "Have you guys ever considered spending more time focusing on your own love lives, or lack thereof, instead of Ollie's?"

Brent stiffened beside Keeton and looked down at his soft drink. I had noticed when they arrived that the familiarity they'd been exhibiting lately was missing. As their sponsor, I was always concerned about budding relationships between members because it could spell disaster and cause relapses. While it was good to be surrounded with people who understood your addiction and the demons you fought, there was still a risk it could cause major setbacks if it blew up in your face. Brent had always seemed so damned level-headed beneath his backward ball cap, but I knew all too well what good actors we addicts could be when it suited us. Keeton, on the other hand, seemed more volatile with emotions simmering much closer to the surface. All of us teased and taunted one another, but there was a rougher edge to Keeton's barbs than there was the rest of ours. I'd hate for Brent to find himself cut and bleeding after getting tangled up in Keeton's barb-wire. I checked myself because I wasn't being fair. I had no idea what Brent's easygoing nature hid and had no way to know he wasn't the one being the ass and causing Keeton to regress back to the surlier man who first showed up at meetings.

I debated whether I should speak to them individually to make sure their heads were in the right place but worried it would cause unnecessary awkwardness between us. As much as I loved these men with all my heart, I should never have allowed myself to get so close to them. It skewed my objectivity and had me second-guessing my motives and decisions which could put their sobriety at risk. Selfishly, I couldn't imagine my life without their friendship and refused to believe I couldn't be both friend and mentor. Hadn't Pastor Randall been both to me? Sure, there were some tough love moments between us, but I never doubted his motives. I would remember that if the time came when I believed a serious conversation with Brent and Keeton was warranted.

"Thank you, Keeton," I said, offering him a kind smile. "I'm glad to see that one of you respects my privacy at least."

"We're just teasing you, Ollie," Adam said. "You know we're pulling for you and Archie, right? Hell, the big sap over there," he gestured to Andy, "has made us all want to find an epic love."

We all looked over to Andy, but his eyes were locked on the stage and he had a faraway expression on his face. We each took turns saying his name, but he didn't acknowledge any of us until I nudged him with my elbow.

"What? Huh?"

"What's wrong with you, man?" Brent asked. "You're shaking like a leaf over there. I've never seen you looking so nervous."

"Are you in the doghouse?" Keeton asked. "I know it's not fair, but there's a lot of pressure on you and Milo to prove to us happiness really is a possibility."

"It's all in how you look at things, kid," Tyler told him. "Whatever you put out into the universe comes back to you. If you have positivity and happiness, then that's what you need to exude."

"Exude?" Keeton asked, rolling his eyes. "I used to be a happy-go-lucky person, and I still ended up with shit kicked in my face."

"Sounds like life to me," Brent said softly. "It's how you deal with your shit that matters."

"So, I just need to swallow a spoonful of sugar to help swallow the medicine life tries to cram down my throat, huh?" Keeton asked.

"You're quoting Mary Poppins?" I asked, leaning forward.

"I have a little sister," Keeton replied, looking surlier than he had a few minutes before. I hadn't meant to embarrass him; I was just shocked. I would've expected him to make a crude reference like life bending him over without using lube or something.

"How's your gag reflex?" Adam asked.

"Adam," I admonished. "You went too far."

"Hey, I'm just trying to help the kid out, Ollie. He's talking about life cramming things down his throat. I was just going to offer suggestions that might help him more than a spoonful of sugar."

"Brent didn't have any issues with my gag reflex, did you?" Keeton asked the red-faced man sitting beside him. Brent swallowed hard but didn't speak. Keeton shoved back from the table and said, "I'm out of here."

Brent stood up so fast his chair tipped over. "Don't go, Kee," he urged, snagging Keeton's forearm before he could walk away. "Please."

Keeton looked at Brent, and for a few seconds, he let down his shield to show the raw emotions he felt. It was so intense that Brent gasped, but he didn't release Keeton's arm. The shields locked back in place, giving Keeton his mask of indifference once more. "Fine."

Adam looked between the two guys. "I didn't mean to start an argument or cause any trouble. I apologize, Keeton."

The younger man studied Adam's face to see if he was being genuine. He must've liked what he saw because he nodded and sat back down. Brent studied Keeton for a few seconds before he returned to his seat. He leaned over and said something in Keeton's ear that must've mollified him because a smirk replaced his scowl.

"Aww," Tyler teased. "You're so cute."

"Don't get the wrong idea, Hannah Montana," Keeton groused, "we're only plotting our revenge on Adam."

"Hey," Adam said, throwing up his hands, "I'm happy to do my part to bring people together."

"Guys," Andy said suddenly. I looked over at him and saw he was pale as a ghost.

"Are you sick?" I asked.

"I'm a fucking wreck, Ollie."

"What's wrong, man?" Brent asked. "What can we do?"

"What if Milo says no?" Andy asked us.

"No to what?" Tyler asked. "That guy wouldn't tell you no if... Ohhhh. You're planning on asking him to marry you."

"Seriously?" Brent and Adam asked at the same time while Keeton only stared at Andy with a raised brow.

"That's awesome, Andy. Congratulations," Adam said.

"He hasn't said yes yet," Andy pointed out.

"He will say yes," Brent said calmly. "The guy is crazy about you."

"When are you going to ask him?" I asked.

"Tonight," Andy squeaked. "On stage. Dressed as Kenny Rogers."

The rest of the world fell away while we studied him to see if he was teasing us. Andy just nodded to confirm we'd heard him right. The rest of the world came into focus again when Andy's sister, Faith, showed up with a garment bag slung over her shoulder.

"Ready, Slugger?" she asked cheerfully. "We need to have you dressed and ready to go by the time Milo takes the stage to perform."

"Why Kenny?" I asked suddenly.

"Milo's performing Dolly Parton songs tonight," Andy said. "I'm going to pop the question after performing a surprise Kenny and Dolly duet with him in front of our friends and family. Our families and some of our friends from Blissville will be arriving soon to witness me making an ass of myself."

Faith smiled up at her brother with so much love in her eyes. "Milo will remember this day for the rest of his life. I'm so excited my brother is marrying my best friend. Let's go find a place where you can get ready and we can hide you until it's time to take the stage. Milo is back there getting ready, so we don't want to risk running into him."

"Archie could help us pull it off," I told Andy. "Do you mind if I go enlist his help?"

"That's perfect," Faith said. "Thank you, Ollie."

"I'll be right back."

I didn't immediately find Archie when I got backstage. There were dozens of queens milling around talking about their performance or going over last-minute changes before they took the stage.

"Have you seen Archie?" I asked Vava Voom who was downing a bottle of water after her lively performance.

"No, I haven't, honey. I'm sorry."

"Well, well, well," a voice said from behind me. "I'd recognize that luscious ass anywhere." I turned around and had to look way up to meet Gracie Lou Fullbush's eyes. "How are you, darling? Volunteering for more of what I gave you the last time?"

"Um, no," I said. "I'm looking for Archie."

"Oh, well, I saw him duck into the prop closet with a tall drink of water." My breath seized in my chest, but she just waggled her brows as if she didn't know my heart was broken. My Archie with another guy? "Honey, the look in Archie's eyes... Whew! They won't be in there long if you know what I mean."

I did know. Bile burned a path up my throat, and I felt like I was going to be sick. "I'll...um...just return to my seat then."

"Should I tell Archie you were looking for him?"

"Don't bother."

I'd just about made it to the exit when I heard Archie calling my name. I couldn't face him right then. I couldn't smell another man on him or see a sated look on his face I hadn't put there, so I just kept walking.

"Ollie, please don't go," Archie said, sounding desperate. I jerked to a stop and pivoted slowly to face him, allowing time for him to catch up to me. He wasn't alone. A tall, blond man with shrewd blue eyes stood behind him. I wouldn't say the man looked smug, but he looked like he was more confident about his role in Archie's life than I was at the moment. "It's not what that *queen* would have you think." Archie didn't stop until we stood nearly chest to chest. He didn't smell like another man, and he hadn't come. There was no sated look in his eyes, only annoyance.

"I'll just be going," Tall, Blond, and Handsome said. "I'll see you later, Arch."

"Not if I can avoid it," Archie told the man without tearing his eyes away from mine. "I can't believe you thought I was fucking around in the prop closet with another guy after what we shared the past twenty-four hours. Do you think so little of me then? Trust is a two-way street, Ollie."

I briefly closed my eyes because his hurt expression and the disappointment in his voice hurt me worse than thinking about him in the closet with another guy. I had wanted to be different than all the other guys he'd known, but I was already letting him down a day after he gave me—us—a chance. "I'm sorry, Archie." I reached up and cupped his cheek. "You're not the only one afraid to believe sometimes." His eyes widened at my admission.

"We have so much to talk about, Ollie." His voice and eyes softened. "What did you come back to see me about?"

"Oh, I can't believe I nearly forgot." I lightly gripped Archie's arm and pulled him away from the queens. "Andy needs a place to get into costume." Archie let out a whoop and did a little dance when I told him about Andy's plans.

"The prop closet is about as good as I can do without much notice," he told me.

"We'll take it. Let me go get Andy and Faith. I'll be right back."

"Hold it," Archie said firmly, crooking his finger at me. "Kiss me, Ollie. I need to know we're okay."

Cupping his face with both hands, I pressed my mouth to his. I wanted to let my lips linger and deepen the kiss so I could show him how he made me feel, but we were surrounded by catcalling queens, his dick was tucked and taped, and Andy was waiting on us to help him make his and Milo's dreams come true. When I pulled back, I saw the dazed and lusty look in his eyes that made my toes curl inside my shoes. "Hold that thought, Trix."

Andy and Faith were waiting anxiously for me to return. "What the heck took so long?" Andy asked. "Or do I really need to ask?"

"Nothing like that," I said, motioning for them to follow me. "I had to wait for him to finish talking to someone before I could ask him to help."

"The hot blond guy who just came through the door like his ass was on fire?" Faith asked.

"Sounds like the same guy," I said, trying to keep the annoyance out of my voice.

"Everything okay, Ollie?" Andy asked. Apparently, I needed to try harder.

"It's fine, Andy. I promise."

Archie greeted Andy with a blinding, brilliant smile and threw his arms around his broad shoulders. "I'm so excited for you. Congratulations."

"He hasn't said yes yet," Andy told him.

"He will," the three of us responded.

"I'm going to leave them in your capable hands, Arch. I'll see you later, okay?"

Archie studied my face to see if any of the doubt from moments before still lingered in my brain. Of course, they did, but not the way he might think. He would think I doubted him, but it was my abilities I questioned. To quiet the unrest I felt in both of us, I pulled him to me once more and pressed my forehead against his.

"We're okay, Archie," I whispered. "I'm not running." Then I pulled back and kissed his forehead before leaving him to help Andy and Faith get ready.

I felt the curious glances from my friends, but I kept my eyes on the stage rather than address their concerns. Things with Archie were too new and still felt too volatile. It reminded me of my first trip to the ocean as a kid. I was fascinated by the miles of sandy, white beaches stretching before my eyes. I scooped up a big handful of the fine sand, and no matter how tightly I fisted my hand, the sand still slid through my fingers until nothing remained. Is that what loving Archie would be like?

I heard Trix's jubilant voice as she returned to the stage to introduce the next act which happened to be Madame O-Feel-Ya-Peach dressed as a splendid Dolly Parton. I set aside my insecurities and cheered and clapped as Peach performed a rousing version of "Nine to Five." Just as the song ended, the curtains parted and out walked Andy dressed as...

"I thought he was supposed to be Kenny Rogers," Adam said. "He looks more like the crazy guy who did all those dirt bike stunts while wearing a leisure suit."

"He's just missing the cape," Brent added.

I grinned because he did look more like Evel Knievel than Kenny Rogers. All that mattered was how happy Peach looked when the music for "Islands in the Stream" started playing. Andy's voice was shaky when he started singing the first verse, but it got stronger as he gained confidence. How could he not when Peach was smiling and swaying to the music and looking at him like he was the best thing ever put on earth? The crowd went wild when Andy started swaying and dancing too. I looked over and saw a large group of people wearing various expressions of awe and love. I'd met several of them either here or at our annual NA chapter picnic for our families.

When the song ended, Andy dropped to his knee and asked Milo to marry him. It came as no surprise to any of us when Milo joyfully and tearfully accepted his proposal. Andy and Milo didn't join the crowd of us waiting to congratulate them for quite some time after they left the stage, but it was understandable they wanted a few minutes to celebrate alone. Knowing Milo, he didn't want to take away attention from the queens performing on the stage either, so it made sense when they didn't appear until after intermission.

They were swallowed up in a sea of love and happiness which was how it should be for every couple who found the person they wanted to spend their lives with. I found myself feeling more choked up and emotional than usual, but this one was personal. These were two people I cared greatly for. It took them several minutes to hug their way over to our table. When they arrived, Milo hooked his arm around Andy's waist and leaned into him.

"Ollie, we'd like to ask you a favor," Milo said.

"Sure."

"We'd like for you to officiate our wedding."

The damn broke and happy tears spilled down my face. "I'd be honored."

Chapter Twelve

Archie

I'D BEEN LEANING OVER HELPING TIGHTEN THE STRAP ON WHET AND Wilde's satiny, pink platform heel when a shadow fell over me. The shadow was too long to be Ollie's and I didn't feel the same crackle in the air that warned me he was near. I was doubly sure it wasn't Ollie when I felt a hand at the small of my back.

"Some things don't change," a deep voice said. "You still have the most beautiful ass in the world."

"Hey," several of the queens said at once.

Most of the ladies were happy to see me make a return to the stage, at least in some part, as Lady Bea Trix, but not all. Some of them were worried I'd steal the spotlight from them, as well they should. Lady Bea was still in high demand and tended to steal the show, but I had no interest in taking anything away from them. The queens I cared about knew it, and I couldn't give a fuck about any of the petty bullshit the others wanted to lob my way. I was, however, more than willing to let either friend or foe take this nuisance off my hands.

I didn't verbally acknowledge his presence or even jerk away from his touch because it would give too much away. I needed a moment to compose myself after the shock of hearing his voice. Years ago, his admiration would've sent thrills up my spine instead of the dread I felt in the pit of my stomach. I waited until Whet's shoe was perfectly secured before I straightened and slightly shifted away from his touch.

"There you go, honey," I said. "You're on in two minutes. Tell Tony that Jim will need to introduce you. I have something I need to address." *Make it someone.*

"I can see you do," she said with a whistle. "Don't you worry about me, Mother." Whet was also one of my drag daughters from years past. I could've told her it wasn't like that between me and my visitor, but it would've just wasted precious time, and she wouldn't have believed me. I could tell she recognized him from previous years when I welcomed his presence.

After she walked away, I turned and faced the nuisance. "Ryder." There was no warmth in my greeting.

"Fuck me," he said in awe. "You're even more beautiful than I remember, Archie." I couldn't help rolling my eyes over his smarmy voice and hands that reached for me like they had a right to. I avoided his grabby hands and motioned for him to follow me into the prop room, realizing too late it gave him the wrong impression.

"Like old times," Ryder said hungrily. "What a way to welcome a man back to town."

I sidestepped him once more. "In town for the weekend and cruising for a good time?" I asked, certain I was right.

"No, I've permanently moved back to Cincinnati, and I wanted to see you. In my mind, Archie White is synonymous to the Queen City."

"You were pretty eager to leave both of us behind eight years ago," I reminded him. "What changed?" Why did I care? He wasn't who I wanted anymore.

"I've changed, and I've grown up, or I've at least outgrown my wanderlust."

"You're joking, right? That isn't something a person outgrows, Ryder." The man dreamed of being the Indiana Jones of the art world. Give me a break. He was apparently in a slump, bored with life, and

was looking for me to light up his life until the need to roam overcame him.

"It is when the person doesn't want to end up old and alone,"
Ryder said, a wry smile tugging on his lips.

"And I'm the one you think will prevent your loneliness?" I asked
incredulously. "Take a look at me, Ryder. I haven't changed." I didn't
need him to know I wasn't a full-time drag queen any longer. He
didn't need to know how much I've grown up since the years we parted. He'd never understood or approved of my relationship with Ryan
and wouldn't be the least bit upset that one of the most important
persons in my life was gone. He wouldn't appreciate my devotion to
Ryan's Place for sure.

"I do think you're the right person, Archie. I've never forgotten
you."

"You just forgot to call or send an email."

"What good would it have done to stay in touch when our lives
were taking us in different direction? The point is," Ryder said, stepping toward me, "you were with me everywhere I went." I kept walking backwards as he stalked forward until there was nowhere for me
to go unless I wanted to topple the prop shelf on top of him. He was
a dick, but he didn't deserve to be maimed for it.

"Stop," I firmly said when he went to place his hands on my
waist. "You don't have the right to touch me like this."

"I don't?" he asked with a frown. "Does that mean someone else
does?"

I thought of Ollie then. My sweet, golden Ollie who lit up a
room when he walked in. I recalled the look in his eyes when he woke
up and found me watching him sleep. I could almost feel the heat of
his hand on my waist as he anchored me in place so he could press
his warm, nude body against mine. I shivered then, and I could tell
Ryder had mistaken it as a reaction to his nearness. "Stop!" I said again
when he began lowering his head for a kiss. "The shiver wasn't for
you, Ryder. It was for my boyfriend."

Ryder looked over his shoulder mockingly then turned back to face me. "I don't see him."

"He may not be in the room with us right now, but he's in my heart. You need to leave."

"Come on, Archie."

I placed my hands on his chest and gave him a hard push. "Go now."

Ryder didn't look like he wanted to move, so I pushed past him and left the room. That's when I saw Ollie walking away with his shoulders hunched. He reminded me of a wounded puppy, and it made me want to shake my fist at the universe and demand it leave me the fuck alone. I could tell by the smirk on Gracie Lou's face she'd told Ollie I was in the prop room with a man. Had she told him it was my ex?

I called his name, and he kept walking, so I trotted after him. "Ollie, please don't leave." He must've heard the desperation in my voice because he stopped and turned to face me. The hurt I saw in his eyes shamed and angered me. How could he think I'd just jump on the next cock that came along after what we shared the night before and again the next morning? He humbled me when he apologized for not having more faith, and the gentle kiss he placed on my forehead was the sweetest kiss anyone had ever given me.

We both knew a lengthy conversation needed to follow, but the backstage at QCD wasn't the place. Then two of our dearest friends, the ones who brought us together, got engaged. I saw the joyous look on Ollie's face when Andy and Milo spoke privately to him after they were swarmed. Saw the happy tears and suspected they'd asked him to officiate their wedding. I still had an hour or longer of the show before I could go spend time with him. I needed to touch him and breathe in his familiar scent. I needed to know he was going to hear me out and believe me when I said I only wanted him.

"Lady Bea," Tony said gently, "why don't you go on out there and be with your friends and your guy. I'll get one of the other ladies to cover for you."

"Tony, I—" His dark scowl silenced my protest. It was going to be a weak one anyway because I wanted to talk to Ollie. "Okay." I kissed his cheek then hustled down the steps and through the door leading to the main floor. The place was packed with dancing and gyrating bodies, so it took me forever to weave my way to Ollie's table. He looked up before I reached him, and I wanted to think he could feel me enter the room like I could with him.

"You clean up nice, Lady Bea," Keeton said when I arrived. He stood up and offered the chair next to Ollie's.

"Thanks, doll," I said, blowing him a kiss. To Ollie, I said, "I've been relieved of my emceeing duties."

"Misbehaving?" he asked.

"Tony could see my heart wasn't in it."

"Oh? Why not?"

I placed my hand on the side of his face and brushed a thumb over his high cheekbone. "I wanted to be with you, especially after the misunderstanding back there."

Ollie slipped an arm around my waist and scooted my chair closer. "Why don't we go someplace where we can talk more privately?"

"Sounds perfect, but I won't be taking you to my mamma's restaurant. I wouldn't be able to get a word in edgewise."

"I think I know a place," Ollie said. "Let's go say goodnight to the grooms-to-be."

Milo hugged me tight after I admired his beautiful band then hugged Andy too. "I can't wait to hear all about the wedding plans," I told them before looping my fingers through Ollie's and tugging him away. "I just need to change my clothes really quick."

"No, you don't," Ollie said. "First of all, I'm guessing taking off all your stuff isn't quick, and second, I like you just the way you are. So, unless you're uncomfortable, you can wear what you have on."

None of the other guys I'd dated had said that to me. They were all too willing to suggest I get changed before we went anywhere, including the ignorant ass who thought he could back me up against the nearest firm structure and fuck me. Like I'd just been waiting around for him to return to me. *Asshole.*

"Wow, your mind must've traveled to an unpleasant place, or you're afraid I'll bolt," Ollie said, breaking through my thoughts.

"Why do you say that?"

Ollie held up our joined hands and saw I had a white-knuckle grip on him. "I'm so sorry," I said, relaxing my hands. "Yes, it's been a stressful night. If you're fine with me wearing this, then I just need to grab my bag with my clothes, wallet, and keys from my locker. Do you want to wait here or come with me?"

"We'll get into mischief if I go with you, so I'll just wait right here for you." I turned to walk away, but he called out my name. "Yes?" I asked, turning to face him.

"I'm driving."

I threw my head back and laughed. "I'll be right back, Golden Boy."

I felt curious eyes on me as I made my way to the locker room, but I didn't make eye contact. I care about ninety percent of the queens but had no use for the other ten. They were mean, nasty, and looked to cause trouble every chance they got. If things started heating up between me and Ollie, I could think of better ways we could spend our Wednesday evenings together after his chapter meetings.

I grabbed my stuff and returned to where I left Ollie. He was leaning against the wall with his arms crossed over his chest while Gracie Lou chewed his ear off. I'm sure she was filling his ears with wild stories about Ryder and me. Her eyes widened when she saw me approach, but she didn't bother hiding the calculating sneer on her face.

"Ready?" I asked Ollie.

"Oh yeah," he replied tightly, reaching for my hand. "See you around, Gracie Lou."

"I sure hope so, cutie."

I didn't bother acknowledging her existence. The only thing I cared about was making sure Ollie knew Ryder had no claims on me or my heart.

"She sure has it in for you," Ollie said when we stepped out into a cool September evening.

"That obvious, huh?"

"She implied you and the blond guy were in the prop room having sex during our first confrontation, and then she basically told me he was the one guy you never got over. She sounded like she felt sorry for me. Offered a shoulder to cry on later if I needed it."

"You won't be needing it," I said through clenched teeth. "Gracie Lou has hated me since the first time she laid eyes on me, and she's pissed I dressed in drag tonight because it pulls some of the spotlight away from her."

"I figured she was," Ollie said. "Can't blame her. No one in there compares to your charisma, beauty, and ability to captivate a room."

"Why, Ollie," I said coyly, "you sure know how to make a girl blush."

"I'm parked over here," Ollie said, tugging me toward the right. "So, I'm taking you to a diner that serves comfort food twenty-four hours a day and seven days a week. I'm not very hungry, but I'd love a piece of pumpkin cheesecake."

"That sounds delicious."

"It's pretty quiet this time of night, so we should be able to talk without someone's adorable mom interrupting us every few minutes." His comment made me wonder once more about his parents, but it wasn't the right time to ask.

When we reached Ollie's car, he opened the passenger door for me. I looked at the door and looked at him like I'd fallen into one of the old movies I adored.

"Too much?" he asked. "I don't want to be like the other guys."

"You're already different than them just being your usual self," I assured him. "I find this cute all the same."

"It's not because you're wearing a dress either," he rushed to say. "I don't think women are so weak they can't open their own doors."

"Ollie," I said, unable to keep from laughing. "Your rambling is even cuter than you opening the door for me." I fisted my hand in his shirt and hauled him to me for a kiss. When I released his shirt, he stood there blinking at me with lust-fogged eyes. "You don't look like you're in any condition to drive, Ollie. Maybe you should give me the keys."

The remark shook him out of his daydream. "Hell no," he said, rushing around to the driver's side of the car like I was about to snatch his keys from him.

"I don't drive that bad," I said once Ollie pulled out of his parking spot and merged into traffic.

"You are the worst driver I've ever seen."

"You wound me," I said dramatically, even though everyone said the same thing about my driving skills.

The diner Ollie took me to was smaller than my mom's pizza joint, but the smells coming from the kitchen were just as incredible. "I smell biscuits."

"The best biscuits you'll ever eat." I turned and saw a statuesque queen making her way toward us. "You look familiar, sugar," she said, appraising me, "have we met before?"

"Sandy, this is Lady Bea—"

"Oh my God!" she exclaimed. "I knew I recognized the seductive, graceful glide. I'm so excited to meet you." She turned to Ollie and mock-whispered, "You never said you knew my idol."

"I never knew you idolized Trix," Ollie countered. "Allow me to make formal introductions."

"Oh my God, my hair is probably a mess, and I probably have lipstick on my teeth," Sandy said. "Oh! Can I get a selfie of the two of us together? Is it too much to ask?"

"Your hair and lipstick look fine," I assured her. "A selfie is fine by me if Ollie doesn't mind." He held up his hand indicating it was fine with him. Sandy looped her arms around me and held the camera up to snap a picture of us.

"I don't like the way my eyes look in this one. Can I take one more?"

"Sure."

She didn't like her smile in the second one, I had my eyes closed in the third, and she sneezed just as her phone took the fourth picture. On the fifth try, she got the picture she wanted. Only then did she ask if we wanted a booth or a table. I realized we weren't going to get much more privacy than if we'd gone to Mamma's pizzeria, so I had to act fast.

"Actually, we only stopped by to get two slices of pumpkin cheesecake to go," I told her. Ollie didn't let on if he was surprised. "Will that be a problem?"

"No, but I'm sad I won't get to spend more time with you."

"There's always next time," I told her. She hummed an agreement as she walked off.

"You're never coming back, are you?" Ollie whispered.

"Not in drag," I replied.

"Your beautiful eyes will give you away."

"I'll wear colored contacts then."

"Please don't," Ollie said, sounding horrified. "You have the most beautiful eyes I've ever seen."

Sandy returned with a small paper bag. "Here you go."

I pulled my wallet out of my messenger bag before Ollie could stop me. I let Sandy keep the change for her trouble and told her I looked forward to seeing her again.

"Where to?" Ollie asked once we were standing on the sidewalk in front of the diner.

"Someplace where we won't be interrupted by another living soul."

Chapter Thirteen

Ollie

"I KNOW A PLACE," I SAID. GOD, I WANTED TO SEE HIM AMONG MY things again. I wanted to hear the awe in his voice when he looked at my drawings and to see his fair skin against my cream bed linens. I wanted to hear the sounds he made when he came.

"Ollie, you know what will happen if I go home with you again," Archie said, a smug smile stretching across his face. "Neither one of us will be satisfied with rutting against each other until we come."

"I know."

"We need to do some talking before we get to the um..." He didn't want to say fucking because he worried he might offend me, and I was certain lovemaking was a foreign word to him.

"We'll talk on the ride there, and we can talk more once we arrive. We can talk all night if that's what you—*we*—need."

"You have church in the morning."

"I wouldn't force you to attend my church service. Is that why you're hesitant tonight?" Knowing he was waiting for me in my house would certainly have me hustling back home as soon as the last member left.

Archie threw his head back and laughed. It was joyful and beautiful; I wanted to find more ways to create the kind of happiness spilling out of him. "It never crossed my mind, Ollie. Besides, I'm not the kind of guy you can force to do anything I don't want to do. I was thinking more along the lines like maybe you don't want to stand at the podium after a night of debauchery. I can see you looking all disheveled and imagine you still smell like me." Archie sobered immediately. "Take me back to my car then follow me to Ryan's Place so I can pack an overnight bag. I need to text my mom."

"You need Maria's permission to stay the night?" I couldn't keep the smirk off my face. "Is it wise to get her hopes up? She clearly loves me and has decided we work together."

"Oh, Ollie. I adore this sassy side of you, and I can't wait to see the other facets of your personality." He shook his head like I might be too much to take, but I was glad he found it endearing instead of annoying. "I need to tell Mamma I can't come to church with her in the morning because I'll already be there."

My breath froze in my lungs. "What?"

"Mamma called me before I left for QCD to inform me she, Esther, and Henry are going to your church service in the morning. She invited me to go along."

"What was your answer?"

Archie tipped his head to the side and gave me a wry grin. "I played hard to get, of course."

"You mean you weren't sure," I countered.

"True," he admitted. "Religion is a touchy subject for me and one of the reasons why I tried so hard to resist you, Ollie."

"I think that's where we need to start our conversation then we can work our way to Ryder."

"He's not important," Archie countered.

"Maybe he's not important to you now, but I didn't need Gracie Lou to tell me Ryder mattered to you once."

"I hate that queen."

"Archie, you might say the guy isn't important—"

"You don't believe me?" All the joy from earlier was gone.

"I believe *he's* not important to *you* anymore, but I can see *you're* still important to *him*. That's all I meant. He's not going to go away, and to be fair, I need to know how hard I'll need to fight to keep you."

Archie sucked in a sharp breath and slowly released it. "Okay. Let's go. We're losing valuable time, and I know you're not going to want to skimp on the talking time to get to the sexy time." He headed for the passenger side of the car. "Tick tock, Ollie."

I unlocked the car with my key fob and hustled to the driver side. I didn't drive as erratically as Archie, but I was tempted to give it a shot. The drive to QCD was too short to strike up a meaningful conversation. I accepted the short kiss Archie gave me before getting out then followed him across town to Ryan's Place. I would've waited for him in the car, but he beckoned me forth with a crook of his long, graceful finger.

"I want to see you in my space," he said when I joined him on the porch. "I want to look at the chaise in the corner of the room and picture you sitting there." I could tell by the intensity in his expression that allowing me into his inner sanctuary was a big deal.

No one was downstairs in the gathering rooms when we walked through the front door, but someone had left the lamp on the foyer table on for Archie. I was again impressed with the homey feel of the place. My pulse increased with every step that brought me closer to Archie's secret lair. I had a hard time imagining what his room would look like because he guarded his privacy so closely. I knew there was so much more to him than the sassy side he showed in public.

"Here we are," he dramatically said after he opened the door and turned on the light. "This is where I do most of my fantasizing about getting you naked." I nearly swallowed my tongue.

"There?" I asked, pointing to his tidy bed covered with a luxurious-looking dark brown comforter and adorned with pillows in earth tones and jeweled colors.

"And there." Archie pointed to the chaise chair he'd mentioned. The overstuffed chaise was covered with a dark teal velvet, making me wonder how it would feel beneath my bare skin. Then I pictured Archie riding my cock in wild abandon. "I know what you're thinking. I promise you it will happen someday." I swallowed hard and looked over at him. His eyes turned a darker shade of green when he was turned on.

"You better release the boys," I said. "I don't want to be the source of your misery, Arch. I only want to give you pleasure."

"Sit!" he said, pointing to the chair. "I'm going to remove my makeup and take a quick shower before we go." I did as he demanded and earned a "There's my Golden Boy," but he said it in a tone I expected him to use if I knelt at his feet and sucked him off at his command. "Stop thinking those dirty thoughts, Ollie."

Archie quickly entered the bathroom of his master suite and shut the door behind him. I realized I'd have one hell of a view into his bathroom from the vantage point of the chaise. I swiftly rose from the chair and crossed the room. Archie answered after I knocked softly on the door. He hadn't even had enough time to remove his wig. "Something wrong?"

"Yeah," I said breathily. "I want to watch you."

"You want to watch me take off my drag costume and makeup?"

I nodded. "Someday, I hope you'll let me watch the reverse process too."

Archie swallowed hard, and his only response was a quick, hard kiss. "Return to your seat," he said in his dominating tone that made my dick twitch. "Enjoy the show, Ollie."

I hustled back to the chaise and got comfortable. Archie waited for me to get into position then took off his wig. Under it, he wore something that looked like a stocking. It came off next, and I saw his dark hair appeared to be wet from sweat. I'd never given much thought to wigs before, but I imagined his body heat was trapped underneath and it could make things uncomfortable. Archie turned to face the mirror then smirked when our eyes met because the chaise was at the perfect angle for us to see each other in the reflection.

Archie tore his eyes off mine after a few seconds to focus on his task. He reached up and removed his false eyelashes and returned them to a small case sitting on the vanity. I never knew false eyelashes could be worn more than once. Next, Archie unscrewed the lid off a short, round jar and dipped two fingers inside it to scoop up a thick, white cream. He smeared a thick layer of it all over his face except for his eyes. Then, Archie pulled wipes out of a purple plastic container and began wiping off his eye makeup while he let the white cream work its magic.

Once his eyes were naked, Archie turned on the sink and allowed the water to warm up before dipping a dark washcloth beneath the faucet. I watched as he removed one section of makeup at a time, rinsing the cloth between each one. When he finished, I saw the gorgeous face of the man who captivated me from the moment we met. Watching him remove his makeup felt symbolic like he was baring more to me than just his clean skin.

Archie smiled wryly then reached behind him and slowly slid the zipper down the back of his dress. It was then I realized he must've taken off his long, satin gloves during the drive home. Archie held onto the bodice of the dress for a few heartbeats then let go, allowing the satin to slide over the perfect swells of his ass, down his long, lean legs, and pool around his high heels. Seeing him standing there in only a pair of ivory lace boy shorts, stockings, and heels was something I would never forget. I wanted to photograph him just like that. Would he let me?

I reached inside my front pocket and pulled out my cell phone. "May I?" Archie took a big shaky breath but nodded. "Stay just as you are."

"I'm a mess," Archie mumbled.

"You're the most beautiful being I've ever seen." I heard the awe in my voice and saw how much it affected Archie. I snapped the photo then set my phone down once I made sure my trembling hand didn't require a retake.

Archie stepped out of his shoes and raised a quirked brow in the mirror. "You can take a few photos, but no nudes." He turned and propped his foot on the closed toilet lid and reached for the lacy band around his white stockings at the same time I picked up my phone. I snapped a few of him carefully sliding the silky stocking down his leg and a few more when he switched to the other one.

"This is where we put the phones down," Archie said with a wry smile. "There's nothing gracious or glamorous about this part."

"Will it hurt?" I couldn't imagine shoving my balls up inside me then taping my dick to my taint.

"It's something you get used to, but it's quite uncomfortable at first." Archie turned his back to me once more and slid his underwear down his legs then spread his legs and reached between them. The vanity mirror wasn't low enough for me to see beneath his belly button, so I couldn't see what his hands were doing. Archie squatted a bit, and I could see his hands moving between his legs. I heard him removing the tape before he tossed it in the trash can. He reached between his legs, and I wondered if he was urging his balls to drop back into his sac. He closed his legs, blocking my view from seeing anything else. "Turned off yet?"

I jerked my eyes away from his ass to meet his gaze. I hated the hesitance I saw there. What had other men done to him to make him so gun-shy? I cupped my aching dick through my jeans, stroking up and down a few times. "Does this look like I'm turned off? The only thing hotter would be seeing your dick and balls through the lacy fabric."

"Ollie," Archie said breathily.

"Get in the shower," I commanded. "Leave the door open so I can watch through the mirror."

Archie turned and walked to the shower, allowing me to see his full, firm balls and semi-hard cock. "I won't take long."

"I won't either," I squeaked.

"Hands off the goods," Archie said with a raised brow before he opened the glass door and stepped inside.

I saw his movements in the reflection of the mirror, and I'd never seen anything as sexy as him washing and rinsing his hair. I was so jealous of the shampoo suds cascading down his body but knew I'd soon get my chance. Archie quickly washed his body with a loofah and shower gel before he turned the shower off and opened the door to grab the towel. I wanted to get up and cross the room to dry him off myself, but he'd told me to stay put. Archie ran the towel roughly over his head, making his hair stick up everywhere. My eyes followed the motion of the towel as he rubbed it across his chest and down his abdomen before drying his arms. My eyes locked on his hard-on and the smooth skin at the base of his cock. I wanted to kiss him there before taking his dick in my mouth.

"You're thinking dirty thoughts again, Ollie," Archie said in a rough voice.

"Can you hear my dick weeping from over there?"

"Is that what I heard while I was in the shower?"

"That was me moaning with the need to touch you," I confessed.

Archie wrapped the towel around his waist and padded into the room, looking sexy, smug, and delicious. "You want to touch me, Ollie?"

"Here? Now?"

"Can you think of a better time?" he asked, standing at the foot of the chaise. He hooked his hands in the towel and waited for me to answer him.

"I thought you wanted to talk first to clear the air and—"

"Ollie, is there anything I can say about religion that will change your feelings for me?"

"No."

"Is there anything I can tell you about my past relationships that will make you want to run in the opposite direction?"

"No."

"Is it the man answering no or is it his dick? I need to know, Ollie."

I thought about what he was asking me for about half a second. "It's me, Arch. All of me wants all of you, but I can wait if you're not sure."

His answer was to open the towel and drop it. I sat up straight, scooted to the end of the chaise, and placed my hands on his narrow hips. I kissed his tightly bunched abs and dipped my tongue inside his navel.

"Ollie," Archie softly moaned as I kissed a path toward his bobbing erection. "You're such a tease."

"Am not," I whispered against his quivering flesh. I stuck out my tongue and licked the smooth skin above the base of his cock. "I deliver." He tried to push my shoulders back so I'd lie on my back, but I wasn't interested in him rutting against me. I dug my fingers into his hips, stilling him. "You're not always going to be in charge, Arch."

He fisted his hands in my hair, rocking his hips so his dick rubbed up against my bristled chin. It could leave marks on his sensitive flesh, but I liked knowing he could look down tomorrow morning and be reminded of this moment.

"Suck me," he demanded. "I've been thinking of your mouth on me forever."

I shifted one hand between his parted legs to gently cup his balls while I lifted his cock to expose its underside with the other. I lowered my head, angling it to the side so I could place my tongue against his ball sac, then I licked a slow, wet trail from his balls to the tip of his leaking dick. "Mmmm," I said when I tasted his precum.

"Ollie," he moaned, sounding as desperate as I felt.

I sucked the flushed, round head inside my mouth and French-kissed the tip, rolling my tongue around and around, then I pushed back his foreskin with my tongue to reach the sensitive spot beneath the crown.

"Yes!" Archie's hands tightened in my hair. He rocked his hips faster, desperate to get inside my mouth, but I tightened my lips around the crown, halting his progress. "You're so mean." I loved how frantic he sounded to have his dick all the way inside my mouth and pleasing him felt much more important to me than teasing him, so I loosened my lips, relaxed my jaw, and lowered my head until my nose touched the bare skin at the base of his cock.

Chapter Fourteen

Archie

"OLLIE!" I WHISPER-SHOUTED WHEN I FELT THE HEAD OF MY dick slide into his throat. I stilled my hips so I wouldn't hurt him. I expected him to pull back right away, but my Ollie was full of surprises. I felt his puffs of air against my pelvis as he breathed in and out of his nose before he swallowed around my cock. "God, I won't last. You feel too good."

Ollie eased off then, slowly letting my cock slide from his mouth. He licked his lips that were wet, shiny, and indecent, matching the hunger in his eyes which looked almost black with lust. The Golden Boy I adored was replaced by someone darker, dirtier, and maybe a little depraved. I craved to know this side of him, wanted to do the dirtiest things to this man who sometimes felt untouchable with his goodness. I hardly recognize the man with the cocky sneer who knew he rocked me to my core and relished every fucking second of it.

"You're wearing too much," I told him. "I need to see your skin—touch it."

Ollie pulled his charcoal gray Henley over his head, baring his dark, olive-toned skin to me. I wanted to touch everywhere all at once, but I started with his hard nipples. I circled the furled buds with my thumbs, feeling them get even tighter. He leaned forward and nipped one of the V-shaped muscles of my pelvis before nuzzling his nose at the juncture of my thigh.

"Lie down," I said. "This isn't fair."

"To whom? I'm happy right where I'm at."

"It isn't fair to me," I said. "I need to be able to touch you and feel you too. I've always wanted to test out the sturdiness of this chair, and I think now is a perfect time."

"Here? Now?"

"Don't you trust yourself to be quiet?" I teased. "Would you like to borrow one of Lady Bea's scarves to bite down on?" I thought Ollie's eyes were going to roll back in his head. "There's a dirty, dirty boy who lives just beneath the surface of your golden goodness," I said, dropping to my knees between his spread legs. "Lie back and let me help you discover him, Ollie."

I kept my eyes locked on his when I reached for the button of his jeans. Instead of stopping me, he reclined back on his elbows to make it easier for me to unfasten and unzip his jeans. He lifted his hips so I could pull them down his legs then I removed his Converse so I could finish undressing him.

Ollie scooted back until he reclined against the angled back of the chaise, allowing me to feast my eyes on his beauty. His dark eyes dared me to take what I wanted, and I wasn't about to pass up on his offer. I'd rushed headlong into relationships before and regretted it, but I knew it was different with Ollie. Everything would be different with Ollie.

I rose swiftly and retrieved the condoms and lubricant from my bedside table. When I turned back toward the chair, Ollie had one hand tucked under his head and the other lazily stroked his cock. I could see the head was flushed and wet, eager to know me just as mine was eager to know him. I couldn't let another minute pass before I knew his taste too.

I set the condoms and lube on the small table next to the chair then lowered myself to kneel on the chaise between Ollie's feet. I leaned forward, bracing my hands next to his hips and lowered myself down until the bottom half of my body hung over the edge of the chaise, and I was up close and personal with his cock. Ollie released his erection and wrapped his hand around the back of my head, gently urging me down lower. This was the boldness I'd seen briefly in the texts he sent and the flashes of heat I'd seen in his eyes. He wasn't a man who struggled to figure out what he wanted; he knew, and he took it.

I licked my lips suggestively to wet them and entice him to lose his mind. Ollie pressed his fingers tightly against my scalp and growled, his bicep bulging with tension. I parted my lips and licked the head of his cock like an ice cream cone, around and around, capturing his essence on my tongue.

"Archie," Ollie whimpered. I loved that I could change him from a dominating man to a moaning, needy slut with a few little flicks of the tongue. "I-I need…" His words trailed off when I sucked him to the root just like he'd done to me. I knew exactly what he needed, and I was going to give it to him. Ollie's mouth fell open for a silent yell and his fingers tangled almost painfully in my hair when I started working his length in and out of my mouth.

Ollie raised his hips every time I lowered my mouth, pushing into my throat. He lowered his other arm so he could trace my lips where they stretched to accommodate his girth. I could tell when he was getting close because his hips lost their smooth rhythm and his thrusts became short and choppy. Ollie grunted with need as he chased his orgasm then pitifully moaned when I pulled off his cock.

"Not so fast. I have big plans for this," I said, stroking Ollie's cock from root to tip. I practically purred as I climbed my way up his body and straddled his hips. "When you come, I want your cock buried deep inside me. Nothing else will do tonight."

Ollie nodded, appearing to be incapable of speech at the moment. I leaned forward and captured his lips in a hot, demanding kiss while reaching for the condom packet off the table. Ollie slid both hands in my hair, holding me in place while he took over the kiss, dominating me as I'd never experienced before. I tore the wrapper open with trembling hands then slid the condom expertly down his length. Ollie hissed when I stroked him with a lube-slicked hand before I began stretching my ass to receive him.

I pulled back from the kiss long enough to align Ollie's cock against my hole. I slowly pressed down against his erection, moaning when the broad head nudged me open.

"Go slow, Arch," Ollie whispered against my lips. His hand went to my hips, slowing my descent. It burned as Ollie stretched me wide, reminding me how long it had been since I'd fucked something besides my fist. It felt so damn good, and I couldn't contain the whimpers of pleasure. "That's it, baby. Nice and slow."

"Ollie," I said, his name falling from my lips like a prayer. "I-I..." My words trailed off when I was fully seated on his cock.

"I got you, Arch." He kissed and licked my neck while I adjusted to him. Ollie ran his hands up and down my back and slid them back into my hair, arching my neck to give him access. He brushed his scruffy chin over my collarbone and my neck, leaving his mark against my skin. Then his skilled hands gripped my hips and rocked me forward just the slightest bit to create friction inside. "You feel so good, baby. So tight."

The slanted back of the chaise made sex a little awkward, and it took a few attempts to find the right angle so I could feel the friction and penetration where I needed it. Reverse cowboy would've worked better, but I wasn't willing to sacrifice looking into Ollie's eyes when he came inside me the first time. Ollie reclined fully against the back of the chaise, and I leaned in the opposite direction, bracing my weight with my hands on the cushions of the chaise. I arched my back and lifted my hips so Ollie could thrust upward inside me, giving him one hell of a show. He could see every inch of his cock sliding in and out of my ass.

Ollie growled and fucked faster and deeper inside me, our skin slapping together to create a delicious sound. "I need you to come,

Archie. I need you to come quick." Pleasure mounted and built inside me from the delicious friction and Ollie's cock nudging my prostate. I was so close, but I needed something to push me over the edge. I braced my weight on one hand and began working my cock with the other. Ollie held onto one of my hips while his other hand reached up and tweaked my nipples.

"Come now, Arch." I came long and hard, splattering his chest and stomach with my cum while moaning his name. I savored the lusty growls rumbling from him as he slammed his hips upward, fucking me harder and chasing his climax.

"Yes, baby!" he said, his sexy body tensing all over as he thrust up inside me once more, spilling inside me. I knew I'd wear bruises on my skin where he gripped my hips, but I looked forward to seeing his marks. "It was even better than I imagined it would be," Ollie said, relaxing into the chair with a sated smile. My Golden Boy had returned, and I was the reason for the serene expression on his face. "You're so beautiful, Archie."

I leaned over him and brushed the wet hair off his forehead. "You're the beautiful one, Ollie. You take my breath away." I dropped a sweet kiss on his swollen lips then reached between our joined bodies to secure the condom while I eased off his softening erection. "Want to get cleaned up before we hit the road?"

I saw some of his satisfaction dim because my question reminded him of the heavy conversation we agreed to have on the way to his house. I owed him an explanation about why religion impacted me so negatively, and he wanted to know more about Ryder. The man from my past had zero impact on my future, but Ollie wasn't persuaded. So, I needed to convince him. "I'm not getting ready to tell you I was molested by a priest if that's what you're thinking."

"I'm not sure what I'm thinking, to be honest. I know you have serious issues with religion and finding out I was a pastor sent you running from me. I don't want you to feel like you need to run from me ever again, Arch."

I extended a hand to him, and he accepted it. We took a quick shower even though we both wanted to linger longer, learning the planes and valleys of one another's bodies while the water ran in rivulets over us. I couldn't think of anything I wanted more at that moment than to make Ollie hard again and finish off the blow job I started earlier before he returned the favor, but it was getting late, and we still had a thirty-minute drive to his house. I suspected sleep would elude both of us, but I knew Ollie needed to get as much rest as he could before his sermon the following morning. I didn't want to be the reason he faltered in front of his congregation.

"I forgot about dessert," I said when I opened the door and saw the paper bag on the seat.

"Pretty sure I forgot my name back there until you moaned it," Ollie said. He reached over and cupped my face tenderly. "Ready?" I knew he meant for more than just the drive through the creepy corn fields.

I nodded. "I called Mamma on the ride over here. At first, she was irritated I was interrupting her *Magnum PI* time, but she got over it when she realized I would be meeting her at church in the morning."

"Is your mom devout?" Ollie asked as he drove through my quiet neighborhood.

"She used to be," I said softly. "I guess you would say she never lost her faith in God, but she lost her respect for the Catholic church." Ollie glanced over at me quickly. "My father was a very abusive man, and my mom sought counsel from her priest when she decided to leave him. You might've heard divorce is frowned upon in the Catholic church."

"They're not the only religion putting ancient words before people, Arch. I'm not making excuses for her priest, but she would've probably received the same advice had she sought counsel from a preacher, a minister, a reverend, or pastor. They're trained to believe the sanctity of marriage comes before a person's needs and wants."

"Even if all the person wants is to live in peace without violence?"

"Of course not, baby," Ollie said softly. It was ridiculous how much I liked hearing him call me baby. "These are the same people who brainwash parents into abandoning their children. It's a good thing God forgives because I can't. Not when it comes to young lives getting destroyed."

"So much passion," I whispered. "It's too bad my mom didn't have a spiritual leader like you."

"What happened, Arch?"

"The priest wanted to counsel my parents to help save their marriage. My mother wasn't a foolish woman. She knew my dad wouldn't be interested in getting help and would be furious she spoke of their problems to a stranger. She told the priest she feared for her life, Ollie. Do you know what he did? He went against my mom's wishes and spoke to my father after mass the following weekend. You see, my dad could sell water to a drowning man. He looked the part of the doting husband and father in public but would beat me for playing with my cousin's dolls and knock my mom nearly unconscious if she didn't have dinner on the table at the right time. He was a fucking monster."

"Baby," Ollie whispered, reaching over and holding my hand.

"Cops were called to our house at least once a week by our neighbors. My mom was too terrified to press charges though. She knew the only way to live was to escape. The thing about abusive spouses is they find a way to alienate you from everyone who loves you. My mom was convinced her family wouldn't want anything to do with her, and she'd lost all her friends. All she had, all she was *permitted* to have was my dad and me. No job. No friends. Nothing but the three of us. It was the only way he could control her.

"Mom must have realized the rage simmering inside my dad was worse than usual. She sent me to my room after mass and demanded I stay there until she came and got me." I swallowed hard because it was still difficult to think about thirty years later. "The screaming and fighting were so much louder, Ollie. I could hear furniture getting shoved aside, things crashing onto the floor and shattering, and my mom sobbing and screaming as she tried to fend him off. This time, the cops arrived during the disturbance instead of afterward. My dad was in such a rage, and I later learned he took a swing at one of the officers with a ball bat. I will never forget how loud the gunshot sounded in our small home."

"Arch." Ollie squeezed my hand. "I want to hold you right now."

"You can hold me when we get to your house." I wasn't ashamed to admit I wanted his affection and gentle touch. "The officer who shot my dad saved our lives in more ways than one. He couldn't walk away from the traumatized woman and her terrified little boy. We had nowhere to go, and he didn't want to drop us off at a shelter. He took us home with him, and it's where we stayed until Mamma found a job and got on her feet. Ryan Lassiter became my mom's best friend, the best honorary uncle a kid could have, and the man I turned to when I realized I was gay. Everything good I have in my life, I owe to him."

"Ryan's Place," Ollie said softly. "Every day you honor his memory the best way you know how."

"I try."

"You succeed," Ollie countered.

"So, you can see why I bolted from you when we first met."

Ollie nodded. "You didn't run too fast, and you didn't run very far."

"Maybe I wanted you to catch me, Golden Boy. My soul knew what my heart was afraid to believe."

"There are no words I can offer to make up for the callous way your mother was treated. I understand why people walk away from churches and religion; I can't blame them. I also know God doesn't stop loving his children when they take a step back. I'm here to offer love, support, and guidance for those who need to feel a connection to something bigger than themselves. I want to be a friend to those who don't believe too. All anyone really wants is to feel love and acceptance, and it's what I offer to my congregation. I don't claim to have the magic answers to the world's problems or a direct line to the man upstairs. I can promise I'd never turn my back on someone like your mom who sought my help."

"I know, Ollie. Mamma knows it too."

The mood was still pretty heavy when we got back to Ollie's place. He held me in his arms like he said he would, and I pulled from his strength. Ollie ran his fingers through my hair and kissed my forehead, my nose, and my lips before leading me into his bedroom and undressing us both because I was suddenly without the energy to do the simplest things. Once we were beneath the sheets, Ollie rested his head on my chest and curled his arm over my waist.

"Don't think I've forgotten about that Ryder guy," he said just as I was drifting to sleep.

"Who?" I asked sleepily. "Pretty sure I was born again tonight." Ollie's warm chuckle followed me into my dreams.

Chapter Fifteen

Ollie

I WOKE LONG BEFORE MY ALARM WENT OFF BECAUSE I WANTED TO WATCH Archie sleep while the sun chased the shadows out of my room. I wished the sun could chase away the shadows inside our souls and the doubts in our minds just as easily, but that wasn't how life worked. Archie reached for me in his sleep like maybe his subconscious needed reassurance I was still there. His hand clumsily bumped into my upper arm before it closed around my bicep, holding me there in case I planned to run. I wasn't the runner in the fledgling relationship though; he was. Would he regret what happened between us? Had things progressed too quickly since Friday night?

"A man can't sleep when you're thinking so hard," Archie said. His voice sounded rough, sleepy, and somehow humorous at the same time. He opened an eye and regarded me. "What has you so worried, Golden Boy? Afraid I'll bolt when you're in the shower?"

"No," I said too quickly for it to be believable. "You don't have a car, so you wouldn't get very far. I was worried you might check out emotionally after such an intense night."

"No way," Archie whispered, scooting closer to me. He trailed his fingers down my arm until he reached my hand. Archie linked our fingers together and lifted my hand to his lips. The innocent kiss on my flesh sent an electric current straight to my balls. The semi-erection

I'd sported while watching him sleep quickly became hard and throbbing. Archie dropped my hand then reached between us and fisted my shaft. "What do we have here?"

My eyes rolled back in my head when he stroked upward and twisted his wrist before sliding back down. "It's m-m-my morning d-d-devotional," I managed to stutter.

Archie tucked me up against him then rolled so I was on my back beneath him and he lay between my spread legs. "There's so much of you I want to worship." Then he kissed me like there was no place he'd rather be, and we had all the time in the world to make love.

We touched and kissed, licked and sucked until my bedroom filled with early morning light. I opened the bedside drawer and handed Archie the condoms and lube. He looked more beautiful than I'd ever seen him as he rose above me, filled me, and completed me. Archie's eyes glittered like jewels, and his expression was so intense it robbed me of the ability to breathe. He wanted me, and he was done running.

Afterward, I held Archie's pliant body against mine and ran my fingers through his hair until I couldn't put off getting out of bed any longer. "Shower with me?"

"Of course."

We brushed our teeth together while waiting for the shower to warm up. I was too busy staring at Archie in awe to notice the hickey he'd left on my collarbone until Archie pointed it out to me in my reflection.

"I got a little carried away," Archie said, not sounding a bit sorry. "I like knowing you'll wear my mark beneath your clergy collar."

"I like you wearing my scruff marks on your chin and neck," I countered.

Archie studied his reflection with a crooked smile. "So do I."

Once inside the shower, we worked together like we'd done it for years. I began washing my hair while Archie started on his body. As soon as I tilted my head back to rinse my hair, Archie asked, "Do you need me to give you some space so you can prepare for your service? I don't want to be in your way and be a distraction."

"You could always help me sacrifice the goat," I suggested once I was done. "Ow," I said when Archie tweaked my nipple.

"That's not funny," Archie said, trading places with me so he could wash his hair while I washed my body. "I'm serious. Maybe you have a routine like athletes and performers have before giving each sermon. I don't want to mess anything up."

"I don't have a routine," I said, "but I want to hear all about yours."

Archie tilted his head back to rinse the shampoo from his hair. "Not me, Golden Boy. I know plenty of queens who do though. Dated a few athletes too. I swear baseball players are the worst. There was this one who—" His words died off when I pressed my lips to his for a quick kiss.

"Can we not talk about other men you've dated? Especially, considering the weekend we've shared together."

"Works fine for me," Archie said happily, and I knew I'd been had.

"Except Ryder," I said. "You already agreed to tell me about him."

"Fine, but there's nothing really to tell," he said stubbornly.

I knew better. I saw the look of determination in the man's eyes backstage. "Then it won't take long, and we can move on."

"We're not discussing it now though. You need to get your game face on."

"Game face?" I asked.

"Preaching face then."

After our shower, I made us both real oatmeal with fresh bananas and blueberries. "Okay, maybe I do have a preaching day routine," I confessed. "I make oatmeal every Sunday just like Millie did for us every week."

"Millie?" Archie asked.

"Millie Givens. She's Pastor Randall's widow. They're the ones who put me on the right path after I got out of jail. Pastor Randall saw something in me worth saving and wouldn't let me give up on myself. They became my family, and the message in my sermon today. I'm really glad Henry is coming because I think he can benefit from hearing my story."

We dressed together after breakfast. Archie surprised me by slipping on silk stockings before he put on his dress pants. "How am I supposed to behave knowing what you're wearing beneath your pants?"

He rose seductively from the bed and crossed the room to where I stood to lean against my dresser. "You can strip them off me with your teeth after church," he offered. "Pastor Ollie, will lightning strike me for having naughty thoughts about you in church?" Archie ran his hand up my shirt and stroked his finger over my clerical collar.

"Have you ever been struck by lightning for having naughty thoughts about anyone?" I asked.

"Not yet."

"Then you won't get struck for lusting after me, Arch." I pulled him closer for a kiss. "I am just a man. This collar doesn't change who I am beneath the clothes."

"Aren't you supposed to be held to a higher standard? Aren't you supposed to sacrifice your wants and needs to serve the Lord?"

"Serving the Lord doesn't mean I have to sacrifice my happiness. What's going on here? Are you worried my being with you will risk my eternal soul? Worried my congregation won't approve? Frankly, my dear, I don't give a damn who approves or disapproves." Archie smiled when he recognized the line I'd borrowed from *Gone with the Wind*. "Only your thoughts on our relationship matter to me, Arch."

I knew I'd hit the nail on the head when he looked down at his feet. "You might feel different once people start losing respect for you because of our relationship. I want to be with you, but I don't want there to come a day when I see resentment in your eyes when you look at me. I couldn't handle that with you."

I lifted his chin so he looked into my eyes once more. "Never going to happen, Arch."

"Never is a long time."

"Do you have any idea how much it means to me that you're standing here talking to me about this instead of running away from me?" I released his chin to run the back of my fingers over his cheekbone. "Other men have let you down and made you feel insignificant, but they're not me. I adore everything about you, Arch. If you want to wear makeup to my church, then do it. If wearing silk stockings beneath your pants gives you confidence and makes you feel powerful, then wear them. I want you as you are; no exceptions. Well, maybe one."

"What?" he asked suspiciously.

"Please don't give me a boner when I'm standing behind the podium. Don't lick your lips or trace the lacy edges of your stockings beneath your slacks or do anything else that will make me linger behind the podium longer than I need to."

"You mean you don't want me to come up there and assist you like I did Friday night?"

"Please don't," I begged, loving the devilish smile curving his lips. "It's hard to believe bingo night was just two days ago."

"Not quite two," Archie countered. "It feels longer, doesn't it?"

I pressed a lingering kiss to his soft lips before pulling back to look into his eyes. "It won't be long before neither of us can remember a time when we weren't in each other's lives."

We walked hand in hand to church, and I wasn't surprised to see Millie had already arrived. She was setting out the weekly devotional pamphlets she printed each week once I identified the message I was going to deliver in my sermon and the songs our musical guests would perform. It was something she did for Pastor Randall each week and continued to do for me. She wore a peach skirt and jacket with a floral scarf around her neck and cream-colored hat on top of her immaculately coifed hair.

"There's my boy," she said, opening her arms wide to hug me. "Good morning, Son."

"Hello, Mama." Oh, how I loved this woman. "Millie," I said, stepping back so I could make introductions. "I'd like you to meet someone special."

"My, oh my, aren't you handsome?" Millie asked extending both hands toward Archie. "I'm Millie, and I'm this beautiful soul's mother."

"It's nice to meet you, Millie. I'm Archie. I'm this beautiful soul's boyfriend."

Hearing Archie refer to me as his boyfriend made me want to do a happy dance, but I managed to maintain my dignity and only slid my arm around his shoulders. "Why don't you find a seat and make yourself comfortable while Millie and I greet the congregation as they arrive?"

"Sounds good to me," Archie said, preparing to sit in the front row on the right side of the altar.

"You might want to move back a row," I mock-whispered. "We're dealing with new snake handlers this week. I wouldn't want you to get hurt."

Archie laughed. "Surely sarcasm is a sin."

"I like him, Son," Millie said as we walked away. I glanced over my shoulder and found Archie watching us. I winked at him, earning a huge grin and a flirty finger wave. I was glad his doubt from earlier had temporarily been laid to rest. I vowed to be ready the next time it reared its ugly head.

I couldn't keep the smile off my face when Maria, Esther, and Henry got out of their car and walked toward the front of the church. "I'm so happy they made it."

"I can tell one of them is Archie's mother," Millie said. "Who's the other lady and the lost lamb?"

"Archie runs an HIV transition home, and Esther is his right-hand lady. The lost lamb is Henry; Archie introduced him to me."

"Good morning, Ollie," Maria said, opening her arms. I couldn't help hugging her longer than usual, because I hated all the pain she'd suffered in her past. I wouldn't squander the trust she was giving me.

"Good morning, Maria. You look lovely." She'd chosen to wear a suit in an amethyst shade similar to the throw pillow on Archie's bed. The purple hue made her eyes look even greener, and I wondered if Archie had a shirt in a similar shade. If not, he would have one soon. I turned to Esther and offered her a hug also. "It's so lovely to see you again, Esther. Thank you for joining us this morning."

"Hey, Pastor Ollie," Henry said, sounding as nervous as the first time he called me.

I placed a hand on his shoulder which seemed to calm his nerves. "Everyone will make you feel welcome here, Henry. We're all as gay as you are," I said sheepishly, earning a slight smile.

"Okay," he said. "I'm glad Archie told me about you, Pastor Ollie."

"So am I."

"Mama," I said when I realized she was waiting patiently for introductions, "this is Maria, Esther, and Henry. Everyone, please meet my mother."

Mama hugged all three of them because that was her nature. The trio went inside and sat beside Archie in the front row while I continued saying hello to members as they arrived.

We closed the doors when it was time to start the service and made our way to the altar. I took my seat off to the side so the congregation could focus on the performers. Millie sat behind her piano while Regina and Abby Thompson and their kids, Sophie, Jack, and Michael, joined her to perform "Love So Great" to open our service. I chose that time each week to thank God for the miracles in my life and ask he give me the strength to reach the hearts of those struggling.

I rose from my seat and approached the podium when the song finished. I could feel Archie's attention on me, so I looked his way and smiled. "Good morning," I said into the microphone, earning the same in return from the congregation. "Thank you, Regina, Abby, Sophie, Jack, and Michael, for such a moving performance to start off our service. Let us bow our heads and pray." I closed my eyes, lowered my head, and recited the words I'd memorized from the prayer I wrote specifically for this service.

"Father, thank you for bringing each of us safely to this place. As we gather, we remember those who aren't here with us today. For those who are ill, we ask for your healing. We invite your Holy Spirit into our hearts. Equip us, challenge us, comfort us, and teach us to be the best version of ourselves. Remind us to love and cherish those entrusted to our care. Let us only evoke your name to spread love and light, not hate and intolerance. As we gather here today, Father, bless us with your love, beauty, and grace. We ask this in your son's name. Amen."

"Amen," the congregation said collectively.

I lifted my head and opened my eyes. I saw that Millie had chosen to sit with Archie and company. Her arm was around Henry, her lost lamb, and he didn't know it yet, but he'd found the mother he never knew he needed.

"Today's message is about family," I said, "and more specifically, I want to focus on the chosen family. The role of family is defined in many verses throughout the Bible, and I firmly believe nothing is more sacred than one's family. Many of us here today grew up in homes where the unconditional love described in the Bible wasn't extended to us when we came out to our families. Some of us found ourselves suddenly alone in a cold and unforgiving world. All of us, whether we know it or not, have found our chosen family." I smiled wryly. "And sometimes they find and choose us, adopting us when we're not even sure that's what we want." I looked over at Millie, and she gave me the same warm smile as the day I showed up on their doorstep following behind Pastor Randall. "Our chosen families are just as sacred, and for some of us, more so than our biological ones. These are the people that see us as we are, warts and all, and love us anyway. How beautiful and sacred is that gift? I know how hard it is to find yourself alone and uncertain, but I also know what it feels like when the family you were meant to have finds you. It opens an entirely new world, everything clicks into place, and you see things in a better light. Your troubles won't magically disappear, but you find people with whom to share them with."

I'd always made it a point to make eye contact around the room when I gave my sermons because I wanted to make sure my message was being received and heard. I hoped that my words gave people optimism and strength, especially those who were so good at hiding their sorrows. I saw tears on the faces of many. While making my congregation cry wasn't an actual goal of mine, I saw it as a sign that my message resonated with them. I received many smiles and nods, as I looked around the room. I saved the front pew on the right for last because their reactions were the ones that mattered the most to me that morning.

Millie looked at me with pride and love, Henry sniffed and wiped his eyes with one of the tissues Millie kept stashed in her pockets, Esther smiled approvingly, and Maria wiped tears and leaned into Archie when he lifted his arm to wrap it around his mother. Then there was Archie. His beautiful eyes glistened with unshed tears, and he looked at me with…adoration and understanding.

I briefly closed my eyes and said a silent, grateful prayer for his presence. I understood at that moment I was looking at my hope, my future, my whole world.

Chapter Sixteen

Archie

WOULD OLLIE EVER CEASE TO SURPRISE ME? FROM THE MO-ment we met, he stunned me time and time again. First, it was the sexuality emanating from him when Milo in-troduced us. I found him irresistible until I discovered he was a pastor. I figured Ollie would take the hint after I bolted, but he knocked me over with his bold texts and sultry stares. I took for granted during those six weeks he pursued me that he'd keep doing it until he caught me. In the back of my mind was the knowledge that I wanted to be caught.

I was ready to give in to our baser needs, but then he said some-thing that no one other than my family, chosen or biological, had said to me before. He told me I deserved better than a quick, dirty romp in a prop closet. I pushed him away, thinking he'd come back like he had the previous month and a half, but he didn't. Ollie's absence from my life rocked me because I'd become addicted to the way he looked at me and made me feel cherished. My world felt cold and dull without his heat warming me up from the inside out. The surprises didn't end there.

He stunned me with his kindness for Henry, a man he'd never met, and his bravery for entering a home where he thought he wasn't wanted. His honesty and openness only made him more beautiful to me. The way he teased the seniors at bingo night was the most adorable thing I'd ever seen, and I was surprised to learn how endearing I found it. Seeing his drawings filled me with an awe I'd stopped feeling a long time ago. Then there was the way he touched me and kissed me as if I was the most precious thing in the universe. It's something every person should feel once in their lives. It was also something I didn't want to live without.

The biggest surprise of all came the night we first made love. Yes, I realized there was a difference from the moment his hands touched my skin and his mouth pressed against mine. The intensity was still the same, but it was…more. I'd bared parts of myself to him, and he showed me how beautiful he found them to be. He wanted me. He craved me. He cherished me.

The wonder didn't stop once we exited our bedrooms though because I got to meet the woman he called mom and his church family. I expected a handful of people to show up, but there must've been close to a hundred. Based on his bingo performance, I expected him to bumble about and be clumsy and cute, but he was…spectacular. His whole demeanor changed when he walked up onto the altar. He spoke with a clear, proud voice that spoke of finding love and acceptance—two things he personified. I was blown away by his commanding presence and charisma, hanging onto his every word. I felt something I hadn't felt in a long time—faith. I believed in Ollie, and his belief that I deserved better from relationships made me want to believe it too. I wasn't going to be healed after one stellar weekend of lovemaking followed by an impassioned sermon, but I was committed to trying. I vowed not to run whenever we argued, and we would because all couples do. I promised myself I'd talk about the things bothering me and listen when Ollie did the same.

If I had to choose a few words to sum up my epiphany while sitting in the pew, I'd call it shock and awe. I was shocked by the depth of my feelings for Ollie and awed that he returned them too. There was no mistaking the look of adoration when he glanced my way.

Him, a man of esteem and respect, who greeted me with a kiss on the cheek when the service was over, and who presented me as his boyfriend to church members who approached to speak with him after the service ended.

Mamma pulled me aside to have a private word when Ollie began talking to the Thompsons about the musical selections for the following week. "I want him for a son-in-law, Archie. Make it happen," she said fiercely, making me laugh softly.

"Mamma, marriage isn't a unilateral decision," I reminded her. "I will take your wishes into consideration."

She reached up and pinched my cheek playfully. "I've never seen you look so happy. Not even the time Ryan bought you the Barbie Dreamhouse for your sixth birthday." Just hearing his name created an ache inside me I knew would never fully go away, but not saying it felt worse. I wanted to feel his presence in the decisions I made, the life I lived, and the family I chose.

"He would love Ollie, wouldn't he?" I asked her. Ryan had disliked every guy I ever brought around because he saw their true selves when I was blinded by lust and my desperation to belong to someone. Ollie would've wowed him just like he did me.

"Ryan would adore him," Mamma said. "He's up in heaven yelling 'finally' and doing the double fist pump he saved for big moments like when you got your driver's license, graduated high school, and got accepted in college."

"Or the Bengals scoring a touchdown. He was a diehard even through the difficult years," I said fondly.

"Oh my goodness," Mamma said fondly. "Maybe he's up there doing the Ickey Shuffle because you've finally found a man worthy of your loyalty and soft heart."

"Please not that," I replied.

Ollie finished his conversation and looked around for me. When our eyes connected, I could see question or concern in his dark eyes, so I sent him a playful wink to let him know that neither Mamma nor

I were upset or uncomfortable. Maybe I'd even tell him the reason Mamma swept me aside was to demand that I marry him, but then again, I didn't want to risk running him off.

"I didn't mean to keep you away from Ollie for so long," Mamma said after looking to see what had pulled my attention away from her. "I just wanted you to know how happy it makes me to see you looking so joyful."

"Thank you." I pulled her into a tight hug, resting my chin on her head and smiling back at Ollie. It felt good to experience this kind of joy. I understood why people wrote sappy love songs and the lines in the movies I adored so much.

Ollie slid his arm around my waist when we rejoined him, Millie, Esther, and Henry. "Would all of you like to join my mama and me for our weekly after-church ritual?" he asked us. "It doesn't involve snakes or sacrificial lambs," Ollie said when I quirked a brow.

"What about virgins?" Henry asked in mock horror. I liked the kid more and more.

"That's only the last service of each year, Henry. It sounds like your previous church was barbaric," Ollie teased right back.

"In more ways than one," Henry said solemnly.

"You're one of us now, Henry," Millie said in an ominous tone. "You won't want to miss out on this weekly celebration." She winked at Ollie and added, "Let me just go grab the black robes." We all laughed at her playful antics. She and Ollie made quite the pair.

"I'm free for the day," Esther said then looked at Mamma and Henry. "What about you guys? Willing to risk the snake venom?"

"Sure," Henry said with a grin.

"I'm game," Mamma said.

"I'll go wherever Ollie does," I said boldly, loving the way his hand on my waist gripped me a little tighter after hearing my declaration.

"Great!" Millie said. "I'll take the lovebirds with me, and you can follow me."

"Sounds good," Mamma agreed. "Oh, and, Millie, never let my

son drive you anywhere."

"Hey!" I said. "I'm a fabulous driver."

"If by fabulous you mean taking corners on two wheels, speeding through yellow lights, and weaving in and out of lanes like a NASCAR race, then yes, you are," Mamma said.

"I have places to go and people to see," I scoffed.

"I'm thankful every day that one of those places isn't a morgue and one of those people isn't an undertaker."

"Maybe I could slow it down a little bit," I offered.

"One of my prayers has been answered," Ollie said dramatically. "I do believe in miracles."

"I'm about to remember something important I should be doing," I threatened.

Ollie removed his hand from my waist and reached for my hand. "I'll play nice." I didn't mind when he played dirty, but I preferred to do that in the privacy of a bedroom.

And if I thought I'd learned all of Ollie's surprises then I was wrong. Millie drove us to a dive in the middle of nowhere called Burt's. "They serve the best beer and wings here," she said when we all stood outside the door. "What?" she asked when she saw my surprise. "A Christian woman can't enjoy a beer and some wings while watching football on Sunday?"

"She absolutely can, and should," I amended, opening the door for her.

"I love manners on a person," she told me.

"That means no belching after drinking a beer, Esther," I teased.

"Wiseass," she muttered under her breath as she followed Millie to a corner booth.

The semicircle booth was big enough to seat all of us and allow us a great view of the game that was about to start. "I'm so glad the game is on the normal broadcast network," Millie said. "I can only take so much of Troy and Joe calling a game before they turn my stomach and ruin my appetite."

"I'll drink to that," I told her.

Millie wasn't lying about the wings and beer being the best. They worked with local IPA brewers and offered the big-name brands as well to provide a stunning array of beer. Millie's dark ale reminded me of something you'd find in England. I was impressed by the bold, crispness of it but still preferred my lighter ale with stronger floral and fruit undertones. Everyone else chose sodas or water instead of beer. We munched on wings, potato skins, and coleslaw while talking about the game and arguing calls until halftime.

"Archie, are you riding home with us?" Mamma innocently asked after we settled the bill and walked outside.

I looked at Ollie, unsure how to answer. I wanted to stay with him longer but didn't want to inconvenience him if there were things he needed to do. We didn't live hundreds of miles apart, but an hour round-trip would be an inconvenience to some.

Not Ollie. "I'll bring him home whenever he's ready. If that's okay with you, Arch."

Mamma smiled broadly. "It's fine with him. Come on, Henry and Esther. We better get going. The Reds have a late start time this afternoon and traffic will be a disaster getting back into the city."

"Be careful," I told Mamma, pulling her into a hug. She'd chosen not to drink, but she wasn't wrong about the flood of traffic into the city. It was always chaos when football and baseball season overlapped. People seemed to lose their minds and drive like...me. "I'll call you soon."

We all hugged each other goodbye and got in our separate vehicles. Neither Ollie nor I said much during the drive back to his house. Millie mostly tsked about the things being said on talk radio. "Why must they be so hateful?" she asked. "I like to win as much as the next person, but I don't feel the need to say such terrible things about these men. Do you think it's because we forget they're men? Does their athletic ability somehow transport them to a higher plane in our subconscious? They're just men who have families who love them and have to hear and read such utter garbage. Why, I'd have to keep my television and radio turned off and cancel my subscription to the Cincinnati Enquirer if I was married to one of them."

"Little young for you, aren't they, Mama?" Ollie teased.

"I wasn't being literal, Oliver. You know Randall still has my heart."

"I know, Mama, but Coach Lewis *is* a handsome man. I suspect there's a reason you like to watch his interviews."

"The man knows football, and he cares about his players," Millie countered. "He gives troubled players a chance when no one else is willing to risk it. I admire that in a person. Besides," she said huffily, "he's not the one fumbling the ball, throwing interceptions, missing tackles, or botching routine field goals."

One could argue he didn't bench players when they continued to screw up, but it wouldn't be me. I wasn't going to upset Ollie's mama. Instead, I said, "You know how fickle Cincinnati fans are, Millie. One day he's Football Jesus, and the next, he's the worst coach in the NFL."

"Isn't that the truth?" she said, nodding her head like I was preaching the word. "They did the same with Dusty Baker when he coached the Reds and now look at them. Tell me how they're better off now. Traded all those talented players to keep one pitcher who hasn't completed a season in years."

"Mama is passionate about her sports," Ollie spoke up. "God, family, and sports."

"Good food ranks above sports. You ought to know this by now, Oliver."

"Millie, did you teach Ollie how to make tomato soup and grilled cheese so fancy?" I asked, suddenly understanding the extra touches Ollie put into his food, including the oatmeal. I saw him adding brown sugar, cinnamon, and a touch of honey to the milk before he brought it to a soft boil and added the oats and fruit.

"I sure did," she answered proudly. "Delicious, isn't it? And such simple touches."

"It was the best I'd ever had."

Ollie squeezed my hand where it rested between us in the back seat. Did he know he was the best I'd ever had in *all* categories? I thought it looked weird when we both got in the back seat to head to the restaurant like Millie was our Uber driver, but I got over it when Ollie slid his hand over mine. The tender way he circled his thumb over the top of my hand reminded me of the way his tongue circled the head of my cock the previous night. I shoved the thought aside and tuned back into Millie's conversation before I got a hard-on.

When we got back to Ollie's house, Millie only got out of the car long enough to hug us both. "I hope to see you again soon, Archie," she said.

"I promise you will. Thank you," I whispered during our hug so only she could hear. She didn't ask me why I was thanking her, because she knew I meant the unconditional love that turned Ollie's life around. Her reply was to squeeze me harder.

I reached for Ollie once we were alone inside his house. "If you want to know, I will tell you the nitty gritty on my disastrous relationship with Ryder, or even the Cliff Notes version if you prefer."

Ollie briefly covered my lips with his finger. "I will listen to anything you want to share, but I already know your past is filled with losers who were too stupid to see and appreciate the gem you are."

He knew this in the same way I knew his family had abandoned him when he came out, forcing him to live on the streets. I didn't need him to rip open old wounds and recount his story, because my instincts and observations told me what I needed to know about his past. I was more interested in his present and future, and I could see he felt the same way.

"Do you believe me when I say neither Ryder nor what he wants now is important to me? Will you believe me when I say you're the only guy I want and need?"

"Yes," Ollie whispered then kissed me.

We'd shared soft, teasing kisses and deep, penetrating kisses. This kiss was…in a class of its own. The need and want were still present, but they were tempered by something deeper that felt like unspoken love. Ollie continued to kiss me as he walked me toward his room and only took his mouth away from mine when it was time to remove our shirts. I watched as he deftly discarded his collar and shirt while I fumbled with my buttons. Our mouths joined once more as we reached out to take off each other's pants. Kisses turned to laughter when we realized our pants were tangled around the shoes we'd forgotten to remove in our haste. It didn't take us long to fix the mess and keep stripping off until Ollie was completely nude and I was left standing in just my silk stockings.

"Did you say something about me removing your stockings with my teeth?" Ollie asked.

My response was to place my hand on his head and gently push until he kneeled before me. Ollie removed both stockings with his teeth, then I tied him to his bed with them while Ollie looked at me with unbridled love and lust. I made love to him until I thought we would both die. Afterward, I untied Ollie's wrists and collapsed on him. He wrapped his arms around me tight and shouted, "Hallelujah!"

Chapter Seventeen

Ollie

"**G**OOD MORNING, OLLIE," CLAIRE SAID WHEN I WALKED through the door. "Usual order?"

I liked that I frequented the coffee shop near Archie's house so much in the month we'd dated to have a usual order. "Good morning, Claire." I heard the bells above the door jingle when another customer entered the café, but I was too busy looking at the muffins and cupcakes in the display case to pay attention to who it was. Did I want the same thing as usual, or did I want to shake it up a little? "Can you add a few of the pumpkin pie cupcakes to my usual order?" I must've missed the Monday lunch rush because there was only one other person in the café besides the person who just entered and me.

"Sure thing," Claire said. "I like that you've waited until the middle of October to choose something with pumpkin in it."

"I associate carved pumpkins and pumpkin seeds with Halloween, but pumpkin-flavored foods with Thanksgiving. The fact I'm eating a pumpkin anything before November first is newsworthy."

"Well, you're normally two months behind everyone else's September first pumpkin spice frenzy then."

"I've never had a problem with being a rogue." I heard a derisive snort behind me and turned to see who so rudely intruded in our conversation. "Oh, it's *you*," I said just as rudely.

"Do you use the same tone of voice with your congregation, Pastor Ollie?" Ryder asked, raking his eyes over my jeans and flannel shirt. His expression said he wasn't impressed by what he saw, but I didn't really care because I was minutes away from seeing Archie, and perhaps talking him into bending over his desk. I wouldn't let this jerk ruin my afternoon. "How much longer do you think you'll keep Archie's attention?"

"Forever, I hope." It was true, why deny it?

"Hope in one hand; shit in the other," Ryder replied. That wasn't exactly how the saying went, but it was close enough. He opened his eyes in mock horror and gasped. "Forgive me for my vulgar language."

"You're forgiven, my child," I said serenely.

Ryder's scowling caused a deep V to furrow on his brow. It wasn't attractive and would cause premature wrinkles, but it wasn't my concern. Not that I worried he would turn Archie's head.

"Heading to Ryan's Place?" he asked. His voice was innocent, but his eyes were a calculating ice blue, a sharp contrast to his black hair.

"I am."

"Archie said you were stopping by and the reason why he needed to cut things short." His lips turned up into a smug smile when I looked at him through unblinking eyes. Could he see my pulse pounding in my throat or hear my heart thudding in my chest? I hoped not because I wouldn't give him the satisfaction of seeing his arrows constructed of words struck me in the heart.

"Then why did you ask me if I was going to Ryan's Place if he told you I was stopping by? Could it be you wanted to cause trouble by implying you had to scurry out of his home so I wouldn't catch the two of you in the throes of passion?"

Ryder threw his head back and laughed like I'd said the funniest thing he'd ever heard. "Throes of passion? Pastor Ollie, the rest of the world refers to it as fucking."

Did he think to shock me? He was bound to be disappointed. I stepped closer to him, closing the distance and inhaled the air around him deep into my lungs. He jerked like I'd tried to lick him or something, but I liked that I had caught him off guard. "You didn't just come from fucking Archie, Ryder. I'd recognize his scent anywhere, and I don't smell him on you." Ryder moved to open his mouth, but I cut him off with a raised hand. "Save your breath before you make yourself look more pathetic than you already have. I know the expression a man wears after spending time in Archie's bed, and that's not it. You'd be too tired to pick a stupid fight with me. You won't come between us, so stop trying."

I wanted him to confirm he hadn't just left Archie's bedroom, but he just smiled and shook his head. "Keep telling yourself that if it makes you feel better, Pastor."

Claire looked torn between throwing him out and not creating trouble with a paying customer. "It's fine, Claire," I said. "I'll let you know what I think about these pumpkin pie cupcakes next time I'm in."

"Have a great day, Ollie," she said, offering me an encouraging smile. "Tell Archie and Henry I send my love."

"Will do."

On my drive to Archie's, I'd convinced myself Ryder was just causing trouble, and there was no basis for the fear that suddenly seized my heart. Archie and I spent every spare moment we could together either at his place or mine. We went on special dates every weekend such as trips to the zoo, a day at Kings Island, exploring the museums that dick face didn't work at, canoeing on the Little Miami River, or hiking at state parks. The passion between us hadn't waned over the past month; it had grown as our relationship got stronger. I wouldn't let the sore loser ruin my day or my relationship with Archie.

When I entered the house, I saw Henry had joined Bart, Douglas, and Jeremy to watch the soap opera. "Hey, fellas," I said, setting the cupcakes, muffins, and coffee on the table in front of them.

"Hi, Ollie," they all said without looking away from the television.

I could hear music coming from the kitchen and knew Esther would be there baking or cooking. I popped my head in really quick to say hello, and she warmly smiled when she saw me.

"Thank goodness you're here," she said. "It chases off the bad juju left behind by the snake who just left."

"Not a fan of Ryder's?" I asked.

"No," she said dryly. "I shouldn't say that because I don't even know the man."

"Then why did you?"

"He upset Archie, and I don't like it." A part of me said Ryder couldn't upset Archie unless he still cared. Maybe I shot myself in the foot when I told Arch I didn't need him to reveal what happened between them because it might've given away clues when he talked about the man. "Wipe that look off your face right now. Archie wasn't mad because he's pining after the fool," Esther said fiercely. "He's mad because the guy implied your relationship wouldn't last."

"Esther, can I ask how you know this? I can't imagine Archie left his office door… Wait. They did meet in his office, right?" Esther responded by putting her hands on her hips and narrowing her eyes. "Okay," I said, putting up my hands in surrender. "I don't see either Ryder or Archie wanting their personal business broadcasted, so I'm certain the door would've been shut."

Esther giggled. "Ryder showed up here out of the blue asking to speak to Archie. When I brought him back to Archie's office, Ryder moved to close the door. Archie told him to leave it open. Ryder objected, of course, because he wanted their business to remain private. Archie told him there was no personal business he was willing to discuss, so he might as well leave. That's when Ryder claimed to be here to discuss business to which Archie said there'd be no need to close the door." Esther picked up a glass off the countertop and held it up for me to see. "I was prepared just in case."

"Esther!"

"I won't have that rude, arrogant man upsetting my Archie and ruining the best thing to ever happen to him. A woman has to do what a woman has to do."

"I appreciate it so much, but I trust Archie."

"As you should," Esther said before returning her attention to the pot on the stove. "I could tell you what they discussed, but I think it's best Archie tells you after he gets out of the shower."

"Shower?" It was a damn good thing I stopped by to talk to Esther first. I can't imagine what would've gone through my head had I found Archie in the shower after Ryder just claimed to leave his bed.

"Dumped an entire cup of coffee on himself after the asshole left. Oops!" she said, covering her mouth.

"He *is* an asshole, Esther. The Lord forgives us both for a momentary lapse."

I let myself into Archie's room and sprawled on his bed, listening to the sounds of the shower. I didn't have to imagine what he looked like naked and wet with water running all over his leanly muscled body because I was blessed to see it several times a week. My heart raced with excitement when the shower turned off because I was moments away from seeing the man I loved. I sat straight up as soon as I thought the L word. Six weeks of lusting and pursuing him, then four weeks of missing him like crazy until we reconnected, followed by the happiest four weeks of my life. Could I possibly love Archie so madly and deeply in fourteen weeks?

Archie opened the bathroom door wearing only a towel. Droplets of moisture dripped from his wet, tousled hair onto his chest. Archie's face lit up with a beautiful smile when he saw me waiting for him. "Well, hello there, Golden Boy. Stopped by for an afternoon delight?"

"I love you, Archie," I blurted. He stiffened and looked at me with wide, unblinking eyes. "Oh my gosh! I've totally misread the situation, haven't I?" I asked in a panic. "You don't have to say it back, Arch. I…um…please don't run." Archie finally blinked but still hadn't moved from the bathroom doorway. I bolted off the bed when I realized I should be the one running. I started slowly backing away from him like he was a wild animal who might pounce on me any second. "I...um—"

"Don't you even think about taking another step," Archie commanded. He pointed back toward his bed, indicating where he wanted me, and I eagerly complied. "You caught me by surprise, Ollie. Let's not mistake it for disinterest." I nodded. "I'm going to go back into the bathroom, and we're going to redo this."

"Okay." I nodded again.

Archie stepped back into the bathroom and shut the door. He waited five seconds and reopened the door, except this time, he leaned seductively against the frame. "Hello, Oliver," he said huskily. "I'm so happy to see you."

I knew what he was expecting me to say, and I opened my mouth to say it, but the only thing that came out was a ridiculous squeak. Archie's lips twitched from fighting back the laughter. "You're looking mighty handsome in your soft flannel shirt. The only place it would look better is on my bedroom floor." He was trying to get me to relax, and I appreciated it, but I worried the moment had passed us by. "You look like there's something very important you want to say to me. Is there?"

I could do this. I could do this. "Clear eyes, full hearts, can't lose."

"You're quoting *Friday Night Lights?*"

"Did I say that out loud?" I asked. Archie nodded with a huge grin. "I was psyching myself up again."

"I didn't know you were a fan of the show," Archie said.

"I was mostly in it for Coach Taylor and Tim," I admitted. "Wow, we've gotten way off track."

"We have," Archie said, sauntering to the bed. "I'll seduce the truth out of you, Golden Boy. Tell me what I want to hear." He placed his hand on my shoulder and pushed back until I lay flat on his bed.

"How will you know I'm telling the truth if I'm shouting it out during sex?"

Archie parted my legs then stood between them. "Because it's you and you'd never lie to me under any circumstances, nor would you say something so important and impactful without meaning it. So, tell me what I want to hear, Oliver." He'd switched to using my full name during sexy foreplay.

"Claire has pumpkin pie cupcakes now. I added them to the usual Tuesday order. Do you know that Claire asks me if I want my usual order now? It means I'm there a lot."

"Is there a point to this rambling?" Archie asked in a bemused voice, placing his hands on my knees.

"Of course, there is. I'm telling you I like Claire and I think I'm going to like her pumpkin pie cupcakes. Did you know I have a rule about not eating pumpkin stuff until November first?"

"I believe you mentioned it once before when I bought a pumpkin spice latte from Starbucks. You looked like I'd worn white shoes after Labor Day."

"Is that a rule?" I asked.

"An old one, but a lot of people still adhere to it."

"Why is the cashmere sweater I ordered for your birthday called winter white?" I asked.

"You bought me a cashmere sweater for my birthday? I wonder what else I can torture out of you," he pondered aloud, sliding his hands up my legs. "Have you started shopping for Christmas already?"

"No," I whimpered. "Not for a few weeks."

Archie's hands slid up over my hips, up my abdomen and chest, and didn't stop until he cupped my face as he climbed on the bed to straddle me. I couldn't look away from the intensity in his green eyes, not even to see if his towel parted enough for me to see his cock and balls. "I love you too, Oliver Knight," he said softly before lowering his head to kiss my lips. "So damn much."

I rolled him over and rose above him, framing his face with my hands. "Never in my life did I imagine I'd find someone to stir emotions in me as you do, Arch. I want to cherish you, I want to protect you, and at the same time, I'm in awe of your strength and independence. You're the reason I never gave up on having a love to call my own. Every broken road led me straight to you."

"First, it's *Friday Night Lights,* and now, you're quoting Rascal Flatts songs?" he asked with a quirked brow.

"Not intentionally, but it's a good song, and the words are true."

"It is a good song, Ollie."

"Why are we still talking when we could be kissing and—" My words were cut off by an abrupt knock.

"Archie, I'm sorry to interrupt," Esther said through the door. "Kerry from HUD is on the phone for you…"

And just like that, the joyful light disappeared from Archie's eyes. "Please tell her I'll be right there." Archie scrambled off the bed and dressed in a hurry. "I'll be back as soon as I can," he tossed over his shoulder on the way out his door.

I didn't wait for him to come back. I followed him and stood behind his chair with my hand on his shoulder to give him comfort. I recognized the acronym and knew it stood for Housing and Urban Development which was the department that oversaw the Housing Opportunities for Persons with AIDS Program. Ryan's Place residents received subsidies to pay for their stay there as long as Archie adhered to the strict guidelines set forth by local, state, and federal laws. Funds from HOPWA were cut considerably during the past two years which was why the owners of QCD put on the weekly benefit for Ryan's Place. Archie had to closely document all money coming in and going out to show he wasn't personally profiting from the subsidies coming in. Since Archie was an accountant, they scrutinized his records even harder. When there was extra money, he'd put it back into the program and offered extra services to the residents. I could tell Archie expected the call from Kerry to be about an inspection or something else equally stressful.

"Good afternoon, Kerry," Archie said cheerfully into the phone. Only I saw how tightly he gripped the pen in his right hand. "Oh, I do have an open room. I must admit I'm surprised you're calling about a resident. Normally Tracy calls me about placement while you call to… Well, you know. Turn my world upside down," he teased. "Ah, that makes sense. I hope she went somewhere fun and exciting. When does he plan on stopping by to check out the place?" Archie nodded and hummed in acknowledgment. "His name? Kaleb Jacoby," Archie repeated back to her as he made his note. "Got it. I'll see him tomorrow at noon."

I sucked in a sharp breath after hearing Archie say the name. My heart stuttered to a stop, and I felt dizzy. It was a name I'd hoped never to hear again, a person I tried my hardest to forget existed.

Archie continued to scribble down whatever she told him. He finally set his pen down and said, "Thanks, Kerry." It was then he must've realized something was wrong with me. Maybe it was my ragged breathing or the way I gripped his shoulder to keep from collapsing. "Ollie?" Archie pivoted in his chair, but I was slow to react in my shocked state and ended up stumbling backward into the wall. "Baby, what is it? You're crying." He leaped from his chair and reached for me, placing his hands on my hips.

Was I? I lifted my hand and wiped it across my cheek then looked at my wet hand like I still couldn't comprehend what was going on.

"Esther," Archie yelled. "Baby, I think you've gone into shock. Sit down." He guided me over to sit in his desk chair. "What can I do?"

Esther rushed into the room. "What's wrong?" she asked.

"I think Ollie has gone into shock. What can we do?"

"I'll make a cup of really sweet coffee and grab spare blankets." Blankets? I wasn't cold. Then why were my teeth chattering suddenly?

It seemed like Esther was gone for an extraordinarily long time. I could hear Archie's voice, but it sounded like it was coming from the other end of a five-mile tunnel. My body shook, and he wrapped his arms around me. His body heat helped chase away some of the chills, and I was able to be more present in my surroundings.

"Here," Esther said when she returned. "Let me help him drink the coffee while you wrap him up in blankets. Coffee isn't your friend today, Archie."

Archie wrapped me up in a blanket burrito while Esther held the cup with the super-sweet brew to my lips. I couldn't manage more than a few sips before I shook her off. "Better," I whispered hoarsely. Why did I sound like I'd been in the desert for a month with no water?

"What happened?" Esther asked Archie.

"I don't know," Archie replied. "I'd just gotten off the phone with Kerry and found him like this." Then it must've occurred to him it happened after he said the incoming resident's name. "Baby, is he someone you know?"

I nodded my head. "He was a boy I met during conversion therapy. I thought he was only going to the classes to get his family off his back like I was. He befriended me, flirted with me, and then betrayed me when I fell for his charms. They put him in the class to bait kids like me, the rogue queer, into revealing themselves. Kaleb was the reason I was thrown out of my house and forced to live on the streets."

"Baby," Archie said, pulling me into his arms. "I'm going to call Kerry back and tell her I won't be able to help her after all."

"No," I said suddenly. "I can't be that person, Arch. My faith won't let me."

"I *am* that person though. This is my house, and I can't bring someone into it who's inflicted this kind of pain on others."

"No, Arch. You're not allowed to turn people away because your boyfriend doesn't like them."

"I can turn homophobic assholes away which could cause emotional stress for my other residents. I can make this place look so unappealing he won't want to stay. I don't owe this asshole and neither do you."

"Let me talk to him first and see what he has to say. Maybe he's repented and sorry for the things he's done."

"How does it give you back the years you lost with your family?

How does it make up for the things you had to do to survive? What can he possibly say that will excuse what he did?"

"I don't know if he can, but I know I have to try. This is for me, not him."

Archie sighed and wrapped his arms tightly around me. "We'll talk to him together then, baby."

Chapter Eighteen

Archie

I DIDN'T WANT TO LET OLLIE OUT OF MY SIGHT AFTER HIS BIG SHOCK EVEN though he recovered fairly quickly. I couldn't be sure if it was genuine or if he was putting on a strong front for me. There was no need to pretend with me. If Ollie wanted to cry and scream about the injustices he'd faced as a young kid, I'd scream and cry with him while holding him safely against me. His calm demeanor lasted until he fell asleep in my bed when the horrors of his past invaded his dreams, making him thrash and cry out in his sleep.

I woke him with a gentle touch then he demanded I chase away the ugly dreams with my touch and kisses. I wasn't sure making love right then was wise, but he seemed desperate, and I wanted to be what Ollie needed. I was glad I'd listened to him because his sleep afterward was calm and peaceful. The next morning, only a hint of the hurt lingered in his eyes because he'd resigned himself to facing down this personal demon. I didn't care what Ollie said; if the guy wasn't genuinely sorry for what he'd done to Ollie, then I'd toss him out on his ass and damn the consequences.

"Good morning, gentlemen," Esther said, entering the kitchen. Ollie and I hovered in the kitchen because I could smell that the cinnamon rolls were nearly done. Ollie had already smacked my hands twice when I reached for a piece of bacon Esther had stowed in the warming drawer. "I hope you don't mind visitors this morning for breakfast. I made too many cinnamon rolls and enough bacon for an army."

"There's an army of two right here," Ollie teased her.

"Visitors?" I asked, although I suspected I knew. "What if I don't want to share?"

"You'll share, or you'll be sorry," Esther warned with good humor.

"Where's my lamb?" Millie asked when she entered the kitchen looking as fierce as any mother bear wanting to assure her cub was safe.

"Mama," Ollie said, brightening up when she entered the kitchen closely followed by my mother. Ollie leaned over to give Millie a warm hug.

"Good morning, Mamma," I said, opening my arms and hugging my mother. "To what do we owe this pleasure?" As if I didn't know. Esther had called the troops last night and convinced them to give Ollie time to recover before they descended on him.

"You know why we're here," Millie said. "Oliver, I know the Lord wants me to forgive this sorry sap who's showing up here today, and I will do my best. There's also a slight possibility I will beat him over the head with my handbag."

"You better not," Ollie said, a crooked grin sliding up the right side of his face. "It feels like you carry around small boulders in it." He kissed Millie on the cheek and added, "Besides, you're better than that, Mama."

"I'm not feeling like a good person right now, Oliver. Are you sure you're okay?"

"I'm getting there. All those years spent in therapy taught me to confront things instead of hiding from them. I sent a text to Drew last night and asked him to meet me this afternoon before the bowling tournament."

"That's a wise decision, Oliver. This meeting will most likely trigger emotions and urges that can wreak havoc on your soul. You are stronger than them, and Drew will help you realize it."

"Is Drew your therapist?" I asked. I knew Ollie had been in therapy after leaving jail, but he hadn't mentioned the therapist by name.

"No, he's my NA sponsor. I should've told you last night that meeting with him today would be imperative to my well-being, but I wasn't thinking clearly."

"It's okay, Ollie." I reached for his hand and gave it a gentle squeeze. I only wanted to help him regain control even if it meant I had to temporarily step aside for someone to give him the specialized support he needed. I understood he needed more than my willingness to listen and my bedrooms skills to get him through the confrontation he was about to face. "Whatever it takes."

"Esther, your cinnamon rolls smell better than I remembered," Mamma said, sniffing the air appreciatively. "I'll help Esther set the table while you go upstairs and rally the guys down to eat breakfast while it's still hot."

"That's right," Esther said. "No sense in wasting daylight. Those who aren't working need to be finding work." She was such a tough nut, and I loved her to pieces.

I also knew Mamma and Esther wanted Ollie to have a few minutes alone with Millie, so I took my time heading upstairs to knock on the doors. Henry and Jeremy were the only two home at the moment, although Reggie would be returning home soon after working third shift.

When I returned downstairs with Henry and Jeremy in tow, the ladies and Ollie were already sitting around the dining room table waiting for us.

"Do any of you mind if I say grace?" Millie asked. No one objected, so she clasped her hands in front of her, lowered her head, and said, "Dear Lord, thank you for this bountiful food we're about to put into our bodies. Let it give us the strength and fortitude to carry us through the challenges you put before us. May you send healing light and love to those who need it, wisdom to those in doubt, and please stay my hand when I want to knock the boy silly for hurting my baby. Dear Lord, the Bengals are playing Monday Night Football, and they need me. I can't be locked up in a jail cell awaiting charges." Ollie cleared his throat in a subtle reproach. "In your son's name, we pray. Amen."

"Amen," everyone said then began digging in. The silence didn't last long.

Jeremy, who sat across from me at the table, raised his brow and asked, "What did you do to Ollie?"

"Me?" I asked. "I didn't do anything to him."

"Who does his mama want to slap upside the head if not you?" he countered.

"Probably the jerk that was here yesterday. What was his name?" Henry asked.

"Ryder Jameson," Jeremy said in an upper crust, stuffy voice.

"Esther told me about Ryder's idea to host a benefit gala or something at The Cincinnati Art Museum as a fundraiser for Ryan's Place. I didn't know Ryder was even back in town," Mamma said. I could tell by her tone she wasn't pleased I'd left her in the dark. I just didn't think it was newsworthy.

"I guess he's been back for a month or so," I told her. "On the scale of one to ten in importance, I'd rank Ryder's return to Cincinnati as a negative ten." I realized with all the excitement the previous evening, I hadn't even told Ollie about Ryder's visit. I turned to look at him, but he was busy shoveling a bite of hot, gooey cinnamon roll in his mouth. "You don't look surprised. Why aren't you surprised?"

Ollie washed down his pastry with a big gulp of milk then wiped his mouth. "I ran into the pompous windbag at Claire's before I came over. He tried to trick me into thinking your meeting was of the personal variety."

"I set him straight right away," Esther said. "Even though it wasn't my place," she scrambled to add when she saw the scowl on my face.

"It's a blessing I talked to Esther first," Ollie told me, reaching over to wipe a smear of cinnamon icing from the corner of my mouth. "I knew Ryder was lying through his teeth, but I might've been caught off guard to find you in the shower after he implied he'd just left your bedroom."

"What a dick," Henry said.

"That's a low blow," Jeremy added.

"Honey, I'm home," Reggie called when he entered the house. "What smells so good?" He stopped at the doorway to the dining room and looked longingly at the food set out on the table. "I should really shower first before sitting down, but it looks so delicious." Reggie got hired as an apprentice with Southwest Ohio Regional Transit Authority to learn bus maintenance. "I'm a little greasy still."

"Don't worry about it, Reg," I said. "It's not like you were working in the sewers."

"How's everyone doing this morning?" he asked, dropping into the open chair beside Henry.

"Most of us are doing great, but Archie has some explaining to do," Henry told him.

"What'd you do, Archie?"

"*I* didn't do anything," I calmly said because I knew they were just teasing me. Ollie squeezed my thigh under the table to reassure me. Had it been anyone other than Ollie, I might've questioned the timing of his declaration of love. "Ryder only stopped by to let me know about a benefit the museum was putting on next month to showcase local LGBTQ artists. There will be a silent auction for the works on display. Ryder claimed he convinced the board to donate a portion of the ticket sales to Ryan's Place."

"I have mixed feelings about this," Mamma said. "On one hand, it's a wonderful thing. The museum charges big money for those events, and they almost always sell out of tickets because it gives the wealthy people in the area a reason to dress up and show off. I can't help thinking Ryder had an ulterior motive for his suggestion."

"Archie told him the same thing," Esther said then grimaced.

"I told him the same thing," I repeated wryly, "and he assured me the offer came with no strings attached. He gave me two tickets to the event, thinking I would be bringing you, Mamma. I told him Ollie would be my guest *if* I attended."

"That's when he got snippy and implied Ollie and Archie might not still be together in three weeks when the event happens," Esther added. "He must have a really big set of balls."

Ollie choked on the bite of roll he'd just swallowed. I rubbed his back while he coughed then took another long drink of milk to soothe his throat. "Well?" Ollie asked once he could breathe without sputtering more.

"Well, what? Are you asking me if he has big balls?"

Ollie threw his head back and laughed. The sound warmed my heart as nothing else could. "I meant are we going to the gala? I'd like to see you dressed in a tuxedo, Arch." If Ollie wanted to see me in a tuxedo, then that's what he would get. I also saw how eager he was to remove the suit from my body. I was pretty keen on seeing how Ollie would look in a tux too.

"Sure, we'll go," I said. I wasn't at all worried we wouldn't be together next month for the gala. "It's a date."

"Well, there goes our morning entertainment," Jeremy said dryly. "Not a single face slap or anything."

"The morning is young, lamb chop," Millie said, pointing to him with her fork. "Eat your breakfast before it gets cold. Miss Esther went to a lot of trouble fixing this beautiful meal to replenish your body."

"Yes, ma'am," he said, tucking into his breakfast.

Millie shot me a playful wink then changed the subject. "How many of you think the Bengals will win tonight?"

"Dalton chokes during big games," Reggie said.

"I think this is his year," Jeremy countered.

"I have no idea what any of you are talking about," Henry said. "I don't follow sports."

AIMEE NICOLE WALKER

"That's okay, lamb," Millie said. "What are you interested in?"

"I'm all about the theater," Henry said passionately.

"Stage or movies?" Mamma asked him.

"Stage." Henry released a long sigh. "Growing up, I was only allowed to act in church plays, but I loved it so much. Luckily, our church put on four or five productions a year, and the man in charge had a lot of theater and music experience."

"I saw in the paper they're having open tryouts for the community theater," Mamma told him. "I know they've already been rehearsing their Christmas show, so this would probably be for the first production of next year."

"I don't know," Henry said. "I'm not sure my talent is worthy of a big production even if it's community theater."

"If you don't get a part in the show, you could always volunteer to help behind the scenes?" Ollie suggested. "I'm sure they're always looking for help with props, costumes, and all the other little things that go on behind the scene."

"It actually sounds like a good idea," Henry said. "I'll never know if I don't try."

"That's right," I told him.

After breakfast, the ladies went into the living room to talk, aka strategize, on what to do with Kaleb Jacoby while Reggie went on up to bed and Jeremy and Henry did the breakfast dishes. I linked my fingers through Ollie's and led him into my bedroom.

"Are you sure you're okay about Ryder?" I asked.

"I knew he was lying, Arch. I know you love me and want to be with me. I want you to know I didn't use the L word because I felt threatened. It just burst from my chest when you smiled at me like seeing me in your room was the best thing in the world."

"I know sincerity when I see it, baby," I said, pulling him into the circle of my arms. "And seeing you in my room was the best thing in the universe. You light up my world, Golden Boy. Some jackass from my past won't change that either."

"We have a few hours before Kaleb arrives." I could tell Ollie struggled to say his name. It might not have been a good idea to use sex as a distraction, but how could I resist him. Ollie had told me about some of his triggers when it came to sex, but this wasn't one he'd described.

"What do you have in mind?"

"Let me show you instead," he suggested.

He slowly stripped off my shirt before removing his. Ollie repeated the process of undressing me then himself until he'd stripped us both bare, and only then did he kiss me. Then the chemistry between us changed from languid to desperate. Ollie's eager kisses and roaming hands spoke of the need to claim and possess, and the way he leaned into my touch said he wanted to be claimed and possessed too.

"We have to be quiet so the entire house doesn't know what we're up to," Ollie whispered.

"Too late," Esther said on the other side of my door.

"Esther!" Ollie and I both admonished.

"It's not my fault the walls and doors need to be thicker in this house," she replied. "I wouldn't bother you if it wasn't important."

Ollie had already scooted off my lap at the sound of her voice, so I rose to my feet and reached for my clothes. "What's up?" I asked, stepping into my underwear.

"Your noon appointment showed up two hours early."

"Eager for his ass whooping!" Millie added.

"Oh my God!" Ollie said, covering his face. "Is your mother outside the door too?" I'd never seen Ollie's face look so red before, but it was better than the ashen white color it was when he learned Kaleb was waiting for us.

"Of course," Mamma said. "I'm as nosy as the rest of them. And really, boys. It's ten o'clock in the morning, and you have a houseful of people. Even though I understand you have to strike while the iron's hard—"

"Hot!" Ollie and I both said then burst into laughter.

"Strike while the iron is hot," I told her. "We'll be out in just a few minutes."

"We can send the twit away if you want to finish," Esther offered. As if we could ever have sex under this roof again.

"It's not necessary. We'll get this confrontation over with and move on with our day. Please show Mr. Jacoby to my office, and I'll be right there."

"Okay," Esther said. I could hear the shrug in her voice.

"And take your two best friends with you," I told her. "I need to have a private word with Ollie before the interview."

"Sure thing," Esther said. "Come on, ladies."

"'Private word,'" Millie muttered. I imagined she used air quotes too. "Who are they trying to fool?"

My mother didn't say anything, but I heard her warm giggles.

"Ollie, are you sure you don't want me to tell him I made a mistake and there wasn't an opening?"

"No, Arch. I won't have you lie. I need to face him."

"Do you want to talk to him privately?"

Ollie shook his head. "We'll do it together as you said."

"Clear eyes, full hearts, can't lose," I said, channeling Coach Taylor.

"God, I love you, Archie."

I gave him a swift kiss then led him across the hall where a tall, slender man sat in the chair facing my desk which meant his back was toward us. His head was bent forward like he was praying or staring down at his hands or perhaps his feet. He straightened and turned his head when he heard us walk into the room. He offered a small smile to me then shifted his attention to the man who entered behind me— the man I'd love beyond my dying breath.

Kaleb Jacoby's eyes widened in shock, and he leaped to his feet. "Ollie?"

Chapter Nineteen

Ollie

KALEB STARTED TO WALK TOWARD ME, BUT ARCHIE STEPPED IN FRONT of him. "Please return to your seat, Mr. Jacoby."

"I...um...sure," he said, looking and sounding as stunned as I felt last night. "I'm sorry."

Archie held out his hand for me to precede him then pulled out his desk chair, gesturing he wanted me to sit down. Like I'd done for him before, Archie stood behind me and placed his hand on my shoulder.

"I want to be very clear about something, Mr. Jacoby," Archie said firmly. "Interviewing potential residents is part of the normal process. I need to make sure I'm not allowing people to move in who disturb the peace at Ryan's Place which includes weeding out self-hating gays who borderline on homophobia. Am I clear?"

Kaleb nodded. "I'm not self-hating or homophobic. I...had a troubled past, but I'm not the same person anymore."

"Before you convince me," Archie said, "you'll have to convince Oliver. I believe the two of you have met before, Mr. Jacoby."

Kaleb closed his eyes and swallowed hard, and for a brief moment, the boy I'd fallen hard for as a teenager replaced the man in the chair across from me. "Ollie, there's nothing I regret more than the way things ended between us."

"Ended between us?" I asked incredulously. Archie's fingers dug so hard into my flesh I almost flinched. "Ended between us?" This conversation was going to take forever if I kept repeating myself. "Kaleb, you pretended to care about me to trap me into revealing I had no intention of converting to a straight boy."

He shook his head vigorously. "That's not true, Ollie." He took a shaky breath and held up his hand. "It's partially untrue. I did initially agree to bait you, but I fell hard for you, Ollie. I kept lying to Skip about the private time we spent together. I told him you were staying true to the mission statement you'd signed. My feelings weren't faked, and I didn't tell the asshole anything."

"He presented my family with photos of us together, Kaleb."

"He must've followed us and took those pictures. I never told him about our alone time in the abandoned subways beneath the city. Please believe me."

"How can I?" I asked. "What evidence do you have to prove you weren't lying to me all along?"

Kaleb reached inside his pocket and pulled out a worn, folded picture and a movie ticket stub that was tattered around the edges. "Do you recognize this ticket?"

"It was our first date," I whispered. *Harry Potter and the Chamber of Secrets.*

"I stole one of the photos from Skip's desk to keep." The picture showed a younger version of myself leaning against a concrete pillar while a young Kaleb kissed me. I tried my best to forget those stolen moments with him, but it only took one picture and a movie ticket for them all to come flooding back. "I tried to contact you to explain and apologize, but Skip told me your parents sent you to live with your aunt and uncle in New Jersey." His words felt like a dagger to the heart.

"Is that right?" I asked, not trying to hide the bitterness in my voice.

"You didn't go live with your relatives?" he asked, brows

furrowing in confusion. I shook my head. "Where'd you go live then?"

"Under a bridge," I said with more calmness than I felt. A part of me wanted to tell Kaleb every sordid event he put into motion, but I couldn't. I wouldn't shame my faith by acting that way.

"No, Ollie. P-p-please, tell me it's not true," Kaleb asked then burst into tears when I wouldn't recant what I'd said. "Oh my God. You must hate me."

"Hate is a wasted emotion, and it destroys a person. I should know because it nearly claimed me. I was one of the lucky ones who survived the streets, but not without scars on my soul. With the grace of God, I have a new life that I love." I covered Archie's hand on my shoulder.

"You have every right to blame me for everything that happened to you, but I never meant for you to get hurt. I am so very sorry." Kaleb rose to his feet and looked at Archie. "It's obvious I'm not a good fit in your home, Mr. White. Do you know the name of another facility that would be willing to take me on?"

Archie removed his hand long enough to pull a business card from his desk. "I don't know if Mrs. Madison has any rooms available at her boarding house, but you can give her a call."

"Thank you," Kaleb said softly, looking at the card in his hand. "This is more than I deserve." Kaleb returned his sorrowful gaze to mine once more. A better person would've put their grievances aside so he could stay, but as I reminded Archie on numerous occasions, I was only human. I believed Kaleb was telling the truth. Why else would he keep those mementos? People tried to avoid the things that made them feel guilty, not hang onto them. I still couldn't stomach running into him when visiting Archie, and I certainly couldn't make love with him living in the same house. "I'm sorry, Ollie. If there was any way I could right all the wrongs, I would. The times we spent together were the only bright spots in my life. I'm so happy you've found love and happiness. I wish you all the best."

"Take care, Kaleb," I said. He nodded then left the room.

Archie followed behind him and closed the door, shutting us inside his office so we could have some privacy.

"Esther is just going to press a glass to the door so she can overhear us," I told Archie.

"I love you so much, Golden Boy. Your goodness blows me away and inspires me to be a better man."

"I love you too, Arch." I wasn't sure how proud he'd be if he knew how badly I wanted to search out the nearest bottle of alcohol or a hit of something to make the pain from the confrontation go away.

"You okay?" he asked, reading me so well.

"I'm not," I admitted. "Not at all."

"What time do you meet Drew?"

I looked at my watch and realized I had five hours before our appointment. "Not until three."

"Why don't you call him now to see if you can meet earlier," Archie suggested. "If not, maybe Andy would be a good choice until you can see Drew."

His understanding broke something inside me. I choked out a sob which was quickly muffled by Archie's shoulder when he held me tight in his arms.

"Let it out, baby," he whispered in my ear. "I'm no expert, but I know it's unhealthy to hold these toxic emotions inside you. I'm here however you need me."

Once I calmed down, I called Drew. He was a freelance writer for several publications and was able to meet me in thirty minutes. "I can't go without talking to Mama first."

"I can't believe they haven't busted down the door yet."

"You had about thirty seconds left," Mama said. "It's a terrible thing to hear your child crying their broken heart out."

Archie released me to cross the room and open the door. The three ladies burst into the room like it was Macy's Black Friday Sale. Mama reached me first, and her hug lingered until she felt me relax.

"I love you so much, Oliver Knight. You're a good man, and

your father would be just as proud as I am right now." Making Pastor Randall proud was my number one goal when I left that jail. I wanted to earn his trust and respect and be worthy of the chance he gave me. "You go on and meet with Drew. Be sure to call me later, okay?"

"I will, Mama." I hugged Esther and Maria too then they followed Mama out of the office, leaving me alone with my guy again. "I'll be back soon, Arch."

"I love you, Ollie."

"Love you too."

Archie's sweet goodbye kiss was the balm I needed for my bruised and battered soul. I wasn't in any condition to drive, so I walked to Claire's. Her big smile dimmed a little when she saw me.

"Everything okay?"

"It will be," I said, and I believe it was true. "I'd like one of those pumpkin pie cupcakes and a salted caramel mocha. That will steer me in the right direction."

"Please tell me you're not upset about the pompous windbag who harassed you yesterday."

"Not in the least. Life just threw me a curveball, Claire. I'm meeting a good friend who will help me process and get back to feeling like myself."

"Okay, Ollie."

I'd just sat down with my treats when Drew came into the store. He took one look at Claire and stopped in his tracks.

"Hi," she said cheerfully. "Can I help you?"

Drew just stood there staring, so I got up to rescue him. "You've seen pretty women before, Drew."

"Not like her," he said.

"Claire, this is my friend I was telling you about. His name is Drew, and he'll take a black coffee and two of your peanut butter cookies. My treat."

"You told her about me?" Drew asked when she turned her back to pour the coffee. "What did you say?"

I snorted. Drew's enamored reaction to Claire chased away some of the chill that had permeated my body. Helping people had always made me feel better which was my favorite thing about being a pastor. "I only told her I was meeting a friend."

"Oh," he said, watching her every move. He stiffened when she turned back around with the cup of coffee and smiled at him. Claire set the coffee down then reached in the display case to pull out three big cookies.

"I threw in an extra cookie since it's your first visit to my coffee shop," she told Drew.

"How do you know it's my first visit?" Drew asked, finally finding his voice in front of her.

"I'd remember seeing you here," she said then shot him a playful wink.

I paid for Drew's coffee and cookies then handed them to him. "Come on, Romeo," I whispered. "I got us a corner table."

Once Drew was away from Claire's beauty, he returned to his usual, unflappable self. "What's up, Ollie?"

Drew patiently listened as I told him about the events occurring over the last twenty-four hours. "That's a huge shock," he said when I finished. "Do you believe he's telling the truth?"

"I do, but the information is too recent for me to process how it changes things or if it does at all. Learning Kaleb didn't mean any harm doesn't change what happened to me."

"It doesn't, but he becomes one less ghost in your past who can pop up out of nowhere and send you into a tailspin."

"True," I admitted. "I know at some point I want to start working on forgiving Kaleb. I'm just not there yet."

"How strong is your need to drink or get high?" Drew asked me.

"It comes and goes. Earlier it was much stronger, but it's better now."

"You know what you need to do right now. Stay away from people and situations that are triggers and avoid places where it's easy to give into temptation."

"Like a bowling alley?" I asked.

"Is this bowling alley a place you normally go to without issues?"

"I bowl there every week in a league."

"You should be okay, but you should leave if you start to feel off."

"My team is made up of recovering addicts, so I'll be in excellent company if I need help."

"I'm also just a phone call away. You've done amazing things with your life since I met you thirteen years ago. I'm proud of you, Ollie."

"Thank you, Drew. Your regard means the world to me."

We lingered at the table talking for a few hours, catching up with one another's lives. We ordered another round of coffees but skipped the desserts the second time around. I didn't get back to Archie's until after three. For once, no one was watching television, and Esther wasn't in the kitchen. I heard Archie speaking to someone on the phone about quarterly returns and other accounting mumbo-jumbo which added to my brain fatigue. I grinned as I let myself in his room because those doors really were an issue. I lay across Archie's bed, planning to let him know I was back as soon as he got off the phone, but I must've ended up falling asleep. The next thing I knew, he was gently kissing me awake. The interior of the room was dark, telling me I'd been asleep for a long time.

"What time is it?" I asked, sitting up so fast we nearly knocked heads.

"Take it easy there, killer. We still have a few hours before we need to be at the bowling alley. I thought you might want to take a shower to wake up while I cook us dinner."

I narrowed my eyes at him because he looked way too happy about cooking. It was his least favorite thing to do. "What are you cooking?"

"Well, I stumbled across this recipe for a fancy grilled cheese sandwich and tomato soup."

"Stumbled across it, huh? Mama didn't give you a gentle push?"

"Millie might've said it was your favorite thing to eat when you were upset. She also said it was the first thing you wanted to make for people who were important to you. People like me," Archie added, recalling the night I'd made the same meal for him.

"It's true," I admitted. "I think a shower sounds lovely."

"Take as long as you need, baby." Archie caressed my face then kissed my forehead before he stood up.

Archie's nurturing didn't make me feel like less of a man or helpless; his attention showed me how much he cherished me. I'd do the same for him if the situation were reversed. I took my time in the shower just like he'd said. I let the hot water cleanse me, relax me, and visualized it washing the ugliness away down the drain with the body wash and shampoo. When I was done, I felt a lot better. I looked at my reflection while I brushed my teeth and took inventory of my emotions. I still felt battered and bruised, but I knew I was going to be okay. I felt stronger than I had that morning and was confident going to the bowling alley was safe. In fact, there wasn't a better group of guys to be around when my chips were down.

Archie's grilled cheese sandwich tasted even better than mine. "You used Gruyere cheese as I did, but I see you've gone an extra step. The outside of this sandwich is pure perfection. Do I see rosemary on this bread?"

"I made a rosemary butter to put on the outside." He looked so proud of himself. "I added a special touch on the inside to make it creamier. Can you figure it out?"

I took another bite and closed my eyes so his smug smile didn't distract me. "Mayo?" I asked.

"Yes!" he said, sounding like a proud teacher. "Millie gave me the basics, but I wanted to step up my game for my man."

"Thank you for today, Archie. Your thoughtfulness and your—" He silenced me with a kiss.

"It's what you do for people you love." Hearing him say he loved me was still so new and thrilling. Looking into his smiling eyes,

I knew the sentiment would never grow old and boring. "Eat up, Golden Boy. The Broken Halos are a few wins away from a championship trophy."

When we arrived at Queen City Lanes, my mood soared even higher when I saw who our opponent was.

"Huddle up, team," I said, gesturing for the guys to gather around me. "Team Righteous Brothers consists of the local homophobic pastors and preachers, including the man responsible for causing Henry's current troubles." The last part was directed at Archie since the rest of them hadn't met Henry. "I know this isn't very Christian of me, but I want to kick their asses so bad they leave here crying."

"Savage," Keeton said. "I like it."

"Let's do it," Milo said.

We all put our hands in the middle and Andy said, "Broken Halos on three. One. Two. Three."

"Broken Halos!" we all said loudly, earning glares and sneers from our opponents.

"Preacher Daily," I said, approaching the lanes with my team following closely behind me. "How unpleasant it is to see you."

"I was just about to say the same thing. Do you pansies think you can beat us?"

"I don't think we can; I know we can."

"God is on *our* side," he said with a sneer.

"We'll just see about that, won't we?"

It wasn't even a contest. All of us threw strikes our first time up to bowl, and it threw them off their game so bad they never recovered. I was so busy focusing on beating those jerks, I hadn't thought about drinking or scoring drugs once. My high came in the form of putting Daily and his hateful crew in their places. It might've been a sin to act so smugly, but he had it coming. I did try to do the gentlemanly thing and offer to shake his hand, but he jumped back like I held a poisonous snake in my hand.

"I don't want to catch something," he said.

"You mean like humanity and kindness?" I asked as he rapidly retreated.

I stopped at the bathroom while Archie returned my shoes. I was surprised when Pastor Daily's son, Geoff, followed me into the bathroom.

"It's not safe for you to be in here with me right now, Geoff."

"Please," he said dramatically, "Father nearly left scorch marks on the floor getting out of here. I didn't know he could move so fast."

"Did you want to talk to me about something?"

"How's Henry?" he asked softly. "Is he doing well?"

"He's doing much better. I know he'd like to see you, and visitors are always welcome."

"I don't know, Pastor Ollie. If my dad ever found out…" His words died off, but I didn't need him to finish.

"I want you to listen to me, Geoff. I'm just a phone call away if you ever need to talk to someone, okay? My cell phone number is on my website and don't hesitate to use it, especially if it becomes unsafe for you to live at home."

Geoff frowned, and I expected him to deny it would ever be necessary, but he didn't. He simply nodded then left the bathroom.

I found Archie leaning against my car when I exited the bowling alley. "Let's go home, Ollie."

"Yours or mine?" I asked.

"Doesn't matter. I only want to be with you."

I ended up driving to my house where we could have the place to ourselves and make as much noise as we wanted. It turned out to be the best decision since neither of us was in the mood to stifle the joy we found in each other.

Chapter Twenty

Archie

I DIDN'T BELIEVE RYDER'S GESTURE CAME WITHOUT STRINGS. I KNEW HIM too well. I'd told him my relationship with Ollie was serious, and he scoffed. He must've assumed Ollie was a virgin, or at least a letdown in bed when he implied I would soon get bored with the relationship and look for something more exciting. This was coming from a man who took cotton swabs and some sort of chemical to methodically and tediously remove hundreds of years' worth of dirt and grime from antique paintings. Don't get me wrong; I thought restoring art was a cool and rewarding job, and it took him to the most amazing museums in the world. In his mind, he was the Indiana Jones of the art world, but in reality, he was more like Mouth from *The Goonies*.

I realized during his visit to my office that he never really knew me. Ryder hadn't taken the time to know my feelings on relationships, or he would've known I'd always wanted to find someone like Ollie with whom to grow old and share a life. I was desperate to belong to someone, and it led me to make horrible choices in men. I let myself believe hookups and clandestine relationships were all I could have—all I deserved. Even after gay marriage became legal nationwide, I wasn't the kind of guy men wanted to bring home to mom and dad. I, and my desire to wear makeup and dress in drag, set the movement back. Blah. Blah. Blah. Then came Ollie, and I found the person God meant for me all along.

I tried to find a reasonable excuse for us to sit out the benefit, but it was wrong to ignore an event that would raise money for Ryan's Place, and Ollie wanted to see me in a tux. Therefore, a few weeks later, I stood in the foyer looking in the mirror while adjusting my black bow tie for the tenth time in five minutes. Ollie was due to arrive any minute.

"Ohhhh," Mamma said, waving her hands in front of her face. "You look so handsome in your tuxedo. I missed this when you refused to go to prom because of old heteropathic something or others."

"Archaic heteronormative traditions," I corrected. "It was true then, and it's still true now. Don't think we don't have issues in the LBGTQ community. Homonormativity is also a thing," I said. "Whenever the community is represented on a television show, it's usually a white, gay male who fits in so perfectly with his straight, white neighbors or co-workers so viewers can all say 'see, honey, they're just like us.' I understand we want straight people to see us as the same because we are just like them in the ways we dream, hope, love, succeed, and fail. However, it sets the movement back when we leave everyone else out of the conversation. Where are the black transwomen and the bisexual Asian men? I could go on, but you see my point."

"I do," she agreed, nodding her head. "I can also tell by your impassioned speech you're nervous." She had me there. "Why?"

"I don't want Ryder causing trouble for Ollie and me. I don't trust him or his motives."

"My love, Ryder can't ruin your relationship with Ollie unless you guys let him. It doesn't matter what the man says or does, only how the two of you react. Ollie loves you and believes in you, and I see you feel the exact same way about him. How could Ryder destroy that?"

"Listen to your mother," Esther said, joining us. "Ollie looks at you the way my Morty looked at me. There were plenty of bimbos who tried to lure my man away, but he only had eyes for me. That kind of love is a beautiful gift, so don't waste precious time worrying someone will take it away from you when you could be enjoying the bounty."

I heard a car pull up in front of the house followed by doors shutting. "They're here." Why was I so damn nervous? Was I worried the reality of me in a tuxedo wouldn't live up to his fantasy? I didn't have time to internally debate it any longer because Millie walked through the door with the love of my life following closely behind her.

My eyes roamed hungrily over Ollie decked out in his black tux which made his olive-toned skin look darker and his eyes warmer. "Wow, Golden Boy. You look…" My words trailed off because I couldn't think of a good enough adjective to describe the way he looked.

"Breathtaking," Ollie said breathlessly.

"Yes, you look breathtaking," I agreed, nodding.

"I was talking about you, Arch. I'm not letting you out of my sight tonight."

"I was just thinking the same about you."

"Good God," Henry said, coming down the stairs. "Are you guys heading to a gala or a GQ photo shoot?" I snorted, and Ollie laughed.

Mamma, Millie, and Esther continued to fuss, making us pose for pictures standing next to the staircase or sitting on it.

"These are looking like wedding photos," Henry teased.

My breath caught in my throat when I saw how badly Ollie wanted Henry's words to come true and knew he saw the same hope in my eyes. We would get there when the time was right. I was sure of it. Right then, I was going to enjoy showing off my gorgeous boyfriend at the event then later strip him out of his tuxedo and worship his body.

We hugged the ladies and Henry then headed out. I noticed Ollie was quieter than normal on the drive over. I looked over and saw his jaw looked clenched in the light from the dashboard.

"Is something wrong, Ollie?"

"Wrong? No, there's nothing wrong."

"You're not worried about Ryder, are you? Esther reminded me tonight that he can't come between us unless we allow it."

"To be honest, I haven't given Ryder another thought."

"Then what's with the white knuckles?"

Ollie glanced down at his hands on the steering wheel then forced himself to relax. "I have something to confess, and I should've done it before tonight."

"I'm listening," I said uneasily.

"Baby, it's nothing bad," Ollie rushed to clarify. "My secretiveness came from a place of humility and wasn't intended to exclude you. Will you believe me?"

"Of course." I wouldn't give many people my blind trust, but I would him. "Tell me your big secret."

"I have artwork on display at the museum tonight. In fact, I've submitted artwork for the past five events."

"Ollie, that's so exciting. Do you normally sell anything?" I asked.

"I…um…do okay."

"You sell out, don't you? I bet they eagerly wait to see your drawings."

"Archie," he said in a voice that pleaded with me to steer the conversation away from his success.

Ollie had once explained pastors of small, non-denominational churches like his often had to work part-time jobs to supplement their income, where larger churches supplied a salary and provided housing for their clergymen. Ollie had inherited his home and church from Randall, who'd bought the buildings with the income he'd earned from the farm where Millie still lived. I was stunned to learn those acres and acres of corn and beans belonged to her, and the bulk of Ollie's annual income came from farming the land.

"I donate my proceeds from the art sale to charities or put it back into my church so we can do fun events, like the annual picnic at Kings Island amusement park."

"Have I seen any of the art you've submitted?" I asked, changing the subject to something he would feel more comfortable discussing. "Are they nudes?" I asked in a scandalized voice.

"No," he said. "I drew these especially for the event because I knew they'd be popular." He sounded guilty like maybe he thought he was a sellout.

"Why do you sound ashamed? Isn't the purpose of tonight to showcase LGBTQ artists who have art to sell?"

"Yes."

"Why wouldn't you bring something people would want to buy? Are you supposed to glue bubble gum wrappers onto canvas and hope someone will like it?"

Ollie snorted. "I guess you have a point."

"What did you draw?"

"You'll see when we get there."

The event at the museum looked like something out of Hollywood. Big floodlights illuminated the old, graceful building with the huge columns and grand steps leading up to the entrance. Photographers were on hand to take pictures of people on the red carpet after they entrusted their vehicles to the valets on hand. I loved posing with my Golden Boy and shamefully hoped our photo made it into the newspaper or the museum's website. I chuckled to myself when I realized Ryder wouldn't let it happen if he could help it.

Once inside, I was wowed again by the breathtaking grandeur of the ornate double staircase in the Great Hall. It wasn't my first time at the museum, but it was my first high-society event there. Waiters wove throughout the crush of humanity dressed in beautiful gowns and formal tuxedos offering flutes of champagne, which Ollie and I both declined. Ollie didn't drink, and I preferred beer.

"Let's go explore. I want to see your art."

"Okay, but please don't make a big fuss."

"Me? Excited to see something you created showcased in a such a grand setting? I can't believe you think I'm going to make a big fuss."

Ollie groaned but led me to the first painting in the far-left corner of the room. I couldn't tell if there was a specific direction we were supposed to adhere to, but it looked like people casually strolled willy-nilly while taking in the art. The variety of submissions from the local artists were vast and jaw-dropping. The arrangement of artwork grabbed my attention and kept me interested in seeing what was next. Modern sculptures and paintings were sandwiched between the more traditional mediums like watercolor, oil paints, and charcoal sketches. They were so different but meshed together to form a beautifully diverse display of talent. It reminded me people could do the same when they put forth the effort.

I didn't need to see the name placard on the easel to recognize my man's work. "Ollie," I said breathlessly. I stared in awe at the sketch of the Roebling Suspension Bridge, my eyes unsure where to look first because I was overwhelmed by its beauty. "This is stunning."

"You know, many people think the bridge was built as a replica of the Brooklyn Bridge, but our bridge was actually constructed first. It opened to traffic on January first, 1867. Construction on the Brooklyn Bridge started two years later. Same civil engineer though."

All Cincinnati natives knew that. "I see you are trying to deflect my attention away from your talent," I teased. "Are you going to strike up a conversation about why the city used to have the nickname Porkopolis instead of the Queen City? Let me just look at this picture, Ollie. I promise not to run up to the top of the stairs and scream my boyfriend made the most beautiful piece of artwork here tonight." Ollie groaned. I put my arm around his waist and pulled him closer so I could kiss his temple. "The drawing is almost as beautiful as you are, Golden Boy."

"I must say, I was impressed when I first saw your submission," said a new and unwelcome voice. We turned and looked at Ryder, who wore a light gray tuxedo and pale pink bow tie that complimented his blond looks. "In fact, this piece of art is the talk of the event. I expect it will sell for a handsome sum."

"I hope so," Ollie said, staring into my eyes. "I'm donating the sale proceeds to Ryan's Place."

"Ollie," I said, sounding as stunned as I felt. "You can't do that."

"Of course, I can. It's my art, and I can do whatever I want with it."

"You need—" Warm, firm lips cut off my words and robbed me of the ability to argue.

"All I *need* is you. The rest is just extra."

Ryder cleared his throat to regain our attention.

"Are you still here?" Ollie asked without taking his eyes off mine. I grinned at his display of irritation.

"Archie, can I talk to you in private for a minute?" Ryder asked testily.

"No," I told him. I finally tore my gaze away from Ollie's warm eyes to look into Ryder's artic ones. "Anything you want to say to me can and should be said in front of Ollie."

"Fine," Ryder said haughtily. "I have something to say to him too." He tilted his head to the left then the right, stretching out his neck then straightened his already perfectly aligned bow tie. These were signs he was nervous which was pretty rare. "I owe you both an apology for my behavior." I would've been less stunned if he told me Elvis Presley was his lab partner. "I was wrong to try to create trouble in your relationship. I've been observing the two of you since you arrived, and it's obvious to see how much you love one another. I'm a big enough man to admit my mistakes and wish both of you the very best."

I narrowed my eyes and scrutinized him closely. "Is this a trick?"

Ryder chuckled and put his hands up in front of him like he was surrendering, his pale eyes twinkling with mirth. "No trick, Archie. I just need to put my energies into finding a man who will look at me the way you two look at each other."

"Apology accepted." Ollie extended his hand toward Ryder. "I hope you find him too," Ollie added when Ryder shook his hand.

"Take care of yourself, Archie," Ryder said, offering me a reserved smile before he left us alone once more.

"That was an interesting turn of events," I told Ollie. "Not at all what I expected."

"Me either," Ollie said, sounding distracted. I turned to follow his line of vision and saw he was looking at a tall, dark-haired man who'd opted to wear a black, V-neck sweater and charcoal gray pants instead of a formal suit like the rest of us. There was an aura about the man which spoke of power and privilege, and it was doubtful anyone would approach him and ask he leave. The man wasn't looking in our direction, so I was unable to tell the color of his eyes, but I guessed they would be dark to match his inky hair and swarthy skin.

"Do you know that man?" I asked Ollie.

"I don't, but it would seem Ryder has picked up the intense focus of a man after all."

I turned and saw the mystery man was indeed watching Ryder circulate around the room greeting attendees. "So it seems. Should we tip him off?"

"Heck no," Ollie said. "There's a lot of fun to be found in the chase."

I pulled him against me and pressed my lips to his ear. "What do you say we finish checking out the other pieces so we can get out of here? The way you look in your tux makes me want to do very naughty things to you, and I don't need an audience."

"And if I assured you I knew of a secluded place we could go? I'm not sure I can wait much longer to find out what you're wearing beneath your tux."

My eyes widened in surprise, but oh, how I loved this side of Ollie. I offered my hand to him and said, "Show me the way, Golden Boy."

Chapter Twenty-One

Ollie

I DIDN'T JUST TAKE ARCHIE OFF TO A DARK CORNER AND RAVISH HIM, NO matter how tempting it was. I wanted to seduce more than just his body. I wanted to engage all his senses until all he could hear over the pounding of his heart was the sound of my voice, the only thing he tasted was me, the only thing he felt was my hands touching and teasing him, and the only smell to tickle his nose was our combined arousal when we finally came together.

I'd been coming to the museum since I was a little kid and knew the permanent collections like the back of my hand. In the African Art section, I slid my hand beneath his jacket to feel the swell of his ass while looking at the various pieces of art collected by Carl Steckelmann during the 1880s and 1890s. While touring the Contemporary Art, I licked the shell of his ear and purred when a shiver worked its way through his body. Archie loved the robot made entirely of old televisions and radios, he loved the way I tugged his earlobe between my teeth more.

"You're really bad," he whispered choppily. "Aren't you afraid we'll get picked up on camera?"

"Have you noticed I've angled my body to hide my roaming hands, and I really don't care if the security guard is up there cowering in the corner because one gay man licked the ear of another."

I ran my hand down the length of his arm until I reached his hand then linked our fingers. "Would you like to see more of my favorite pieces?"

"This does end well for me, right? Is this payback for me teasing you during bingo?"

I tilted my head to the side as I was considering it. "I would be justified to get even, don't you think?"

"Maybe a little."

"It's not what I'm doing, baby. I'm just a man who's enjoying spending time in one of his favorite places with his absolute favorite man. If I could strip you bare and ride you in the middle of the American drawings, I would do it."

"Oh God," he whispered. "I'd love it too. How much money do you think we'd need to donate to have the museum to ourselves for a night?"

"More than either of us will ever have," I replied dryly. "We'll settle for the next best thing."

The tour continued with long French kisses among the European paintings, drawings, and sculptures and teasing strokes along the rigid length of his cock while taking in the Musical Instruments Collection.

"I have something for you to blow, Golden Boy," Archie whispered darkly in my ear while we read the information about the Raven Rattle from 1914 originating from Queen Charlotte Islands, British Columbia.

In the Fashion Art and Textiles, Archie temporarily forgot about me when he laid eyes on the Chanel, Dior, and Vionnet collections. "Does Trix see something she likes?"

"These gowns would go great with the stockings I'm wearing beneath these trousers." Archie looked at me then, and I realized he hadn't forgotten about my being there while he lusted over sumptuous fabrics. He was biding his time to get even. "I even wore a garter belt for the special occasion."

A quickie in a dark corner was no longer an option. I needed privacy and a bed. I didn't want to utilize the horny, cow-like sculpture labeled a Rhyton Vessel. "He's as horny as I am," I said pointing to the long, curving horns.

"It appears to have a saddle on the back of it," Archie said. "Do you think it's strong enough to support our weight. I could straddle Rhyton, and you could straddle me."

Archie pulled me in front of him and pressed his dick against my ass. I reached up and slid my hands through his thick, dark hair. Sex between us was always explosive, but I knew it would be off the charts by the time we finally got back to my house.

"What I wouldn't give to pull your cock out and stroke it right here."

I pressed my ass harder against the bulge in his pants. He was harder than I'd ever felt him before, and the need to feel him buried inside me made me moan out loud.

"Time to go, don't you think?" I asked.

"Yes, but let's walk casually so we don't look like we've hidden ancient artifacts in our jackets."

It was harder to act normal than I thought because I was so in tune with Archie and how badly he wanted me too. It felt like we were emitting a strong enough current between us to cause a fire. We made our way back to the main staircase and had just rounded the final curve before we reached the bottom when we almost ran into the man who had been watching Ryder so intently.

"Pardon me," he said. He had a melodic British accent and a warm smile, but his dark eyes seemed cold and calculating. "I'm looking for someone. I saw him speaking to you earlier. Tall, blond hair, and blue eyes. His name is Ryder Jameson."

I suddenly had a bad feeling about the guy and shockingly felt the urge to keep Ryder away from him. "We haven't seen him since we spoke to him down in the Great Hall."

"Damn," he said, sounding irritated. "Thank you, anyway."

"No problem," Archie said, shrugging at me when the guy just continued up the stairs at a quick pace.

"What do you suppose that's about?" I asked once we reached the ground floor.

"It's not my concern," Archie replied, leading me toward the exit. "You are my concern. The things I want to do with your body are my concern."

I handed the valet ticket to the attendant then slid my arm around Archie's waist. He was absolutely right and thinking about Ryder would just be a damper on our perfect evening. I was so excited to get Archie naked I considered getting a hotel room, but I hadn't been inside one of those since my last customer booked a cheap room the day before my arrest. I didn't associate hotel rooms with lovemaking and happiness, so it was probably a trigger.

Archie wasn't in the mood to play fair. Once we were in the car, he traced his fingers over the straps of his garter belt and around the lacy band of his stockings on his thighs. He reached between his legs and massaged his balls, moaning and telling me how full they felt. Then he stroked his cock and teased his nipples through his crisp, white shirt.

"You're starting to drive as erratically as me," Archie teased in a voice darkened by lust and raw need. "I must be a bad influence on you, Golden Boy."

"I'm glad you finally admit you're a horrible driver, Arch. I think we both know why I'm driving twenty miles over the speed limit and switching lanes like a race car driver." At last, I saw my exit sign, turned on my signal, and cut across three lanes of highway to get there just in the nick of time.

The trip once we left the interstate wasn't very long, but Archie never let up on his seduction. Luckily, he kept his hands to himself, or we'd end up in a plowed field or crashing into a tree. I turned into my lane on two wheels and kicked up rocks and dust as I sped toward my house.

We were out of the car as soon as I put it in park. We rounded the hood at the same time and crashed into each other, hands groping and sliding over hard planes and curved butt cheeks. Our kiss was scorching and feverish with teeth bumping and tongues tangling. I nearly tripped up the steps, and Archie caught my startled gasp and laughter with his mouth. My hands shook so bad I dropped the keychain twice before Archie took it from my hands and unlocked the door.

"These clothes have to go," I told Archie, pulling off my jacket and tossing it to the ground. "I can't go another second without knowing what you're wearing under your pants."

"I can't wait to see your reaction," Archie replied, cupping his swollen cock through the fabric.

I dropped to my feet and pressed my face against the front of his pants. "You're leaking." I inhaled the smell of his arousal deep into my nose then went to work on his buckle, button, and zipper. "Oh dear God," I whispered when I revealed the matching lavender lacy underwear and garter belt. I slid his pants down his legs and waited as he kicked off his shoes and stepped out of his trousers. "Archie," I reverently whispered as I ran my finger from the curve of his arched foot, over his toned calf, along the back of his knee where he was ticklish, and up his inner thigh until I reached the top of the soft gray stockings. "You're so beautiful and sexy."

Archie slid his hand into my hair and tilted my head back so he could look into my eyes. "You're the sexy one. I could come from the way you're looking at me right now."

"I can do better than that," I assured him, loving the way his hard dick looked beneath delicate underwear. I leaned forward and tongued his balls through the lace then licked a path up his shaft until I teased the sensitive foreskin around the crown of his cock.

"That *is* better," Archie said, pushing against my tongue.

"Not as good as you taste, baby."

I reached beneath the garter belt to pull his panties down far enough to release his cock. It sprung forward and landed eagerly on the tongue waiting for it. I wasted no time working him in and out of my mouth knowing he had to be close to exploding by that point.

"I won't last long if you keep it up, baby," he said huskily.

"I suppose it's my fault," I said, leaning back to sit on my heels. Archie's cock jutted proudly from his body, looking flushed and angry from being hard for so long. I took my time working open the buttons of my shirt while he ripped his open, sending tiny buttons scattering to the floor. I rose to my feet so I could finish undressing until I was completely naked and Archie wore only his stockings, garter belt, and panties pushed to mid-thigh. I retrieved the supplies we needed from the drawer in the coffee table then shoved it out of the way like a man possessed. I climbed onto the couch, rested my forearms on the back of the sofa, and jutted my spread ass cheeks toward him. "Enough foreplay."

Archie chuckled while he rolled the condom on his dick then squirted lube onto his fingers. I sluttily moaned when he worked me open because I was moments away from getting what I'd craved all night long. "Feel good, baby?"

"Divine," I said when I felt Archie line the head of his cock to my hole and push against it.

I earned another warm chuckle, but it died the minute my greedy ass pulled him in deeper. "This will be fast and hard," he said which was the only warning I got before he pushed in to the hilt, pulled back out until only the tip of his cock remained inside me, and drove his hips forward again hard enough to rock the couch slightly. Archie pulled my hair, curving my neck back just how I liked it and started a pounding rhythm which had me coming so hard and fast my vision dimmed. Archie's orgasm was only a few strokes behind mine, and he hoarsely shouted my name when he filled the condom.

"Now that we've taken the edge off," I said when he pulled out of me and flopped down on the couch, "perhaps you'd like to see the surprise I have for you."

"Surprise? What surprise? Is this an anniversary or something?"

I thought his panic was endearing and adorable. "I knew how

you'd react when you saw the drawing at the museum and thought I'd surprise you with a piece of my art you can hang on your bedroom wall."

"Why not the dining room or living room?" Archie asked with a furrowed brow. "There's nothing inappropriate about a bridge is there?"

"I didn't draw a bridge for you, Arch. I drew something a little bit more...personal."

I was suddenly overcome with nerves. What if he didn't like it? I thought it was my best work to date, but he might take one look at it and feel appalled. What if he felt objectified?

"Well, where is it?" he asked excitedly.

"It's in my bedroom."

Archie leaped from the couch, pulled his underwear up for better mobility, and extended a hand to help me up. "No one has ever created a drawing just for me. I cannot wait to see what you've done." Archie hopped onto the bed and crossed his legs seductively, almost distracting me from retrieving his gift. "I want my present," he demanded like a diva.

I crossed to my closet and pulled the framed drawing out and carried it to the bed, so the front was facing me. "I won't be upset if you don't l—"

Archie leaned forward and snatched the frame then turned it around to see the drawing. "Oh my God," he whispered in awe. "Did you draw it from the picture you saved on your phone."

I nodded. "Do you like it?"

Archie looked at the drawing I made of him removing his stockings the first night we made love. His foot was arched elegantly on the toilet lid as he pushed the stockings toward his knee. I tried so hard to capture all the facets of him that I loved so much, the masculine tone of his gorgeous body, the feminine frills that made him feel powerful, and the hunger in his eyes when he'd looked at me.

"I love it," he whispered in awe, tracing the line of his back. "It's the most beautiful gift anyone has ever given me." He looked at me with tears in his eyes. "I don't just mean the drawing, Ollie." Archie rose up from the bed and gently set the frame down like it was a prized treasure. "I'm talking about your love, and the way you see me—all of me. I love you so damn much."

"I love you too, Arch." *Always. Forever. Until death do us part.* I looked forward to adding those words to our declarations someday.

Chapter Twenty-Two

Archie

I KNEW WHERE I'D FIND OLLIE WHEN I STEPPED OUT OF THE SHOWER THE next morning. He was going through his preaching day preparations which basically just included making oatmeal for breakfast. I noticed the extra ingredients he added to the oatmeal base changed with the season. His fall combinations included cranberries, cinnamon, nutmeg, and pecans. I looked forward to seeing how he changed it up for winter and spring. There was a new aroma wafting down the hallway, one I was quite familiar with and was accused of being addicted to. Bacon!

I dried off and grabbed a pair of my sweats and a T-shirt from the dresser drawers Ollie assigned me. I loved having drawers at his place, just as I loved seeing his things in the dresser at my house. I loved how our lives became more and more entwined every day. Ollie was never far from my mind, and I knew he felt the same way from the texts he sent when we were apart. We had the love I'd always hoped to find, and I belonged to him in ways I never dreamed possible.

"Changing things up, I see," I said when I entered the kitchen. Ollie had just slid the last piece of bacon on a plate lined with paper towels to soak up the extra grease. "That's the best-looking bacon I've ever seen."

"This is the secret to creating the best of anything," Ollie said, gesturing to his ancient-looking cast iron skillet. "Ole Bessie never lets me down."

"You name your skillets?"

"The name came with the skillet when I inherited it. I did tease Millie by saying I would change the name. She threatened to take the skillet to my head."

"She'd never do such a thing."

"I don't know," Ollie said. "I saw her chase a fox with Ole Bessie when it tried to get her chickens." I laughed at the image springing to mind while Ollie chuckled over the memory. "She's something else, my mama." He shook his head and smiled ruefully. "She also told me to eat food while it's hot. Can you grab plates and bowls, Arch?"

I was very comfortable in Ollie's kitchen in ways I wasn't in my own. The kitchen at Ryan's Place was Esther's domain, and I often felt like a naughty kid when I dirtied a dish or prepared a late night snack. She'd never said anything to the residents or me to discourage us in the kitchen, but she made it clear we had to clean up after ourselves. Esther and Millie had similar personalities and believed in tough love, where Mamma tended to handle things with a gentler approach. I think it had to do a lot with the violence I witnessed during my first five years. She worked hard to show me a person didn't need to raise their voice, and certainly not their hand, to mold and teach a child. Still, I think their bolder, more self-assured personalities were a wonderful influence on my mom. She seemed more confident and assertive, and I liked the changes. For Esther and Millie, my mom softened some of their sharper edges with her graceful demeanor. The three ladies' personalities combined to create a mighty team worthy of superhero status. We never knew what they would think up, say, or do at any given moment.

I looked forward to attending services each week with them and Henry who was blossoming before our very eyes. I felt like a proud parent watching my child gain confidence and strength. I still saw shadows under his eyes on occasion and caught a lost expression now and then, but I also saw him dust off his pants and keep moving. It took a lot of courage sometimes. He'd found a part-time job at a bookstore and tried out for a community theater role and was chosen to star as one of the four main characters. He walked around on a cloud for days afterward before nerves set in once rehearsals started. The three women in his life offered encouragement through pep talks and love. He soaked it in, and I knew he fully understood what Ollie's sermon about the chosen family truly meant.

"You're extra reflective this morning," Ollie said when he sat across from me at his table. "Is everything okay?"

"Better than okay, Ollie. I'm still amazed at how much my life has changed since I met you. I'm just feeling grateful."

"I'm grateful for you too."

For church, I put on the dark purple dress shirt Ollie bought me because he said it made my eyes look greener. I wanted him to see me in the front pew and know I dressed for him. Millie, Esther, and Mamma all showed up wearing their Sunday finest, which now included hats and gloves for Mamma and Esther. Henry wore a sweater and trousers and a rueful smile on his face.

"The ladies are in rare form this morning," he cautioned. "Esther and Maria discovered a new show on Netflix they couldn't stop talking about, and we met Millie in the parking lot who was fired up over the sports talk radio show she was listening to before we arrived."

"Uh-oh," I said softly. "Lunch at Burt's should be interesting."

"You have no idea."

Ollie's sermon was about forgiveness, and how much better it is for us to forgive those who trespass against us to have a fulfilling life free of burden, but admitted it was something he had struggled with his entire adult life.

"If you're open to forgiving, the opportunity and the ability will come to you when it's time," he told his congregation. "Forgiveness isn't something you can force, and offering meaningless platitudes does nothing to heal the hurt inside you. It's never wrong to tell someone forgiveness is something you want to achieve but haven't yet. It's okay to insist on time to put distance between the person and events that have caused grief in your life. It's okay to feel conflicted about forgiving people because you're human, and you don't have to decide your entire life this very second. Today, I simply ask you to open your mind up to the possibility of forgiveness and a life un-encumbered by sadness, grief, and grudges. Imagine yourself living each day with the knowledge you've been hurt and you've moved past it by forgiving the ones who've trespassed against you.

"In my mind, holding onto grudges gives those people power over you; power they don't deserve. Forgiveness is freeing and power-ful and uplifting. It's knowing someone wronged you, but you're no longer willing to let it rule you. That, my friends, is the best part of forgiveness. It's not about making the other person feel better about what they did, in fact, most of us don't have the opportunity to look them in the eyes and say they're forgiven. In many cases, the person you need to forgive hasn't even apologized to you, but it doesn't mean you can't forgive and move on. Don't do it for them; do it for your-self." As with all of his sermons, I could tell the words he spoke were personal to him. Had he reached the point of forgiveness with Kaleb and his biological family?

After his sermon, Ollie sat in his chair off to the side of the al-tar while Millie and the Thompson family performed three songs with lyrics matching the tone of Ollie's sermon better than Bea Trix could match her pumps to her dress. They put so much energy into the service each week, and their efforts were greatly appreciated and enjoyed.

Once the congregation left, we headed over to Burt's for our usu-al lunch. Henry hadn't exaggerated about Millie. She was all worked up.

"Thank you for reminding me I need to work on my forgive-ness skills, Son. These talking heads on the radio have one purpose each day, and it's to rile up Millie Givens with their exaggerations, half-truths, and outright lies. Their behavior is just disgraceful. When in the world did sports radio merge with shock radio? It's like these guys get up each morning and ask how they can be the Howard Stern of sports radio."

"Mama, maybe you shouldn't listen to the programs if they upset you so much."

Millie threw her head back and laughed. "On the contrary, getting mad at these silly men makes me feel alive."

"Then maybe you should call the show," I suggested, earning an elbow jab from Ollie. "What? She knows more about the Cincinnati sports teams than those two idiots combined. Better yet, they should have you on the show!"

"They couldn't handle all of this," Millie said, turning into the parking lot of Burt's, "but I love the way you think, love." Millie pushed her door open after she put the car in park and turned off the engine. "Guess what?" she asked her friends. "Archie gave me the best idea."

Mamma and Esther looked about as enthused as Ollie did when Millie told them my suggestion. "What?" I asked them too. "She'd be fabulous! Those callers would eat her sass up with a spoon."

"I'm not sure it's good for her blood pressure," Mamma said worriedly.

"Or, it could improve her blood pressure because she's getting the frustration out of her system," Esther said.

"It's just a fun idea," Millie said, waving the notion away. "They wouldn't want to waste time with an opinionated old woman."

I looked around the parking lot and along the sidewalk in front of the restaurant. "I don't see an old woman."

"Oh, I just love you to pieces," Millie said, squeezing me. "Let's get inside and order our food. All this yelling at the radio has worked up an appetite."

We headed to our usual corner booth where the waitress took our usual order. Why mess with a good thing when it worked so well for us? The pregame show had just ended, and we expected the broadcast to change from the studio to stadium, but they pitched it to the local news affiliate instead.

"Oh look," Mamma said. "It's the art museum. I wonder if they're going to say how much money the event raised."

"I wonder how much your drawing sold for, Ollie," I said.

"You submitted a drawing?" Millie asked. "Was it something I've already seen or something you drew just for the event?"

"It was—"

"Hold up," Henry said, raising his hand and cutting Ollie off. "There was a theft from the museum last night."

I looked back at the screen, and sure enough, there was a breaking news banner at the bottom of the screen followed by the words: Artifact Heist at the Cincinnati Art Museum. "Oh my God!"

"Can you turn the volume up?" Ollie asked the waitress when she returned with our drinks. "We were there last night."

"Sure thing," she said then hurried off.

The male anchor led off the broadcast with, "Sometime in the middle of the night, someone disabled the elaborate alarm system and jumbled the security cameras long enough to steal a twelfth-century fangyi ritual wine vessel belonging to Wu Ding, a king of the Shang dynasty." A picture of a tall bronze box-like structure with a lid shaped like a roof appeared on the screen. The wine vessel was green in places from oxidation, but it didn't detract from the intricate symbols all over it. "The museum says, due to its rarity, the vessel is valued at two hundred and fifty thousand dollars."

The camera shifted to the female co-anchor, who said, "Police are looking for information about the man you see in these photos." A picture of the guy who was interested in Ryder, the same one who nearly knocked us over on the steps, appeared on the screen. The next photo showed him casually accepting a champagne flute from a waiter, and the final picture showed him speaking to us on the staircase. The images changed once more to show agents from the FBI entering the museum. "If anyone recognizes him please call the hotline number at the bottom of the screen."

I felt the attention from the table shift from the big screen television and onto Ollie and me.

"Uh-oh," Ollie said. "I bet the police will want to speak to us."

My cell phone rang as soon as the words left his mouth. The caller ID said it was an unknown caller, but I had a pretty good idea who it might be.

"Hello," I said more calmly than I felt.

"Hello, may I speak with Archie White, please?"

"This is he."

"Mr. White, this is Agent Hugh Kiphart with the Federal Bureau of Investigation. I wondered if you could come down to the federal building this afternoon to speak with me. I went to your home, and one of the residents said you are out of town."

"By out of town, he meant thirty minutes away. I stayed with my boyfriend and attended his church service. I can be downtown in about an hour if that works for you."

"It's fine, Mr. White. Is your boyfriend Oliver Knight?"

"Yes."

"Would he be available to speak with us too?"

"Of course, Agent Kiphart. Neither of us has anything to hide."

"Thank you, Mr. White. I'll see you in an hour." He hung up without saying goodbye, but it wasn't a social call.

"You're wanted for questioning?" Mamma asked, wringing her hands.

"Mamma, we didn't do anything wrong. The picture was very misleading. We don't know the man. He only asked us if we'd seen Ryder."

"Interesting," Millie said with a gleam in her eyes. "You think Ryder is on the take?"

"I really don't know Ryder anymore, but the man I knew eight years ago loved art above all else, including money." And me. "He didn't just love art; he revered it."

"I don't believe Ryder was involved," Ollie said.

"You don't know the man," Millie pointed out.

"Just the feeling I get," Ollie said with a shrug. "Should we head there now?"

"I bought us an extra thirty minutes so we could grab a bite to eat first. I don't see why we should go to the station hungry."

"How can you think of your stomach at a time like this?" Mamma asked.

"Easily. I didn't do anything wrong, so I don't have anything to worry about. My conscience is clear, but my belly is empty." Okay, so empty was an exaggeration after the breakfast Ollie had made, but nearly four hours had passed since then.

Ollie had a harder time eating, but I knew his nervousness had nothing to do with guilt. We hugged and said goodbye to Mamma, Esther, and Henry then climbed in the back of Millie's Cadillac, so she could drive us back home. I clasped Ollie's hand between both of mine, attempting to chase away the chill permeating his body.

"I love fall, but I don't care for the cold, November rain," Millie said. "You boys be careful." We leaned forward between the front seats to kiss her cheek, so she didn't have to get out in it.

I knew Ollie was upset when he handed me the keys to his car and said, "You drive."

I wasn't about to question him in the cold rain, so I got in on the driver's side and waited until we shut the doors before I said anything about it. "Baby, why are you so nervous?"

"The last time I talked to someone from law enforcement it didn't go very well for me, Arch. The arresting officers made no secret about how they felt about gay men. I realized I'm not the same strung out, homeless guy I used to be, and the set of circumstances are completely different, but I..."

"You can't help feeling the way you do. There's nothing wrong with it either, baby." I leaned over and kissed him softly. "All you need to do is tell the truth. If they make snide remarks about our sexuality, we'll turn their lives upside down with complaints and legal action. We should not and will not put up with any crap from them or anyone else."

Ollie nodded and released a shaky breath. "Will you do one thing for me?"

"Anything."

"Keep all four tires on the road at all times."

"Okay, but just this once."

"And maybe keep your speeding to only five miles over the limit," Ollie suggested.

"That's two favors, but for you, I will even drive the speed limit today."

I tried to keep the mood light by singing along with the music and even coaxed Ollie to do the same a few times. His tension returned once we parked and walked to the federal building. We were shown to separate interview rooms which we both knew would happen. We'd seen enough law enforcement shows to know they would want to trip us up and pit us against each other if we knew something of value.

I wasn't in the room long before a male and female agent entered the room. Both of them looked to be my age until you looked into their eyes. The things they'd witnessed on the job aged them. I figured Ollie broadcasted his nervousness, so they wanted him to stew a little longer to make him squeal faster. It was a good strategy, and one I'd employ if I were them.

"I'm Agent Hugh Kiphart, and this is my partner, Danica Marshall. Thank you for coming in so promptly, Mr. White."

"I have nothing to hide, Agents," I said, leaning back in my chair to show how relaxed I felt. Kiphart's crooked smile said *we'll just see about that.*

"What were you doing at the benefit last night?" Agent Marshall asked, jumping right in.

"A portion of last night's ticket sales are getting donated to my HIV transition home. I believe you visited it earlier today, yes?" She nodded. "One of Ollie's drawings was featured in the silent auction, so we decided to attend."

"How do you know Lucien Clarke?" Kiphart asked.

"I don't know a Lucien Clarke, Agent." He pulled a photo from the file he'd brought with him and slid it across the table. It was the one they showed in the breaking news broadcast.

"This picture indicates you know him."

"Wrong, Agent. This picture indicates we spoke to him. You and I both know they aren't the same. Besides, if this were captured on a live video feed, then you'd know damn well our conversation lasted for less than a minute after he nearly ran us over. You'd also know we didn't speak to him before or after the image was captured."

"Fine," Kiphart conceded. "And I can assure you the security cameras did indeed capture your tour through the museum." He raised a brow, but I didn't see censure or disgust in his dark eyes. Did he think I would blush or cower? I might've if we'd been caught with our pants down, but the most the cameras picked up was two men hopelessly in love. "What did Lucien Clarke say to you?"

"He was looking for Ryder Jameson," I told them. "He'd seen us talking to Ryder earlier in the evening and wanted to know if we'd seen him since. We hadn't because, as you noted, we were preoccupied with other things."

Marshall chuckled and asked, "Ryder Jameson is a former boyfriend, right?"

"Yes," I confirmed.

"Have you been in touch with him at all since he left Cincinnati eight years ago?" she continued.

"No. I hadn't talked to him until he showed up at Queen City Divas—"

"That's where I know you from," Kiphart said, interrupting me. "Lady Bea Trix."

"Can we focus here, Hugh?" Marshall asked him.

"Yeah, sorry. Continue," he said, gesturing his hand in a circular motion.

"He showed up out of the blue back in September. I told him I wasn't interested, but he didn't believe me right away. In fact, he didn't believe me until last night when he saw Ollie and me together. He apologized to us both for trying to cause trouble, and it was the last we spoke to him. It was then Ollie noticed Lucien Clarke's intense focus on Ryder. He watched him as he made his way through the room."

"Did Mr. Jameson indicate he was aware of his presence? Acknowledge him in any way?" Agent Marshall asked.

"Not that we saw," I told them. "We weren't there long, as you can tell by the footage."

Kiphart nodded and exchanged a glance with Marshall. "That's all we have for you today. We ask that you give us a call right away if you learn anything new."

"Sure," I agreed.

I sat on an uncomfortable plastic chair and waited for Ollie to finish his interview. I couldn't help but worry about him since he'd been so nervous, but he offered a crooked smile when he finished.

"It wasn't so bad," he said sheepishly.

"Let's get out of here," I said.

When we exited the police station, I noticed it had finally stopped raining. I also saw that Ryder was standing on the corner like he was waiting for the crosswalk sign to change so he could cross the street.

"Is that Ryder?" Ollie asked.

"Yeah," I said. "He looks like he's still in his tuxedo from last night."

"Do you think he was here all night?"

"It sure looks like it," I admitted.

I was about to call out to him when a black sedan with darkly tinted windows pulled up and stopped in front of him just as the crosswalk signal changed. The window rolled down, but I couldn't see who was behind the wheel. Ryder looked alarmed at first but ended up getting in the car. It sped away before I could memorize the license plate number.

"Not our business," I told Ollie. "You know everyone is waiting to hear about our big adventure with the feds. Let's get it over with and make the best of our day."

"Does making the best of it involve nudity?"

"Without a doubt, baby. Without a doubt."

Chapter Twenty-Three

Ollie

THE MISSING WINE VESSEL STAYED A HOT TOPIC ON THE NEWS FOR A few more weeks, but eventually, the excitement died down when all the tips, speculation, and rumors couldn't turn up the missing item. It wasn't long before the latest political scandal rocked the nation and became the top story everyone discussed online or gossiped about over coffee. I thought it was too bad because the longer the wine vessel went without being found, the unlikelier it became the museum would recover it. The person with the skill to bypass complex security systems and jumble the video feed surely had the resources to get the item to its destination which I figured was a private collector with too much money and too little morals.

The day before Thanksgiving, I stopped by Claire's to pick up my usual order on my way to Ryan's Place. Esther had plans to teach me the proper way to make yeast rolls for our big dinner, and I was going to teach her the secrets to the best pumpkin pie they'd ever eat. I checked my phone while I waited for Claire to fill my order then looked over to the corner of the room when I felt someone watching me. I hardly recognized Ryder Jameson as the same man I met months before. He looked gaunt, exhausted, and barely hanging on.

I walked to his table, unable to resist the sadness I saw in his blue eyes. "Ryder, are you okay? You look…" I let my voice trail off while I searched for the right thing to say.

"Like hell?" he suggested, his mouth tipping up at the corner. "It's because I feel like hell. I've felt this way ever since the night of the gala." He ran both hands through his hair, leaving it sticking up in spikes all over the place. I noticed he was dressed too casually to have come from work.

I pulled out a chair and sat down without waiting to be invited. "Did they fire you?" I asked hesitantly.

"Put on paid leave until they can be sure I wasn't the one who helped Lucien Clarke steal the wine vessel." He looked at me with earnest, pleading eyes. "It wasn't me, Ollie. I don't know why I care what you think, but I'm telling the truth."

"I believe you, Ryder." And I did, even though I didn't have a reason to believe him. "Do you have a past with Lucien?"

"You could say that again," he sneered. "Of course, I never knew him as Lucien Clarke back then. He was Sebastian Deveraux. We met at a bar in Paris and had a torrid affair for weeks. He was so urbane, worldly, and sexy. He was so knowledgeable about art, and we spent many nights sharing wine and discussing my favorite subject. I didn't realize he was using me until a valuable piece of art was stolen from the museum at the same time the man I'd started to fall in love with disappeared. It was a gala similar to the one here, and he'd told me he wouldn't be able to make it because he had to travel for work. I was crushed when I saw footage of him at the event. He was careful to stay where I couldn't see him while keeping me in his sight. God, I was such a fool, Ollie. I went to the museum director with my tail between my legs and told him about the man who introduced himself to me as a British businessman working in Paris who loved art, opera, and wine."

"I'm really sorry, Ryder. Did you get in trouble at work?"

"They were extremely suspicious but couldn't prove I'd given Lucien information to help him. He hadn't used my employee ID to access any of our databases or mess with security alarms and cameras.

They determined I was a stupid sap he used to get information. I bare-ly held onto my job." He scrubbed his hands over his face. "Art is my life. What will I do if I lose my job?"

"Fight for your job, Ryder. Don't roll over and play dead." I re-called the black, luxury sedan with the tinted windows. "Was he the one you got into the car with after you left the police station?"

Ryder's eyes widened in alarm, and he looked like he was going to deny it, but instead, he said, "It was him."

"What did he want?"

"To convince me he was innocent," Ryder said, sounding con-flicted. Surely he didn't believe him.

"Which time?" I asked. "Priceless artifacts were stolen both times he appeared in your life." Ryder groaned. "Wait. Did this happen more than twice?"

He nodded. "Lucien showed up one day at the museum I was working at in Egypt. He was so convincing, and I was so...."

"Horny?" Many a man suffered after listening to his dick.

"Lonely, Ollie. I was so damn lonely. I was desperate to believe him because I wanted to, and it backfired. The second time around, I kept my mouth shut about recognizing him when photos were pre-sented to us. They had no idea we'd been fucking for weeks, and I wasn't about to tell them. Lucien and I hadn't discussed a single thing about the museum in Cairo, so there had to be someone else giving him information. Same as Paris and Cincinnati."

"I assume you came clean to everyone about the theft in Cairo too?" I asked.

"It didn't take them long to find the connection. My time work-ing for the museums was in my bio, and directors tend to remember the dates when priceless items turn up missing."

"I don't mean to sound cruel, but if the museum knew you were working at both the museums at the time these items were stolen, why did they risk hiring you? Wouldn't you be too big of a risk? I'm sure a paintings conservator is an important job, but aren't there ones with less...baggage?"

Ryder sat up straighter and looked at me with bright, alert eyes when moments before they were dull and sad. "Ollie! I think you're onto something. Why the hell would they hire me? Two thefts from the museums I worked at and neither of the items were recovered. Unless..."

"They wanted a scapegoat."

Ryder shook his head in disgust. "There's no other explanation. Regardless of what Lucien says, he must be involved with someone on the museum board. How else could he have gained access to the event?"

"You need to talk to Agents Kiphart and Marshall."

"I already have," Ryder said patiently. "I'm not convinced they care."

"They care about the truth, Ryder. You just have to make them see you're not guilty. Offer to take a polygraph. Wait," I said, thinking back to the movie I watched over the summer. "Surely, there's an insurance adjuster assigned to investigate the theft." Ryder nodded to confirm my thought. "There's the person you need to get on your side and make them hear you."

Ryder got to his feet so fast he nearly knocked the chair over. "Thanks, Ollie. You've helped me sort things in my brain and stop moping. Congratulations, by the way."

"For what?" I asked.

"I heard your Roebling Bridge painting sold for five thousand dollars. It's the largest amount any piece of art has sold for since the museum started the event. It really is a stunning piece."

"Thank you."

"Did you donate the money to Ryan's Place?" He shook his head. "Never mind. Of course, you did."

"Of course, I did."

"See you around, Ollie."

When I repeated the conversation to Archie after hanging with

Esther in the kitchen, he wasn't too impressed with Ryder's excuses or the idea he was being used as a scapegoat. It wasn't that he believed Ryder or didn't believe Ryder, he just didn't care. "Not our business, Golden Boy." It was the last time we discussed Ryder and his capers— intentional or otherwise.

One of the coolest things about building a life with someone was combining individual traditions and creating new ones as a couple. Millie and I had a tradition of serving Thanksgiving dinner to the homeless, where Archie, Maria, and Esther shared a big dinner with the residents of Ryan's Place. Our new tradition was volunteering to serve food early in the day followed by a family feast in the evening. I didn't expect all the guys from Ryan's Place to go with us too, but they piled into vehicles, and we headed over.

A few of the guys served drinks, a few others handed out the mittens and hats donated to the shelter, and the rest of us served food. I remember being on their side of the table, grateful for the food, warmth, and drink. Some would say their pride would prevent them from taking a handout, but they'd never been homeless. They'd never sold pieces of their soul one drink or hit at a time. They'd never lived beneath a bridge or sat outside a stadium with a sign asking for change only to get hit, kicked, or spit on. It's so easy for people to say what they will or won't do until they were actually faced with the challenge they claim to know so well.

Serving the Thanksgiving meal was bittersweet. I was happy I overcame the odds thanks to Randall's fortitude while I was in jail, and his and Millie's unconditional love when I was released. A person had to be numb not to feel the sadness for the souls overlooked and forgotten. Every day, I tried to show my gratitude by paying it forward.

I heard the sound of a pending scuffle, so Archie and I hurried down the line to break it up. "Come on, guys," I said firmly, gripping each of them by the bicep. "This is Thanksgiving. Can we please put aside our differences and break bread together?"

The man on my left jerked his head in my direction, and I looked into the startled eyes of Kaleb Jacoby. He was covered in dirt and grime with matted hair and a scruffy beard. The clothes he wore were two sizes too big and just hung on his frame. "Ollie?"

"Kaleb, what are you doing here? I thought you'd moved into the boarding house Archie told you about."

"What happened, Kaleb?" Archie asked firmly. "Did she turn you away?"

Kaleb shook his head. "I moved in for a few days, but I couldn't stay there. A few of the other boarders made me uncomfortable."

"You've lived on the street since then?"

"Why do you sound horrified, Ollie? You did it, and you were only a kid."

"Kaleb, are you taking your meds? Do you even have access to them?" Archie asked. Kaleb shook his head. "We have to fix this right away." Archie and I looked at one another and silently agreed about what needed to be done.

"You're coming home with us, Kaleb," I told him. "Archie still has an available room."

"No," he said, shaking his head. "I can't. Not after hearing what happened to you."

"Kaleb, I forgive you."

"It doesn't matter. I don't forgive myself, Ollie."

"Kaleb, if you ever really cared about me, then you'll come home with us. I cannot and will not live with your death on my conscience, especially if I could prevent it. Right now, we need to get you off the street, and we can sort everything else out later."

"Ollie—"

"Listen here," Millie said, muscling in. "He's not taking no for an answer, so you might as well give up. We have hundreds of people who need to be fed and no time to be arguing over something when the answer is so obvious. Now, are you going to hang around and come home with us, or are you going to make an old woman walk the streets at night hollering your name until she finds you?" God, how I loved my mother.

"I'll come peacefully," Kaleb said, fighting off a smile.

"Smart boy. Get back to work, fellas."

"Yes, ma'am," we both said.

I looked over my shoulder on the way back to our stations and saw Millie had switched from her tough love to a tender talk. I knew the expression and body language better than I knew my own. She was laying down the groundwork for Kaleb to find a better life, just as she had for me.

"Mama's found a new lamb," I said.

"I'm totally singing that in my head to the tune of 'Mary Had a Little Lamb,'" Archie said.

When we got back to Ryan's Place, the first thing Kaleb wanted was a shower. Henry let him borrow some of his clothes since they were about the same size, and the rest of the guys worked hard to make him feel comfortable. I spent a lot of time in the kitchen with Esther and Maria while the guys and Mama watched football.

"I'm proud of you, Ollie," Maria whispered, pulling me into a hug. "My son is so lucky to have you in his life."

"I'm lucky to have him too." He was my greatest gift, and I loved him with everything I had.

"Before we can eat," Maria said once we were seated around the tables in the dining room, "we're each going to say something we're thankful for."

A few of the guys groaned but were silenced when Esther raised a brow. Most of the sentiments were heartfelt, and we expressed gratitude for having each other in our lives, and some were humorous and silly to lighten the mood. Henry nearly brought me to tears when he said he was thankful for his chosen family, and Kaleb, who'd only lived there a few hours, expressed his gratitude for second chances. Archie and I kept our declarations PG, but we both sappily included one another in the list of things we were most grateful for.

Once we were alone, things were different. I straddled Archie's lap so I could stare into his eyes and whisper how much he meant to me against his lips and tell him how excited I was to celebrate the Christmas holidays and ring in the new year together. "It's going to be the best year of our lives," I told him.

"It'll be pretty hard to top this year," Archie challenged. "I can't imagine our lives being any more perfect than they are now."

I could, and I knew just how to make it happen.

Epilogue

Archie

Five months later…

"**W**HY HAVE I NEVER HEARD OF FRENCH PARK BEFORE now?" I asked Ollie as we strolled down one of the winding, wooded hiking paths. "It's so green and lush in the springtime. Jack is dying to play in the creek," I warned. "Those waterfalls would make perfect spots for taking pictures too." Jack, our newly adopted German Shepherd, eyed the creek so pitifully.

"We'll stop soon. There's a shelter house a little way down this trail," Ollie said, sounding distracted.

"What's going on? You seem edgy," I told him.

"Nope. I'm just hungry. I have fried chicken and all the trimmings inside this basket."

"Then let's get moving a little faster," I said.

We came around a curve, and I was stunned to see Milo standing off to the side holding something in his hand. The elated joy on his face distracted me from seeing what he held in front of him. When I got closer, I realized he was holding one of Ollie's illustrations. It was something he must've sketched from memory from the night we met. In the drawing, my eyes appeared to glitter with attraction, and a flirty smile teased my lips. I had wanted him so much.

I stopped to take the drawing, but Ollie squeezed my hand. "We'll collect them later."

"Them? There's more? What's going on?" I asked.

"You'll see," Milo said. He kissed me on the cheek then tucked in behind us to follow.

We walked quite a bit further before we came across Andy leaning against a tree, smiling ridiculously. "Love looks good on you, Arch," he said, gesturing to the drawing he held in his hand like Vanna White. This one was a picture of the two of us kissing beside Ollie's car in the bowling alley parking lot. Andy joined Milo, and I heard them exchange a smacking kiss.

The next person along the trail was Henry, and he held a drawing of Ollie and me at bingo. We stood behind the podium lost in our own little world. Henry too joined our entourage.

We came along Millie who held a picture of me sitting on the front pew on my first visit to his church. Millie took the arm Henry offered.

Then it was Esther who held up a picture of Ollie and me sharing a quiet cup of coffee together in her kitchen. We leaned into each other while I looked at the paper and Ollie looked at something on his tablet. Esther looped her arm through Millie's, and we marched on to our final destination.

Mamma was waiting for us in the center of the shelter, and she held up a sketch of my favorite photo of us as a couple. It was taken the night of the museum gala. Archie and I sat on the stairs smiling at one another, and the love we felt for each other radiated off the page just as it did in the photo.

"My Archie," Mamma said, coming forward and hugging me. She reached up and wiped away the tears spilling down my face. She kissed my cheek and hugged me tightly. "My Ollie."

Andy took Jack's leash, and Milo took the picnic basket. Our friends and family formed a half circle around us when I turned and faced Ollie. He reached into his pocket and pulled out something circular, but I didn't have a chance to see it before he dropped to one knee.

"Archie, will you do me the greatest honor and be my husband?"

"I will," I said eagerly. Ollie slid the band on my ring finger, and I got my first look at it. It was a dark, rugged-looking titanium metal inset with delicate pink diamonds. My man knew me so well. "It's so beautiful."

Ollie rose to his feet, and we exchanged our first kiss as an engaged couple while our family, biological and chosen, gathered around and cheered.

"How are you guys going to work out the names?" Milo asked. "I'm not sure hyphenating is going to work."

"Why?" Henry asked.

"They'll either be known as White-Knight or Knight-White," Andy said. "One sounds like something out of a fairy tale and the other sounds like a kid trying to say night light."

"Good point," Henry said.

"We have plenty of time to decide that," Ollie said. "Right now, I just want to celebrate this joyous occasion."

"When are you fellas going to get married?" Millie asked. "I'm not getting any younger."

"Soon," Ollie said. "We're not getting any younger either."

The three ladies started up a conversation about the best months to get married while I looked into Ollie's smiling eyes.

"I'm so happy you caught me, White Knight," I whispered against his lips.

"I'm so happy you slowed down long enough for it to happen, Knight White."

We burst into laughter, both of us knowing two things: there was no way we were hyphenating our names, and we both had new nicknames for each other. In my mind, there was no debate to be had. I would be honored to take his last name as my own. When I looked at Ollie, I didn't see a man with a broken halo; I saw the best man I'd ever known. He would forever be my Golden Boy.

The End!

Want to be the first to know about my book releases and have access to extra content? You can sign up for my newsletter here: eepurl.com/dlhPYj

My favorite place to hang out and chat with my readers is my Facebook group. Would you like to be a member of Aimee's Dye Hards? We'd love to have you! Click here: www.facebook.com/groups/AimeesDyeHards

Acknowledgments

First, I need to thank my husband and children for their constant support and encouragement. It's not easy living with a writer who often disappears into a fictional world for long periods of time. They do so many things to help me out so that I can realize my dream. I love you guys more than words can ever express.

To my creative dream team, thanks seem hardly enough for all that you do. Miranda Vescio of V8 Editing and Proofreading, thank you for your tireless work, feedback, and many laughs while editing. Jay Aheer of Simply Defined art is an incredible artist, and I love how she brings my words to life. Stacey Blake of Champagne Formats is also an amazing artist who does incredible interior formatting, illustrating, and designing for e-books and paperbacks. Let's not forget Judy Zweifel of Judy's' Proofreading. She does an amazing job of finding the tiniest details that make a book shine.

To my lovely PA, Michelle Slagan. I'm not sure how I ever did this without you. I love you to the moon and back!

Lastly, I am so grateful for my beta readers and the honest feedback they provide me. Thank you for all that you do, Racheal, Kim, Dana, Jodie, Michael, Michelle, Brittany, and Laurel.

About
AIMEE NICOLE WALKER

Ever since she was a little girl, Aimee Nicole Walker entertained herself with stories that popped into her head. Now she gets paid to tell those stories to other people. She wears many titles—wife, mom, and animal lover are just a few of them. Her absolute favorite title is champion of the happily ever after. Love inspires everything she does, music keeps her sane, and coffee is the magic elixir that fuels her day.

I'd love to hear from you.

You can reach me at:

Twitter—/twitter.com/AimeeNWalker

Facebook—www.facebook.com/aimeenicole.walker

Blog—AimeeNicoleWalker.blogspot.com

.

www.ingramcontent.com/pod-product-compliance
Lightning Source LLC
Chambersburg PA
CBHW021244260626
47155CB00004BA/1316